I0584089

ISBN:978-1-64456-338-0
Library of Congress Control Number: 2021941062

INDIES UNITED PUBLISHING HOUSE, LLC
P.O. BOX 3071
QUINCY, IL 62305-3071
WWW.IDNIESUNITED.NET

# Books by Vera Jane Cook

## Southern Fiction
*Dancing Backward in Paradise*
*The Story of Sassy Sweetwater*
*Where the Wildflowers Grow*
*Pleasant Day*

## Women's Fiction
*Lies a River Deep*
*Marybeth, Hollister and Jane*

## Historical Fiction
*The Fourniers: Book One, When Hannah Played Ragtime*

# As Olivia Hardy Ray

## Science Fiction & Fantasy
*Pharaoh's Star*
*Annabel Horton, Lost Witch of Salem*
*Annabel Horton and the Black Witch of Pau*

For my mother, Vera Leona Ray
And for Alice Henry Thomas Henry Decker,
My Alice

# GLAMOR GIRL

## The Fourniers

# VERA JANE
# COOK

INDIES UNITED PUBLISHING HOUSE, LLC

Sheela Fournier
1920 - 1976

# Chapter One

Sheela did not remember her aunt's motel in Clearwater very well. She and her sister had been so young that summer back in 1926 when Wade showed up out of the blue and insisted on driving his children to Aunt Rena's for the summer. It had been the only time her father ever wanted to take her anywhere. She had a vague recollection of her mama staying behind in Jacksonville because she was waiting on the new baby, begrudgingly allowing Wade to take Sheela and her sister, neither of whom wanted to part from their pregnant mother. But Wade got his way, as usual.

Sheela remembered her Uncle Charles more clearly than her father's sister, Aunt Rena, and sometimes even more clearly than her father. Uncle Charles had been a funny man who sang the silliest songs she had ever heard. He taught the children how to put their fingers in the dirt and plant flowers. During that summer trip, he'd often take them to the beach, and he'd blow up big colorful beach balls for them to play with. Neither her aunt nor her father ever came to the beach that summer, but her Uncle Charles loved to stand in the water and watch her swim. He would tease her with lots of splashing. But she'd swim away from him. Sheela swam out much too far for Uncle Charles to follow, even though she could still touch the bottom when she stood. He "swam like a duck," she told her sister, and it used to make them laugh like crazy to watch their Uncle Charles waddle over the waves.

She heard Uncle Charles fell down the stairs and broke his neck about a year after the Depression set in. Rena used the insurance money to keep the motel running. Wade Jr. told his sisters there was a rumor all over Clearwater that Rena had pushed Charles to his death so she could use the insurance money to get her through the Depression. Rena married less than six months later, but according to Wade Jr., her new husband lived only a year. He had a fatal heart attack while repairing the roof of the Sea Spray, and of course, more insurance money followed.

Sheela's aunt was on her third husband by the time she picked up the girls from St. Stanislaus Catholic Orphanage in 1938. Sheela felt sad thinking about showing up in Clearwater and not seeing her Uncle Charles and his funny handlebar mustache, soft and unruly as the fur on an old teddy bear. She hadn't seen her aunt since that summer when they'd been so young. Her mother was still alive back then. After her mother died, the only person to ever visit them at the orphanage was her older brother, Wade Jr. Sheela had some fleeting memory of a short woman with dark hair who liked orange neck-scarves and spoke English like her father with that French dialect. Wade Jr. never talked about where their father was or what he was doing. Sheela never asked, and she certainly never saw *him* walk through the doors of the orphanage.

Their Aunt Rena was more remote and stern than the nuns she had left behind in Jacksonville.

"Don't talk while I'm driving," she told them. "It makes me nervous listening to the chatter of young girls."

Sheela and her sister Leda sat in the back seat and gave each other wide-eyed stares and winks that almost made them laugh aloud. They had to put their fists into their hands to keep back the laughter. It was as if laughter was something no one ever wanted them to do. Back at the orphanage, they were always sneaking it behind their hands, or else biting their lips so hard to stifle it their lips stung all day. The only nun at St. Stanislaus the girls ever saw laugh was Sister Vincetta and Sister Mary Veronica, who left so abruptly. Legend had it Sister Mary Veronica had a giggling fit during a church sermon because of the way Father Timothy said "Jesus." Sister Vincetta told them that Sister Mary Veronica was just a child herself and prone to giggles. Sister Vincetta laughed as loudly as Sister Mary Veronica when she told the girls about Father Timothy's constant referral to "Jaysus" and the hysterical nun in the quiet church on Sunday morning.

Sheela identified with Sister Mary Veronica that day, unable to stop herself from feeling silly. She and her sister stuck out their tongues at passing cars and each other while they slid down as far as they could in the back seat and made faces at their aunt behind her back. Rena Soldar hunched over the wheel, her two hands clutching it, both of those large hawk eyes of hers riveted on the road, talking about the Sea Spray and what chores the girls would have before and after school. But neither Sheela nor Leda paid much attention to their aunt that afternoon. They were too busy trying not to break up into hysterics while the miles slipped by, and all those yellow and green houses peered back at them from the road, looking so sadly neglected and worn. But the sky was so blue that day it made them too happy to notice, and there is nothing like a warm blue sky to make two teenage girls feel kissed by paradise, just by being under it.

# Chapter Two

Darryl Jordan met them as they pulled up the drive. He stared at Sheela so hard, he tripped up the walk.

"This is your Uncle Darryl," Rena said.

The young man put both their bags under one arm and held the door open. Two large teeth fell over his lip which made him appear harmless and jovial.

"Never would have known you had such pretty nieces," he said with a wink.

The back of Sheela's neck turned hot as she followed her aunt up the stairs.

"Thank you," Leda said shyly.

Rena's new husband, Daryl, appeared to be a lot younger than Rena and somewhat dim-witted. But he was strong and able to run errands and attend to chores while Rena ran the motel. Sheela surmised that most of the time, the guests never even saw him.

Their room was in the attic of the house because the bedrooms were only for guests. The girls stopped short at the top of the stairs and stared around them. With only two small windows to let in air and light, it was so hot they might have gagged. The ceiling was low enough to touch. The twin beds were set in an L-shape around an upright support beam, where a small cross bearing the crucified body of Jesus hung from a nail. A chest for their clothes completed the sparce furnishings, and a bathroom down a small flight of stairs led to the third-floor landing. Their aunt's private quarters were on that floor.

"You will clean my bedroom before any of the others," Rena said with a threatening stare. "And then work your way down to the rest of the rooms, as well as the guesthouse in back. In the winter months, the motel is almost always full of people who still have money, so all the rooms and baths have to be attended to daily."

"Yes, ma'am," they said in unison.

The girls quickly got into a routine, cleaned the rooms for an hour before they left for school, and then finished their chores after 3 P.M. when they returned. For the most part, their aunt ignored them. They'd catch her staring at them, especially when Darryl was about, but Rena didn't speak to them directly unless they had left an ashtray unwashed or wrinkles on the beds. If they needed anything, they got it themselves or went without. Mostly, their aunt spoke into the air and never looked directly at anyone, not even Darryl. Sometimes, the girls nodded or answered back in quick sentences while their Aunt Rena offered a noncommittal grunt and continued to fill the atmosphere with her monologues and gestures, as if it didn't matter at all what she said or to whom she said it.

But Sheela's Uncle Darryl never left her alone, constantly winking at her and laughing as though she had just said something funny. Lots of times, he'd show up after school and tease her.

"Want me to carry your books, Sheela?"

"Drop dead, Darryl."

One time he cornered her near the toolshed behind the motel and reached his hand inside her blouse. Sheela screamed and jumped back.

"If you let me do it, I'll take your rooms for you. I'll clean them every day for a week."

He looked at her with a wet sneer on his face, his fleshy lips perspiring, talking in some low whisper as though he had an ache somewhere.

Sheela pushed him aside and ran back to the motel. She told her sister that Darryl had cornered her back where they kept the tools and to not go back there ever because he could get her alone real easy, too.

The morning of a school holiday, during Sheela's junior year in high school, Darryl attempted to force himself on her once again. Her aunt had taken Leda into town to see a doctor because of an outbreak of rashes over the girl's entire body.

"*Mon Dieu*, it does not look good for our guests to see the girl sitting around with some hideous outbreak," she whispered to Darryl as she hurried Leda out.

Sheela was just beginning to clean her aunt's bedroom when Darryl walked in and threw her on the bed.

"Don't say nothin' about this, you hear? You do, and I'll hurt your sister, you understand?" he said as he ripped her clothes and tore at his own.

But Sheela put up too good a fight. She kicked up her leg to throw him off her and managed to push her knee up hard against his groin. He yelped like a wounded dog and grabbed himself between the legs. She'd never seen tears come to anyone's eyes so quickly. He took short, quick breaths while he curled up on the bed holding his testicles with both hands.

"You little cunt," he sneered.

Sheela seized the opportunity and ran out of the Sea Spray like lightning and down the stairs so fast she almost fell. She rushed out into the street wanting to scream bloody murder. Instead, she walked to the park across the street and sat under a tree. Families were having picnics. Sheela thought about her mama. She bit her lip to stop her tears from falling. "Toughen up," she thought she heard her mama say through the clouds.

# Chapter Three

No one saw Darryl again in Clearwater, Florida, for several years. Rena never said a word when Sheela came back from the park with red eyes and torn clothes. She just stared at the girl and nodded.

Her sister's elbow jabbed her in her ribs. "Oh, shit," Sheela heard her whisper.

Their aunt picked up a hammer from the kitchen drawer and dashed up the stairs. They heard the yelling and took off toward the back, where they crouched behind a trellis and stared up at their aunt's bedroom. They never saw Daryl again after that day. Although it was a relief not to have him lurking about, Sheela was constantly afraid he would show up again and kill her.

"Oh, don't worry," Leda said. "I'm sure Aunt Rena has hammered him to death by now and fed his body to the fish."

Rena must have divorced Darryl at some point because she found a new husband within three months of his disappearance. Chester Moody was a beefy man who liked to sit on the front porch and take naps in the rocker. He brought the girls to fierce hysterics because he snored so loudly the guests raised their eyebrows and politely glanced in another direction. Rena talked to him constantly, even when he appeared to be asleep. She put him to work in the kitchen, along with Leda and Sheela, and hired a girl to clean the rooms. A much nicer arrangement for Sheela and Leda_because even though they had to clean up after him, they got to lick up all the chocolate sauce from the pots.

Sheela had a boyfriend in her senior year named Calvin Woods. He was always holding her hand and carrying her books, and he would come by every evening to sit with her on the porch of her aunt's motel.

"Come on, Sheela, let's go down to the beach," he'd say.

Sheela would check to see whether Aunt Rena was around and quickly jump the porch railing to run off with Calvin.

She thought he was the best-looking boy she'd ever seen. His hair was a fine soft brown that hugged his neck in wisps that fell onto his collar, and best of all, he had deep dimples that showed up in his cheeks every time he smiled.

Every boy in Clearwater thought Sheela was the prettiest girl they'd ever seen up close and envied Calvin the luck of winning her heart.

"What do you see in him, Sheela?" they'd shout. "He's a weirdo, so shy he stutters."

"That's precisely what I like about him." Sheela

wasn't so young she couldn't tell the difference between a bunch of roughnecks and a true gentleman.

She found it endearing that Calvin blushed around her so much of the time. He was a bookworm, too. He liked to read her chapters from favorite novels, passages he would underline in red. Calvin Woods wrote her so many love letters, they filled her chest at the motel. Sheela loved that he was so tall and lanky he had to duck through doors, and his knees were so high when he sat that even the cats didn't know where to find his lap.

"Marry me, Sheela," he whispered in her ear, then fell to his knees on the sand, and searched her eyes. "Be mine forever."

Sheela contemplated the ocean and a boat so far away it looked as if she could hold it in her hand.

"I can't," she whispered. "But I love you, Calvin. Don't ever forget that."

He looked at her sadly and rose to his feet. "Okay," he said. "I'll wait."

Most everyone thought they would get married after graduation. So it came as quite a shock when Sheela disappeared. Pensive and despondent for a while, Calvin eventually wound up marrying a girl from Orlando whom he'd met on a trip. There was a rumor in Clearwater that Sheela wrote Calvin a letter right after leaving town, telling him that she'd never come back to marry him. There was another rumor going around as well. People said that Sheela went and met herself a millionaire in Miami and didn't have the time of day anymore for a poor boy like Calvin.

# Chapter Four

Sheela had seventy-five dollars in her pocket the day she slammed the door of the Sea Spray Inn for the last time and hitched a ride to Miami. She'd been saving the money ever since that first time with Eugene Howe.

"I'll have dinner in my room tonight." Eugene smiled at Rena. "Do you think I can have some company? Perhaps your pretty niece, the tall one?"

Rena snapped her fingers, quickly turning her neck to find Sheela.

"*Oui*, my niece is quite beautiful, isn't she?" And the unstated negotiations began as Eugene put one hand on his wallet, and the other quite close to his fly.

"I'll see what I can do," she told him.

Eugene Howe had been vacationing at the Sea Spray Inn for years but started coming more often once he retired. He always took the best room and requested thick steaks and rich desserts. Rena always ordered a special case of whiskey when he came to town, and she spent many hours with him in the parlor, re-filling his glass and increasing his tab.

"Mr. Howe is one of the most prominent men in his home state of Alabama. Take special care of him, Sheela." Rena leaned close and looked into her eyes. "He has a certain fondness for you. Why don't you serve him in his room tonight? You remind him of his daughter." She smiled with an absence of effort.

Sheela did not dislike Mr. Howe. In truth, he encouraged her to talk to him about school and what she liked to do with her time. Sometimes he brought out photographs of his wife and children. With a despondent sigh, he mentioned that his wife had died several years before, and he was very lonely.

"He has something special to show you tonight," Rena said. "You be nice to him. These are hard times."

Sheela looked at her aunt's face. "And perhaps I have something special to show him, too?" she said with a sneer.

Sheela watched as Eugene uncovered a wine-colored folder that looked as if it were made of satin. He brought it to the edge of the bed and patted the space beside him. "Come sit by me," he said as he carefully unwrapped it.

Sheela sat close to Mr. Howe in case he cried

over more family photographs. The poor man's hands were shaking, and he was breathing so heavily, the bed moved. But it wasn't a picture of his wife that he showed her. Neither was it a picture of his daughter, Delia. He showed her, instead, photographs of naked people engaged in all sorts of odd behavior. She particularly wanted to laugh at the one with all the bare-assed ladies dancing with one another; but she intuited laughter would be inappropriate because Mr. Howe was so intensely serious. She felt him put his hand over hers, and she quickly stood up. He cocked his head at her for a moment, then he reached in his inside pocket and counted out bills. There must have been at least twenty bills that he counted and forced into her hand.

"Your aunt said you would be nice to me," he said.

She stared at him. He was heavily bearded. She didn't like that. His stomach rolled over so many times, he looked deformed. She didn't like that, either. She noticed the jowls in his cheeks. He was running his tongue over his lips, looking up at her as if he would pounce like a hungry lion if she gave him the slightest provocation. She stared at the money. It made her think of what her aunt had said to her. *You'd be surprised how good he'd be to you if you grant him a favor or two.*

"Are you a virgin?" he asked her.

"That's for me to know and for you to find out," she said.

He laughed at that. "I know you have a

boyfriend. This won't interfere."

Sheela pushed Calvin from her mind. Aunt Rena was always telling her that Calvin would never get out of the trailer park. She stared back at Eugene Howe. She wanted money. Her witch of an aunt didn't give her a dime. She just needed a little money to get out of Clearwater forever, and away from all those damn dirty dishes and smelly toilets.

"If I turn out to be a virgin, it's going to cost you more than this." She stared into his eyes and put the money on the bed.

Eugene stopped licking his lips. He also stopped his deep breathing. His mouth drooped a little as he watched her.

"You're made for this." He grinned as Sheela's fingers traced the buttons on her blouse.

# Chapter Five

Throughout Sheela's final year in high school, Eugene sent her gifts: garters and lace brassieres that he told her to wear for him on his next trip down to the Sea Spray Inn. He visited Clearwater at least once a month to see her. One month he sent down a friend, Wes Monroe, a boisterous, handsome man at least six feet tall. With his striking mane of thick black hair and a dramatic mustache, her Aunt Rena said he was a dead ringer for Clark Gable. But though he gave Sheela even more money than Eugene, he never touched her. He only wanted her to watch him while he slowly disrobed, paraded himself in front of her, and pulled on himself until he ejaculated all over his hands and fell to his knees, groaning and sobbing.

Sheela was generous with her money. Her aunt took most of it, but she had enough to take her sister to the movie theater whenever they could sneak away from the motel. She sent money to both her brothers, and she promised Leda she would send her money from Miami.

"Find a place of your own, Leda," she said, handing her a fistful of ten-dollar bills. "Leave that bitch in the dust."

It was just one week after her high school graduation that Sheela took Leda by the arm and led her off toward Cleveland Street.

"I've got enough saved now," she excitedly told Leda. "It's time for me to get the hell out of here."

"Out of here to where, sister?" Leda asked, looking at Sheela like she'd lost her mind.

"Miami."

Sheela had no concrete plan. Miami was a random choice because it sounded like the most exciting place to be. She knew by now that she'd never starve: that there would always be a man around to fill her purse.

"What about Calvin?" Leda asked.

Sheela looked away. Calvin respected her. When he got carried away and tried to touch her in all her secret places, he would stop himself and apologize. He begged her forgiveness over and over until she finally told him he didn't have to worry about his hands anymore. But being with Calvin was like leading two lives. After the time with Eugene Howe, it all changed. She couldn't think of lying down with Calvin and accepting his tenderness, not after Eugene.

"I don't know," Sheela said, taking in her sister's shock.

"I thought you loved him," Leda said, her confusion apparent.

Sheela had become distant with Calvin after

Eugene soiled things. She pretended to have stomachaches and leg cramps. Calvin would bring two aspirins out from his mother's cupboard and hand them to Sheela with a cup of water.

"Feeling better now?" he'd ask while the crinkles over his nose deepened.

"Uh-huh," Sheela would tell him and watch the way the sun played on his hair with a halo of streaks that turned the brown to gold.

Sheela took her sister's hands and sat her down on a bench.

"Sometimes I dream that Calvin and I are married, and we're so happy we never stop laughing. But then the dream changes and Calvin turns into Eugene Howe, and the walls in our house suddenly fill up with Mr. Howe's dirty photographs. I try to escape, but then Papa shows up and puts wax in the keyholes so I can't jimmy the lock. I scream and beg to be let out, but Papa ignores my cries. Then Aunt Rena appears with a salacious sneer on her face. She locks me in with Mr. Howe and throws the keys to all the rooms into the sea."

Leda looked into her gaze. "I understand," Leda said tearfully. "I'll pray for you, Sheela, every day."

Sheela didn't say goodbye to Calvin the day she left Clearwater. She hitched a ride from Cleveland Street with a traveling salesman, feeling as free as a fish in water. It was an adventure for Sheela to ride out of town, knowing she was never coming back. It was like digging a hole in the sand and really discovering China.

# Chapter Six

The house had a silver dome and stood majestically on three quiet acres of land. The ceiling curved and gently rested on beveled columns with gilded posts. The marble floor was almost nude in color and captured footsteps in its shine. The deep rich mahogany staircase lifted with a grand sweep, like an arm in reach. The upstairs rooms were carpeted in muted tones and lit by Tiffany-shaded lamps. Chaise longues covered in satin nonchalantly stretched before drapes of silk and stared back at beds smothered in velvet.

Sheela had been greeted at the front door as if she were someone's best friend or, at least, a relative not seen in years. The tour of the mansion lasted half an hour. Overwhelmed, Sheela breathed in the perfumed air and followed Kit Malone into the "afternoon parlor."

"I call it my 'afternoon parlor' because of this wonderful light."

Sheela looked past tall windows and onto trees that shaded rose bushes and tulips.

"Please be seated." Kit pointed to a couch that looked as if it had been spun with gold.

Sheela sank into pillows that seemed to hug her body from all directions. Kit sat across from her in a chair with long, clawed arms and legs that stood on point like prima ballerinas frozen in motion.

Sheela guessed Kit was her Aunt Rena's age, at least forty-five, though it was hard to tell. Kit was still beautiful. Her golden yellow hair wound around her head in a crown of waves; her hands and legs were long and slender, and her breasts round and curved up from her low-cut blouse, revealing skin that looked as soft as a baby's cheek. She smiled at Sheela.

"We're going to work on that accent. You're a bit *too* Southern."

Sheela nodded. She would do anything Kit told her to do. It hadn't been an easy decision to enter the house, but now she was inside, she was sure she had made the right choice. She had almost turned back. She had circled the property three times before she decided to ring the bell. The man who had told her about the mansion said she'd be a fool not to hitch her horse to Kit's wagon. He told her she'd make more money than she ever dreamed possible. Word had it that Kit Malone was good to her girls, and her clients weren't street scum, either. Kit's client list included some very well-known, wealthy men about town. The man had spoken to her like a school adviser suggesting a course of study. Then he had put his hand in hers, kissed her on the cheek and told her to get out of that two-bit bar they were in and cash in on her class.

"Though men do like a bit of a Southern drawl, you'll find that my men like a refined, well-spoken woman." Kit leaned forward and reached for her afternoon tea. She stared at Sheela and smiled again. "You will have men eating out of your hand." She laughed, and the sound of her laughter was as lighthearted as morning birds.

Sheela tried to maintain focus on Kit's eyes as she spoke and not to stare at the paintings that hung on the walls like rectangular paper coffins, revealing effigies of naked women, unnerving the beholder with their sad and seductive stares.

Kit sipped her tea and continued, "Pleasing men is an art that can be cultivated and learned. For God's sake, listen to everything they say, or pretend to. Stroke their egos even more tenderly than their genitals." She sat back in her chair. "And remember, beautiful women are feared as much as they are desired. Power is always with a woman if she knows how to use it. I tell you this so you can have everything you want in life. Most people don't know how to get what they want. It's so simple. First, you must be committed to it with all your heart, and then ask yourself how you're going to attain it. Are your assets in place?" Kit leaned forward and placed her tea on the table. "Beauty and brains, my dear, those are the assets of choice for a woman. You must have both, and clearly, you do. You will use your assets wisely in this house. Exercise your sense of humor, listen with rapt attention, and never disagree with a man unless you do so as softly as melting butter. Always tell men what they want to hear. Build your fortress!"

Kit got up and went to the window.

"We do not work before 4 P.M or after 2 A.M." She drew back the drapes and turned to Sheela. "I want you to meet someone."

Kit's tone changed as she called out toward the yard. It took on an uncharacteristic excitement. "Alice! Bring her inside!"

Alice entered with a confidence that made Sheela take notice. She was a serious young woman who appeared no older than seventeen. Her skin was a cocoa brown, and her loveliness was apparent even in her unflattering black uniform. In her arms, she carried a tan-and-white King Charles spaniel. Kit quickly fell to her knees and held out her arms.

"Sweetie Pie, come to Mama."

The puppy ran around in splendid circles kissing and licking his mistress with the exuberance of a crazed lightning bug, her little tail ticking from side to side like an over-wound clock. Sheela let out the first laugh she had had since she left Clearwater.

"Come on, Sheela," Kit called to her. "Come, say hello to Sweetie Pie."

Sheela fell to her knees and let the puppy jump up and nip at her nose. Kit arched her back, squared her legs, and then chased the dog around on all fours, while Sheela followed. They scuffled around the "afternoon parlor" after Sweetie Pie, as the puppy leaped on and off chairs and flew over small tables. Alice looked on in quiet amusement and Sheela laughed so hard, her sides hurt.

"Miss Kit was a Ziegfield girl," Alice told her while Sheela unpacked a small bag she had brought back from the rooming house over the bar. "She's well over forty. Shouldn't be crawling around the floor like that at her age."

"Really?"

Sheela easily imagined Kit in a chorus line with her hair touching on her shoulders and her long shapely legs strutting across a stage as if she were Queen of the Nile.

"Where you from, girl?" Alice asked as she reclined in the chaise and stretched her legs out with a deep and tired breath.

"Jacksonville," Sheela said quickly. She would never tell anyone she was from Clearwater. That was just a place haunted by senescence and speckled with little hotels like her Aunt Rena's. Home was the little two-story house on Cherry Street with the long yellow wall and the torn wallpaper that had followed her up the stairs with tiny, faded roses opening and closing. It was where she lived when her Mama was alive.

"Jacksonville? That's my home. My daddy and brothers are still there. I send them money. Guess what? I make more money than my daddy."

"No kidding?" Sheela looked at her and smiled politely. "I wonder if we ever passed each other on the street."

"I doubt it," Alice said with a tilt to her eyebrows.

Sheela felt the blush on her face appear. The

only time she ever really saw any colored people was when her mama took her to see a Baptist choir at the old cathedral on Third Street once.

Alice smiled and lit herself one of Sheela's cigarettes.

"You know, she brings that little dog out every time a new girl comes."

"Why?" Sheela put the last of her belongings away and jumped onto the bed. It gently moved to the bounce and then settled back. "Oh, what a bed," she said as she let out a sigh that might never have ended if Alice hadn't interrupted her.

"You don't have much, do you, girl?"

Sheela didn't answer. Her hands back over her head, she settled against a large plum pillow.

"No matter. Miss Kit going to buy you some clothes."

"Why does she bring the dog out?" Sheela asked as she stared up at the vaulted ceiling and smiled at the cherub mural.

"If a girl don't take to the dog, she don't get hired."

Alice rested her hands back under her head, too, and kicked off her slippers.

"Why not?" Sheela crawled to the foot of the bed and stared at her new friend.

"Miss Kit says if a girl don't like the dog, she's too cold to be worth anything. She says men like to marry cold women, but they like their whores warm and friendly."

Sheela rolled over in laughter. Alice was startled at first, but she welcomed the chance to share the humor and soon joined Sheela in her fit of hysterics. By the time their ten minutes of complete loss of control ended, they were both curled up on the Persian rug and holding their sides.

"Are you one of the girls?" Sheela finally asked her.

"Shoot, no." Alice sat up and wiped the tears from her eyes. "Ain't no colored girls working here. I take care of things for Miss Kit."

"I bet she'd take you on. You're real pretty."

"She did once ask me if I was interested." Alice produced a warm round smile, and the memory of the moment made her laugh again.

"What's so funny about a proposition?" Sheela leaned back on her hands and rested her feet up against the bed.

"I said, 'Miss Kit, with all due respect, I don't want to work in your whorehouse. I'm saving myself for love.'"

Sheela sat straight up and giggled. "You said what?"

"Hell, girl, ain't enough money in whoring to make me deliver used goods to my man. And besides, there's more money in running a brothel than spreading yourself all over the place. That's where there's real money. You getting thirty percent, she's getting seventy."

"Where did she get this mansion?" Sheela asked. Her curiosity was piqued now, and she wanted to know everything there was to know about Kit Malone.

"This was a gangster's house during prohibition.

He got himself killed in 1928, and they tried to turn the place into a hospital, but it never happened. So it just sat around doing nothing till Miss Kit bought it in 1932."

"Where does she come from?"

Sheela wondered how anyone could accumulate enough money to buy a place this big. But the door opened then, and Kit entered. She smiled at the girls on the rug. Sweetie Pie hung from her arms in a pant, her regal little face looking oddly childlike and affable. Alice stood up quickly and dusted off her uniform.

Miss Kit pointed her finger at Alice and slowly moved it from side to side.

"What's the rule of the house, Alice Henry?"

"Colored help don't mingle," she answered with her head bowed.

Alice kept her eyes to the floor. Sheela noticed the deep glow to her cheeks.

Sheela stared at Kit, her own face turning color.

"What else, Miss Henry?" Kit asked her sweetly and softly.

"Colored girl here to serve," Alice answered slowly.

Kit held out the dog and told Alice to take it to bed. Then she said goodnight to Sheela and nonchalantly added that she'd make friends with the other girls soon enough and not to distract the colored help.

# Chapter Seven

Sheela could always find Alice in the late mornings cleaning the upstairs rooms. The girls were all outside taking the sun if they weren't sleeping in. Sheela had only seen a few of the girls around the pool, and they had stared at her with a curious gaze from under large hats as they sat around sipping tall cool glasses of iced tea. Sheela was there three days before Kit finally introduced her as the newest "pearl in the oyster." The girls laughed and shook her hand. They told her their names one by one. She felt shy around them, but she looked them square in the eye anyway and said she was pleased to meet them.

"Look at that face," said the one they all called Helen of Troy. "What a looker!"

"She looks to me like she belongs in high school. Hey, how old are you, kid?" yelled out a woman with hair as white as Jean Harlowe's.

"I'm eighteen," she lied.

"Eighteen? Why I was fighting to protect my virginity in the back seat of my daddy's Cadillac when I was your age," laughed another while she covered her visible skin in a thick white cream.

Sheela knew she was younger than all of them. Soon they would come to regard her as "the kid," and they would give her advice on how to purse her lips in a pout because men thought it was sexy.

"Walk like there's nothing but Champagne bubbles under your feet, and never let your shoulders stoop," they told her.

But it was Alice she really wanted to talk to when the house was quiet, and the other girls were resting up for the evening.

"They have to be watched," Alice told her. "They hard as nails. And you the prettiest."

"What do you mean, 'hard as nails'?" Sheela wanted to know.

"Business is business. You know what I mean?"

Sheela looked back at her blankly.

Alice laughed. "Don't turn your back on a-one of them and don't trust them, neither. This ain't no ladies boarding house. Keep your money hidden. They'll run over you twice if they can make a nickel doing it."

Sheela wanted to laugh, but Alice met her eyes with such firmness that it stopped her.

"And one other thing, Sheela Fournier."

"What?"

Sheela sensed that a serious mood had invaded Alice's jovial nature, and it made her look almost tearful.

"I don't care what I said in front of that witch, but I don't really believe that colored people were put on this earth to wipe any white asses. You hear me?"

Sheela stood for a moment, letting the tears well up in her eyes and feeling her heart beating in her chest like a drum. She walked up close to Alice who stared back at her with a relentless glare.

"You're my friend, Alice Henry. I think you're always going to be my friend."

Alice's face relaxed a bit, and the gentleness returned.

"We'll see," she said.

The grandfather clock in the hall chimed an afternoon hour, and the sun rested in the room like unexpected warmth in a cold place.

"We'll just see," she said again.

The two young women stared at each other; the silence between them bordered on some inherent sadness.

"Well, you will." Sheela insisted softly.

Quite unexpectedly, the sadness faded, and the promise of trust hinted at the edges of Alice's frown as she watched Sheela turn and skip down the stairs.

# Chapter Eight

Sheela worked at Kit Malone's house for six months before she met Jack. He picked her immediately. He'd called at Kit's mansion for an escort while he was in Miami on business and noticed Sheela on the rear lawn. She saw him behind the window, staring at her and offering a smile on one side of his face. She pretended not to notice as she turned her head in the other direction.

Jack tapped on the window and waved.

Sheela took off her straw sun hat as she looked back in his direction and twirled the hat around her finger.

He waved again.

Sheela crossed one of her long, slender legs over the other and tapped her bare foot to a tune she was humming in her head. The man continued to stare and wave, and she continued to pretend not to notice. Jack turned back to the room.

"The one outside."

Kit stared past him.

"Sheela? You'll like her. Quite a sense of

humor."

"Dress her up and have her ready by nine. I'll be back for her then."

Jack Eric Stanton was worth millions. His family had owned small drilling companies that hired themselves out to drill for oil. When Jack inherited the company, he sold everything his father had owned and bought up land. He leased the land out for construction. In 1936, by the time he was forty-nine years old, he was one of the richest men in America.

Stanton was a collector of fine art. He was also a collector of women. Kit Malone and her girls referred to him as "Uncle Jack" and fell over backward to please him. He came to Miami often and usually seen around town with two, or even three, of Kit's girls. When he excused himself for the evening, at least two girls accompanied him back to his hotel. He was difficult to please, but he prided Kit's eye for beauty. His favorite pastime was flaunting his women before other men and offering his business associates the "pick of the litter." He then enjoyed the ensuing battle between the women for the pleasure of being picked, because the winner was always handsomely rewarded.

Kit dressed Sheela in a white low-cut dress with open shoulders and a white-sequined design that ran up the sides. She threw a white ermine stole over her shoulders.

"Ah, *le coup de maître*," she said.

Jack Stanton let out a long, low wolf whistle

when she entered the room.

"Beautiful, isn't she?" Kit rearranged her hair and winked at Jack.

Jack nodded. "Are the others ready?"

He had also instructed Kit to ask "the canaries," Lulu and Dakota, to join them. They came down the stairs, trailing their stoles behind them.

Lulu and Dakota were striking women, and both were almost as tall as Sheela. Jack Stanton liked his women tall even though he was only five-foot-six. Jack didn't weigh more than a hundred and forty pounds, but his voice carried, and people were usually surprised when he stood up and barely reached the shoulder of most men.

Jack was partial to Lulu and Dakota because they had both been cafe singers and he liked to hear them sing. He enjoyed listening to the girls grappling for the lyrics, and he always tried to trick them and come up with tunes they didn't know. He would give them ten dollars for every song they could sing straight through without messing up the lyrics or the melody.

"Do you sing?" he asked Sheela.

"Sure," she told him.

"Sing for me, dear. You pick it."

They were in his hired Cadillac on their way to the Chez Belle on Miami Beach. Sheela started singing her rendition of "All of Me." Her voice was nasal and hit the air like the moan of an animal. But she wailed with all the confidence of Ethel Merman. Lulu laughed, and Dakota held her ears. Jack reached into his pocket and came up with a ten-dollar bill.

"Here's ten bucks, dear. Stop singing."

"All of me... Why not take all of me," Sheela warbled in a flat monotone that went every which way but on key.

Jack handed her a twenty. "Please, spare me," he pleaded. "I'll pay you anything to shut up."

"Lalala. I simply adore you," she wailed.

"I don't think you've got the lyrics, dear." Jack sighed. He then reached into his pocket again and came up with two twenties, but Sheela didn't stop singing until she had made herself one hundred dollars. Jack laughed along with the others as the Caddie pulled up in front of the hotel.

The Chez Belle was not the best restaurant on Miami Beach, but Jack liked it because everyone knew his name and the maître d' always kept his table ready for him. The room was large and usually crowded. On any given Saturday night, murmurs of conversation filled the air, the waiters always busy. Long-legged women sold cigarettes for a dime, and one could smell the sizzle of steak and get their picture taken for a buck.

Just about the time they were all settled at the table, Jack noticed a familiar face easing through the crowded room, heading their way. The tall, broad-shouldered young man walked right up to Jack and smiled.

"Why, Jack Stanton." Leroy St. James extended his hand, and Jack reached out and shook it. Leroy was a business associate of Jack's who analyzed land value and sold his projections in neatly packaged portfolios.

"Evening, St. James," Jack said politely.

"Why, you pick the sweetest flowers on earth," Leroy said as he bent and kissed Dakota's hand and grinned at Lulu. "Nice to see you again, darlings."

The women smiled demurely and turned their attention back to Jack Stanton. Even though Leroy had been a client of Miss Kit's for two years, it would have been in poor taste to acknowledge him too demonstratively when Stanton was the evening's paying customer. But Jack Stanton surprised them.

"Are you alone, St. James?"

"Yes. I just finished a business meeting in the bar. I saw you come in."

"Why don't you join us? No sense eating by yourself."

Jack called over a waiter and asked for a different table. The waiter nervously gazed over the crowded room. His worried expression amused Leroy, and he handed the boy a five-dollar bill.

"We're very busy tonight," the waiter said apologetically. "I don't know if I can..."

"Just bring me a chair," Leroy cut him off.

The relieved waiter hurried over with a chair, and Leroy snapped his fingers.

"Place it there between those two lovelies." Leroy watched as the waiter placed the chair between Lulu and Dakota.

Jack took Sheela's hand as Leroy settled himself and grinned at the girls.

"What do you think of this beauty?" Jack beamed.

Leroy looked at Sheela as if she were the menu.

"I don't believe in robbing the cradle... and personally, I like blondes." He turned back to Lulu and winked.

Leroy St. James was of towering height. He had jet-black hair and large blue eyes. His shoulders were very wide, and his skin was deeply tanned, as if he'd spent a lot of time under the Miami sun. He was at least twenty years younger than Jack Stanton.

"You two could be siblings," Jack said, looking from Sheela to Leroy. "Don't you think so, girls? Couldn't Leroy be Sheela's brother?"

"I can't tell who's prettier," Lulu said sweetly. Dakota giggled.

"Well, I can," Jack said firmly.

"Are you Irish like Sheela?" Dakota asked him.

"I'm Indian and Irish," Leroy said as he bent toward Lulu and lit her cigarette.

"Where's your tomahawk?" asked Sheela with a grin.

Leroy chuckled. "In my pocket," he said, staring into her eyes.

Sheela liked his good looks, but she felt that if she turned her back on him, he'd skin her alive and sell her shrunken head on Biscayne Boulevard for a fin.

Leroy sat back in his chair and put his arms around Dakota and Lulu. Ash fell from Lulu's cigarette and landed in the crease between her breasts. Leroy stuck his finger in the water glass.

"An Indian to the rescue," he said. He put his finger in the crease and slowly rubbed the ash away.

Lulu squirmed as if it tickled. Leroy showed his white teeth and a long-dimpled dent on the left side of his face.

They ate shrimp cocktails and steamed lobsters. Sheela sipped white wine, and Dakota and Lulu had martinis. Leroy and Jack showed the girls how to crack the lobster shell and scoop out the meat, even though both Dakota and Lulu appeared expert at it. But it was always proper form to appear helpless. It was one of Kit's most stringent rules.

As Leroy dunked his fork into the melted butter, some of it fell to his lap. He stared at his fly and frowned, "Wouldn't you know? A new suit."

Sheela stuck her finger into the water glass and held it up.

"An Irish lassie to the rescue?" She laughed.

Leroy laughed back while Dakota slipped her napkin in the water as well.

"Just press it on the stain, sweetie," she said as she handed him the napkin.

Leroy showed a broad grin. He held up his knife and fork. "My hands are full."

Dakota pursed her lips and slipped her hands under the table. Leroy sipped on his scotch while Dakota rubbed the stain out of his trousers. His eyes peered into Sheela's.

"She found my tomahawk," he said sheepishly.

Jack surveyed the room and noticed how many heads were turned toward the women. That's why he appeared in public with more than just one beautiful babe. It always turned heads to see him with more than one beauty. They must wonder how he did it. He was envied. He was envied much more than a man like Leroy St. James, even though he was no beefed-up jock with wavy hair. Granted, he was a small middle-aged man who had never been particularly good-looking, but he made real money, and when he walked into a room, people stood off to the side and let him pass. He sneered at St. James while he flirted with Lulu. *Overblown schmuck. No real class.*

Stanton had married into real society. He owned a mansion in Connecticut, and his wife had given him five sons. *Nothing but hotel rooms and whores in this jerk's future.* He chuckled to himself as he stared at Leroy.

Jack was sure that St. James barely cut five figures. And even if he did make six, it couldn't buy him sophistication. Jack Stanton was an educated man, a respectable man. Aside from his wife and family, he had an estate in Palm Beach and an art collection that rivaled the Frick. *That jerk, St. James, wouldn't know a Manet from a Gauguin. Probably why he's throwing himself all over Lulu and Dakota. Why that's like passing over French wine for a slug of cheap beer,* thought Stanton as he smiled at Sheela.

Lulu was a real head-turner all right, but all a man had to do was look closely and he'd see that hard cynicism. Jack didn't like that in a woman. Stanton didn't believe a whore was worth much after the age of twenty-five unless she was doing something real special to earn a buck.

It was clear that St. James sat on his taste. Stanton looked at the ridiculous design of an alligator on Leroy's tie and the odd color blue of his suit. *Hell,* thought Jack, *the bastard must shop off the rack down on First Street.*

Jack watched as Leroy took some thin Dutch cigar out of his breast pocket. *Can't even buy himself a good cigar.* Jack reached out and snapped open his 14-karat gold lighter and lit the fire for him. Leroy blew the sweet-smelling smoke over his left shoulder and raised his eyes to the ceiling.

*Well, long as it's Lulu Leroy has his eye on.* Jack smiled to himself as Leroy flirted with the girls. He didn't altogether like this Leroy St. James, but couldn't deny his talents. He had advised Jack on a land deal in 1935 that had practically doubled in value, and was currently checking out a buy in Miami for Stanton, a parcel of land that Jack wanted to lease back for a golf course.

Jack figured he'd offer Lulu to Leroy and take the other two back to the hotel with him. He might even send Dakota back to Kit and keep Sheela all to himself. He just wanted to stare at the girl. He found her so lovely and amusing, and besides, he was getting tired and had been uncomfortably aroused watching Dakota rub out the stain on Leroy's fly. He wondered if Leroy was sitting across from him with a dick as stiff as his own.

The women went to the powder room just about the time the waiter brought the check. Jack reached for it, but Leroy slipped it out of his hand so fast Jack didn't know it was gone.

"Waiter!" Leroy called out.

Jack stared at him in amazement.

"This is on me, St. James."

Leroy looked at him and shook his head. "The broads are on you. Dinner is on me."

Jack certainly liked the way this man did business. "All right. Fair enough. I owe you, so go on and take your pick. Lulu or Dakota?"

Leroy took out a coin.

"You're a gambling man... aren't you, Mr. Stanton?"

"So formal? Call me Jack."

"Heads or tails, Jack?"

"What are the stakes, St. James?"

"Tails, I get the pick of the litter."

Jack Stanton laughed loudly.

"Sure, go ahead."

Jack put his hands on the table and stared at Leroy. *Your idea of the pick of the litter is some old whore that will ride you like an old mare. What the hell have I got to lose?*

"Ready?"

"Flip your coin, St. James."

Leroy St. James flipped the dime in the air and caught it. Then he smacked it over on his hand.

Tails.

"Lulu will be thrilled." Stanton winked as he crossed his hands over his chest.

Leroy smiled. "Lulu?"

The women returned from the powder room. Stanton wore a grin on his face a mile wide. *No taste in women. What an ass.*

Leroy St. James slipped the ermine off Sheela's chair.

"I believe you've won, Beauty," he said.

Sheela looked at Stanton helplessly as Leroy placed the stole over her shoulders.

"Shall we?" Leroy whispered.

Sheela glanced back quickly at Jack Stanton. He was staring blankly after Leroy St. James as he briskly led the evening's prize out of the Chez Belle restaurant and into the cool Miami air.

# Chapter Nine

"You in trouble with Miss Kit," Alice told her as Sheela dragged her feet down the hall toward the bathroom the next morning.

"He won me in a bet. Uncle Jack let me go," Sheela said sleepily.

Alice followed her into the pink-and-white mirrored room and sat on the edge of the large square tub.

"Do you mind?" Sheela put her hands on her hips and stared at Alice.

Two knocks quickly followed on the door, and Sheela let in Dakota and Lulu.

"Can't a girl go to the bathroom?" Sheela scowled.

Dakota joined Alice on the tub, and Lulu put the toilet seat down and sat on the john.

Sheela threw her towel in the sink and pointed her finger toward the door. "Out. Now!"

"Coulda' fooled me. I thought for sure Leroy didn't even like you. Uncle Jack wasn't happy. He's the client, ya know. Leroy... he's just a big jerk,"

Lulu said from the john as she took a cigarette out of her robe and lit it. She threw the match in the tub and told Alice to run the water so it would go down the drain.

"Uncle Jack brought both of us back here and spent about an hour talking to Miss Kit," Dakota said. "I hope she doesn't throw you out on your rear."

"Hey, I didn't do anything. Leroy flipped a coin... told me Jack lost and I was the prize." Sheela leaned against the sink and softly exhaled.

"The old coin trick, huh?" Dakota shook her head and smiled.

Leroy had laughed so hard the bed shook when he showed her the dime back at the hotel. It had two tail sides.

"Stupid old bastard," he said to her. "Now what would I want with two old whores when I can get myself a schoolgirl like you? Stupid bastard."

He was quick and, not surprisingly, rough, but in the end, he had sat on the edge of the bed and stroked her face.

"Pretty girl," he murmured. "A man could go crazy for you." Then he laughed real hard as if he had just thought of something funny.

He didn't call a car the way Stanton might have done. He showered and dressed. He drove her back to Kit Malone's and held her hand the whole way. *Odd thing to do,* thought Sheela.

Both sides of her face felt raw from the tight jagged facial hair he had rubbed over her skin, and his saliva left an aftertaste, like tobacco juice.

"You could be my lucky charm," he told her.

"Um," she said, hoping he wouldn't be back for more.

Sheela turned her attention to Dakota, who was reaching out for Lulu's cigarette. "Leroy's younger than Jack," she said. "That's a plus."

Dakota laughed. "Now don't go falling for Leroy St. James. He works for the Mafia."

Sheela's eyes opened wide.

"The Mafia?"

"That's right, sweet girl. Stanton doesn't even know it. But I do." She stared at Lulu. "And so does she."

"Does he, Lulu?" Sheela asked her.

Lulu got up and threw her butt in the john.

"Aw, hell, that's all we've got in Miami... Mafioso and millionaires."

At that moment Kit rapped on the door and told Sheela she wanted to see her in the library at two sharp. Dakota and Lulu both bit their lips and promised Sheela they'd vouch for her and tell Kit they had witnessed the bet. Alice looked up toward Sheela and opened her eyes half-dollar round.

"Lord have mercy," she said to no one in particular.

# Chapter Ten

Sheela did not expect to see Uncle Jack standing in the library when she entered. He was looking out of the window toward the gardens.

"Magnificent roses." He looked energized, as if he had just won a tennis match. "You'll find that my gardens are not as prolific. I have a fine hand for chrysanthemums, though, and the property is filled with lilies. I do love lilies, but I simply don't have enough roses. What is your favorite flower, Sheela?"

"I don't have one." Sheela stared awkwardly at Miss Kit. She was sipping tea from the large wing chair that faced out toward the gardens.

"Surely you have a favorite flower, Sheela?" Miss Kit's smile was a reprimand. Sheela knew that because her eyebrows peaked right after she showed her teeth.

"The rose, I would say," said Uncle Jack. "Red, of course."

"My mother loved gardenias." Sheela was confused but played along. "I would say gardenias."

Jack Stanton came around the desk and into the

room. He sat himself down and reached out for the other cup of tea.

"Fragrant. Very fragrant." He sipped on the tea. "I will remember your favorite flower," he said with a wink.

"Sheela," Miss Kit began, "Uncle Jack would like to take you back to Connecticut with him."

Sheela stared at Miss Kit and then back at Jack Stanton.

"Connecticut? But why?"

"My dear, that is obvious. Jack likes you."

"You mean I am to leave here and live there?"

"Precisely." Jack beamed. "I love to have beauty around me."

Sheela stared at him in disbelief. She did not trust this situation; it was another moment in time in which the world changed too abruptly. It felt precisely like that moment she found out her mama had killed herself and nothing was ever the same again.

"Don't you have a wife in Connecticut?" she asked him.

Jack Stanton laughed. "Yes, I do. But she has had five children and no longer attracts me. We have an understanding."

Sheela continued to stare at him. She'd found his comment distasteful.

"Don't look so shocked. My wife and I have an arrangement, and she's quite happy with it. She won't bother us. I am going to move you into the house on the far end of our property. We call it a guesthouse, but it's a reasonably sized house. I live there. My wife lives in the main house."

Sheela said nothing. She kept waiting for someone to mention Leroy St. James, but Miss Kit and Uncle Jack merely sipped their tea and resumed their conversation. They did not ask her if she wanted to move to Connecticut. The matter seemed settled. They were talking about the care and maintenance of rose bushes.

"Excuse me," Sheela interjected.

"What is it, Sheela?" Miss Kit asked sweetly.

"What am I to get from this?"

Jack Stanton put his arms across his chest and gave himself a squeeze. "Culture," he told her. "I will teach you things. You will get a college education from your Uncle Jack."

"A college education?" Sheela realized he was serious. "Why, life is already enough of an education, Uncle Jack, and I prefer the Miami sun."

"Oh, I forgot to mention that you will have three thousand dollars a month at your disposal, to do with what you will," he said casually.

Sheela walked to the table and poured herself a cup of tea. She then sat down in the large silk chair with the wide, round yellow arms.

Jack stared at the girl with a nervous grin.

Miss Kit's breath rose and fell in the sunlit room, like the sweetness of a bashful first kiss. Sheela noticed a check under the saucer on the side table. She watched as Kit nervously fondled the edges of it.

Sheela listened to Miss Kit's breath, aware of the tic in Jack's left eye. She smiled out of the window at nothing in particular and took a long, slow sip of the warm lemony liquid. She carefully returned the cup to the saucer and stretched her long legs out before her.

"When do we leave, Uncle Jack?" she drawled demurely.

# Chapter Eleven

Leroy St. James showed up at Kit Malone's two days before Sheela was scheduled to leave for New York. Jack Stanton had booked a room at the Waldorf Astoria for the weekend of her arrival. He told Sheela that he wanted to show her the city before driving to Darien and settling her into the large white cottage at the far end of his twenty-two-acre estate. Sheela was anxious about the move, but she had her future to think of. She knew she could never make the kind of money Stanton had agreed to give her as long as Kit Malone owned seventy percent of her. Now she was free of Kit, and the expectation was exhilarating. She calculated how much money she could save in three years if she banked only thirty percent of what Stanton was paying her. Dakota and Lulu told her that Stanton tired of women easily and that his sexual appetites were peculiar, so she should just save the money and try to get in his will. Sheela had laughed heartily at that.

"I intend to retire in three years and buy a

house," she told them. "Then I will get married and have a baby. I won't need Stanton's money anymore."

Dakota put her hands on her hip like a mother in protest. "Men are only good for one thing. No, not sex and no, not marriage, but it buys both and lasts longer, and guess what? It's made of paper."

Sheela tossed a shoe at her and called her a cynic. She didn't bother telling them that they were wrong about love. They would have fought her on it anyway. She tried not to think about Calvin Woods anymore, and she never talked about him. She did write and ask her sister whether he had stayed in Clearwater or moved up to Jacksonville to go to college. Sometimes at night, right after her head hit the pillow and the room was so dark she didn't know where she was, she'd think about Calvin, but then it made her so sad she'd have to force herself not to. The memories of her and Calvin together triggered anxiety and emptiness. Emotions that made her want to curl up in a ball and pray for oblivion. It felt almost as hollow as when she thought about her mama being in the earth.

Leda wrote back and told her that Calvin was married and still living in a trailer park. She said Calvin worked over at the grocery store, but still talked about moving to Jacksonville. Sheela sometimes wrote his name over and over again on a piece of paper. Sometimes she drew a big heart and included her name inside with his, the way she used to.

Sheela's bedroom window in the mansion faced out toward the back where the pool was, so she saw Leroy St. James walking toward the large square sun patio. She wondered if he were there to see her. They had had their night together, and she didn't really care if she ever saw him again. Her face still stung from the way he had scratched her with his bristly skin. She didn't dislike Leroy, but something about the guy depressed her. She casually wondered if he had heard about her deal with Stanton and wanted to buy her time for one more night.

Leroy settled into a deck chair and asked Alice to bring him a scotch on the rocks and tossed a long manila envelope onto the table. Kit Malone sat under a large sun hat and peered at him over candy-striped sunglasses. Sweetie Pie lay curled under her chair and glared at Leroy. Occasionally, the dog would lift her eyes and let out a series of yelps while she turned her little regal head around and surveyed the space around her mistress.

"It's only a bit easier to get past the dog than that thug you have guarding the mansion," Leroy told her.

Kit's property was fenced around all three acres. A john could get to the front door from the driveway, but then he had to get past Bull Sardone. The rumor was that Bull had come with Kit from Chicago when she bought the property. The girls were sure Kit and Bull had been married at one time, and rumor was that Bull had done at least thirty hits for the mob. The girls affectionately referred to him as "Killer Bull," a name that always produced a big toothy smile from the Bull's enormous face and even an occasional hug.

"We girls have to protect ourselves." Kit smiled sweetly. A sandal hung from her right foot and dangled precariously as she moved her leg up and down.

Leroy stretched his tall body and put his hands over his head. His short shirtsleeves were rolled up and his legs hung over the sides of the red-and-white chaise. The sea breeze gently tousled his hair as he reached for one of the long thin cigars he kept in his shirt pocket.

"What can we do for you this afternoon, Leroy?" Kit asked.

Leroy tossed his match into an unfinished cup of coffee. The stained white cup smiled back from a silhouette of raven lips, left capriciously on the rim. The used match floated in the brown liquid. Leroy puffed on his cigar and grinned at her.

"Want to see something, Miss Kit?"

"Sure." She shrugged her shoulders.

Kit watched as Leroy took two matches and broke them off. He separated the bottom to make the match look as if it had little arms and legs. He did the identical thing with the second match. He removed the cup from the saucer and carefully put the two matches on top of one another.

"Watch this." He was nearly giggling with excitement.

Kit had seen the match trick a hundred times.

Every john in town wanted to show the girls the match trick. She smiled at Leroy. He lit the matches. They moved in a tiny passionate merge, as if in the throes of intercourse, and then fizzled out. Leroy laughed loudly.

"Ooh, very amusing, Leroy," Kit said haphazardly. "Now back to business. What can we do for you?"

"I'm going to do something for you. I'd like to see Sheela."

Kit sensed that her latest business acquisition was about to be challenged. She was sure that either Lulu or Dakota had called Leroy and told him about Stanton's offer. Her eyes went to the manila envelope he had tossed on the table.

"Perhaps we should discuss this before I summon her?"

"What did Stanton give you for her, Kit?"

Kit stared at him, silently. *A dangerous man.* She sat back and reached for a cigarette. Leroy leaned over and lit a match under it. He flipped the match into the used cup and slid his hand into his breast pocket.

"A blank check, Kit," he said as he held it up. "Go on and double what you got from Stanton."

Kit remained silent and took long deep swallows of smoke into her lungs. Leroy sat up as Alice brought him the scotch.

"Alice, tell Sheela to come out here. I want to speak to her," Kit said softly, her eyes on Leroy. "We'll listen to you, Leroy," she said as she dragged on the Chesterfield that peered out of a long red holder.

Leroy lay back in the chair. Kit noticed his clean white nails. His pants were an odd color, and she smiled at the lizard design on his tie. His shirt was the same color green as his socks. The thick black lashes around his eyes were almost unnatural, and were it not for the rugged, handsome features, he would have looked oddly effeminate. He waited quietly now for Sheela with his eyes closed and his face to the sun.

Sheela finally approached the patio and took the chair beside Kit. Kit winked at her from over the round candy-striped sunglasses.

"Leroy was showing me the match trick."

Sheela contemplated Leroy. Leroy sat back in the red-and-white chaise and laughed like a schoolboy who had just heard about the girl down the road who was letting every boy in town peek up her dress.

Sheela watched the dent in his cheek as it narrowed and the wide grin that revealed a mouthful of small, perfect white teeth. His hair fell on his forehead in long wavy strands that he brushed back with his fingers. He was practically giggling, and it seemed to her as if he were slightly intoxicated.

Kit Malone sat up straight in her chair and played with the ends of some magazines piled on the table. She called for Alice to clear off the area and bring an ashtray for Mr. St. James and a pitcher of iced tea. Leroy didn't take his eyes off Sheela. He puffed on his cigar and blew the smoke out of one side of his mouth without even blinking. Sheela picked up a copy of *Look* Magazine and started humming.

"How much is Stanton giving you to leave the luxury of Miami and torture yourself with the Connecticut winters?"

"Enough." Sheela smiled at him. "News travels fast." She turned to look at Kit who stared back into her eyes and continued to smoke.

"I have a deal in San Francisco I'm working on. Now there's a city. Ever been there?"

"Nope."

"I want to take you, Beauty. You'll love San Francisco."

Sheela looked at his mouth as it moved over the cigar the same way he had suckled and pulled on her breasts with his lips. She almost sneezed as the pungent odor of his smoke tickled her nose. He licked his cigar enthusiastically, leaned back further in the chaise and picked the tobacco off his tongue.

"So, Beauty?"

"I'm not going to San Francisco with you. I've got a flight to New York in two days." She looked back at Kit quizzically.

Leroy blew some smoke out of the side of his mouth and sat up. He gazed at Sheela as she flipped through the magazine. She hummed a few stanzas from "Ain't Misbehaving."

Alice came back to the patio with the pitcher of iced tea and two tall glasses.

"Take Sweetie Pie back inside, Alice. It's too hot

for her," Kit said.

The little spaniel had to be chased around the chairs until Alice, having tripped and fallen, scooped her up and carried her off. Leroy laughed so hard he had to sit up and rub the tears out of his eyes.

"Dumb little nigger," he said.

Sheela glared at him, she wanted to call him a shanty Irish bum, a cheap Chief Cherokee, but Kit would have had her head on a platter.

Leroy looked at Kit through pinched eyes. "I have a dilemma, Miss Kit," he said. "Now perhaps you can help me solve it."

"I'll try, Mr. St. James," Kit said slowly.

"I have taken a liking to Beauty here and I want to bring her out to San Francisco, but Mr. Jack Stanton has gone and bought the girl right out from under me."

"I accepted a business deal, Leroy. No one *buys* me. I go where I want to go," Sheela said methodically.

"A business deal?"

"That's what I said, Leroy."

"I'll tell you how I do business, Beauty." Leroy turned to Kit. "I'm a gentleman, and I don't want to take a lady anywhere she doesn't want to go. I merely want to suggest a proposition that is better than the one she has." He turned back to Sheela and raised his eyebrows.

"Okay, I'm listening," Sheela said slowly, while the sun invaded her skin and brought tiny beads of perspiration to the surface. "But make it quick,

Leroy, I want to take a swim."

Leroy reached inside his pocket and produced a tiny velvet box. Kit's mouth opened and she quickly looked at Sheela. He reached out for the manila envelope on the table and handed it over to Kit.

"Open it," he said.

Kit quickly opened the envelope while Leroy handed the tiny box to Sheela.

"For you, Beauty."

Sheela looked at Kit, who was reading from a stack of bank statements.

"Go on, open it," Leroy said.

Sheela opened the tiny green velvet box. "Are you insane?" she asked as a diamond engagement ring glittered back at her.

"Marry me, Beauty." Leroy turned from Sheela and peered intensely at Kit. "Go on, read her my net worth, Miss Kit," he said without waiting for Sheela's reply. "I told you I was offering the better deal."

Sheela sat up quickly and threw her legs over the side of the chaise.

"Marry you?" Sheela shook her head.

Kit stared at Sheela, her mouth so open she might have caught flies. Kit managed a smile before she started to read. Sheela listened intently.

"Well, he's got what looks like three million dollars in cash and bonds, and it says here that his business income in 1936 was over two hundred thousand. He owns a white 1934 Cadillac and a cabin in Ellenville, New York."

Kit took her eyes from the papers and looked at

Sheela oddly. She turned to Leroy St. James. He reached for his thin cigar and leaned back on the chaise. Sheela slipped the ring on her finger and shrugged her shoulders at Kit.

"Well, Beauty, what will it be? Me or that perverted little Stanton? You do know he's perverted, don't you?"

"I'll think about it, honey," she said sweetly, giving Kit another puzzled look.

Leroy rested his head back as he puffed and licked his cigar. As he closed his eyes against the sun, Sheela stretched her hand out before her. The clear alluring stone gave every appearance of a confident smile from its perch of white gold.

Sheela stared at the diamond and wished it were from Calvin, suddenly anxious in the same way as in the middle of the night when she thought about what it might be like to live in the trailer park with him. The anxiety lingered the way it did when she first saw the flesh on Eugene Howe's naked body, or when she thought about her mama locked away under the lid of a coffin. She waited for the bad feeling to pass, but it didn't, so she reached for Leroy's scotch.

The flash of heat in her chest was just what she needed. It burned away her despair and hopefully erased it altogether.

# Chapter Twelve

After Leroy St. James left that afternoon, Sheela and Kit Malone devised a plan. They had agreed to accept Leroy's offer, over a quick surreptitious wink, and now they needed to make sure that Sheela could get out of it at the proper time. As handsome as Leroy was, and as rich as he appeared to be, he was still unstable, unpredictable, and quite capable of altering his bank records. He was also with the Mafia, a connection Kit advised Sheela to avoid.

"Jack Stanton is class. Leroy is a schmuck," Kit told Sheela. "Stanton will introduce you into high society. Leroy is liable to drag you to the gutter."

Sheela agreed that she'd feel more secure with Stanton, and Kit breathed a sigh of relief. One thing she couldn't afford was to have Jack Stanton displeased with her. But they weren't going to let easy money from Leroy get that far away from them either.

"Call Stanton and tell him you have to delay your flight to New York," Kit said.

"What will I tell him when he asks me why?"

"Tell him you want to visit your brothers in Jacksonville. After all, living as far north as Connecticut, who can tell when you might see them again? He'll certainly fall for that. He's sentimental."

"Then you want me to go to San Francisco with Leroy?" Sheela asked, still unsure whether that was the smartest move, given Leroy's Mafia connections.

"I'll cash Leroy's check for thirty-thousand dollars, thirty percent of which is yours. The moment Leroy's check clears, I'll wire you a plane ticket straight up to Idlewilde Airport in New York."

"But what if he wants to get married in San Francisco?"

Kit stood up and poured herself more iced tea. "Stall him. Tell him that you want to be married in Miami with friends around you and not in some strange town where you don't know anyone."

Sheela presumed they'd get away with it. "I guess it will work."

"Sure it will. Just remember not to let him get you drunk and talk you into any fly-by-night justice of the peace. Stall the big fool long enough for his check to clear."

"Leroy will be mad enough to kill me," Sheela said.

"You just leave Leroy to me. I'll take care of him." Kit put her arms around Sheela. "Look, a girl can change her mind, you know. And besides, you'll be safely tucked away in Connecticut and I've got

Bull to protect *me*. Don't worry about Leroy. He's all mouth."

Kit expected that Leroy might pound his fists into a few walls but as far as she was concerned, her end of the bargain would be honored the minute Sheela accompanied him to San Francisco. Kit would just tell Leroy that she had been confused about his deal and thought it was only the trip that was worth the thirty thousand. After all, marrying him was really Sheela's call, not hers. Kit knew that Bull would keep Leroy out of the mansion until he cooled off. She was surprised that Leroy would make such a stupid deal, but maybe he had genuinely fallen for the girl and didn't think she'd con him. In any case, she could live without Leroy's business but not Stanton's.

Sheela wished she could get excited about going to a city as alluring as San Francisco, but it felt too much like a business deal—a damn good business deal at that—worth nine-thousand dollars in her pocket. She looked through all of Kit's magazines and read everything she could find out about the city just in case she got some time to herself. San Francisco seemed like such a fascinating place with its long, sweeping bridges and hilly streets, not at all like the flat terrain of Florida.

Unfortunately, she knew Leroy would be an obstacle to the fun she wanted to have. She assumed that he would probably want to scratch his bristles over her body all day and go to nightclubs all night. She thought how differently she would feel if she were to be walking up those high streets with a girlfriend, taking a real trip.

"Can I take Alice?" she asked Kit.

Kit looked at her as if she'd lost all her good sense. "Of course not," she said. "Alice is needed here at the mansion."

# Chapter Thirteen

"I guess I'm never going to see you again, am I, girl?" Alice asked sadly while she helped Sheela pack her things. "Seems like you weren't here long at all."

"See this ring?" Sheela held Leroy's diamond up to Alice's eyes. "It's yours, if you come to San Francisco with me." She grinned and dangled it in front of her.

Alice looked at Sheela like she'd lost her mind. She let out a swift flow of air that gave sound to her breath and caused her lips to swell out.

"Shit, I'm not going clear across the country for some fool piece of glass may not be worth more than fifty dollars."

Sheela couldn't believe she didn't recognize a diamond when she saw one. "Worth hundreds," she said. "Well? Take it or leave it."

"*Hmph.* Leave it," Alice said confidently.

Sheela plopped down on the bed.

"Doesn't money mean anything to you?"

"Not enough to make me leave Miss Kit and take

off with the likes of you and that big jerk, Leroy."

Sheela lay back. She thought about making conversation with Leroy St. James and how boring that was going to be. She hoped she wouldn't have to spend more than five days with him. He shook Kit's hand on the patio to solidify the deal, and then had taken Sheela in his arms and kissed her. His mouth was almost too soft as he covered her face in his tobacco-wet saliva. His tongue was like some invading weapon that darted around her mouth as though on a secret mission looking for enemy submarines. His heavy breath was immediate, and he pressed his body against hers, ready to consume her.

"I'll go ahead and book the flight," he said.

And she heard him laughing like a crazy man as he walked off.

Sheela watched Alice carefully fold her blouses and pile them on top of one another in a small suitcase.

"You don't like Leroy, do you, Alice?"

"Don't matter none who I like or don't like."

Sheela enjoyed the company of the other girls, but she could walk right out of Kit Malone's and never think about them again. But Alice was different. Sheela had never known any colored girls before. Never did in Jacksonville or Clearwater. Her Aunt Rena had told her that they weren't worth knowing, but her mama always said that color didn't mean a damn thing to Jesus.

"You can see a person's character in their face,

Sheela," her mama always said. "It's all there before you, child, everything you want to know, and color is the least of it."

When she looked at Alice, she saw something that reminded her of her mama. She couldn't tell exactly what it was that they had in common but when Alice talked about her daddy, it was almost like sitting on her mama's lap again and hearing about Grandpa Reilly and his favorite sheepdog that lived for twenty years, or how she and her sister Anne read all those books together by the big stone fireplace in the kitchen. Listening to Alice talk about her daddy was like imagining the dark, damp sky against the rocky Irish Sea, the way her mama saw it. In the same way, she imagined Alice's daddy and his big old, hearty laugh reverberating clear down the block.

"Ever been to the colored section of Jacksonville?" Alice asked her.

Sheela knew where it was, but no white kids ever went there. It was some mysterious dark road that would have taken her to a place where children ran barefoot in the street and old colored folk slept on rockers all day. She remembered hearing people tell her that colored people were usually up to no good, drinking beer or harming white people.

"We live in a big gray house," Alice continued. "My mama kept the house real nice while she was alive. Now my daddy lives there with my two brothers, and it's still nice. Our house is real pretty. We have a vegetable garden out back and a big, square red-and-white tablecloth in the kitchen.

Mama went and put all kinds of pretty pictures on the walls. She brought them home one day from the Five and Dime, and Daddy went and nailed 'em up in all the rooms. What was your house like, Sheela?"

"I hardly remember. Just a house." Sheela abruptly walked over to Alice and put her arms around her. "Take me home with you and let me meet your daddy?"

Alice's round, beautiful face beamed, and she laughed.

"When are you going to have time for this little colored girl when you running from coast to coast with gangsters and millionaires?"

Sheela looked into her eyes sadly.

"I'll give you two thousand dollars if you come to San Francisco with me. Cash!"

Alice stared at her in disbelief.

"How will I get back from San Francisco? Miss Kit don't want me to go. She won't give me a plane ticket."

"But if I give you two thousand dollars in cash, you can buy your own ticket."

"Or hock that ring you give me."

Sheela suddenly had an idea. "That ring could be our friendship ring. What do you think about that?"

"I don't know, Sheela. This here is the best job I ever had. Miss Kit won't take me back if I run off with you. We can write to each other, though, still be friends."

"If you come with me to San Francisco, you won't come back here, Alice. You'll come with me to

Stanton's in Connecticut."

"You crazy. What is Stanton going to want with me?"

"The hell with what Stanton wants. You'll be *my* maid. You'll work for *me*. I'll insist on it."

Alice's eyes seemed to tear over, and her brow got all wrinkly. She turned to Sheela and glared at her.

"Shoot, I ain't no white girl's maid. I ain't ever going to be no white girl's maid."

Sheela stared at her friend and tried to understand her anger.

"What the hell do you do for Miss Kit then?" she asked.

"I tend to Miss Kit."

"What does she pay you?"

"Twenty dollars a week," Alice said proudly.

"I'll pay you twenty-five dollars a week to tend to me, Alice Henry."

Alice looked at Sheela for a long time. She knew she shouldn't be putting her future in some white girl's hands, but it was frightfully exciting to think of herself flying in an airplane clear across the country and back again. Sheela was gazing into her eyes, sadder than anyone she'd ever seen, except her little brother when their mama died. Sheela was certainly the nicest white girl she'd ever known, and with twenty-five dollars a week, she'd be able to send her father even more money. He'd be so proud of her.

"I'll take the night to think about it," she finally said.

"Alice Henry, if you're going to go with me, we've got to get you a ticket. You don't have all night to think about it."

"All right, Sheela. All right! I must be crazy, but all right. I'll go!"

Sheela called Leroy that evening and told him that if he didn't secure Alice a seat on the plane and a room at their hotel, the deal was off. She heard his breath seeping through the tiny little holes of the phone, landing on her ear like the air in a seashell.

"I don't want that little tar baby coming with us, Sheela," he moaned between his bursts of breath.

"Then I'm not going any place with you," she insisted.

Leroy took himself a long silence. The air in his lungs continued to hit her ear the way it had that first night he had covered half her face in saliva.

"There may not be any room on the plane," he told her.

"Use your connections, darling," she said and abruptly ended the conversation.

Miss Kit told Alice she'd never be welcome back at the mansion if she ran off with Sheela and left her on such short notice, without any reliable help.

"Where do you think you're ever going to make the money I pay you?" Miss Kit asked.

Alice found the tip of her shoe and stared at it.

Kit turned to Sheela and brought her fine narrow eyebrows together.

"Are you out of your mind, bringing a little colored girl clear across the country with you?"

Sheela thought better of explaining to Kit that she had offered Alice a better deal, and quite fairly, stolen her away. After all, she didn't much feel like walking off into the unknown by herself, so she used her resources. No harm in that.

# Chapter Fourteen

Nervous about flying for the first time, Sheela felt better when she pretended it was Calvin who would show up at her doorstep to marry her, with his head all stooped over so he wouldn't bump it on the frame.

She didn't tell Alice that Leroy's ring had been stolen when she went for her bath. She had put the ring back in the box because she was afraid it would slip off her finger if she wore it in the water. But there had been so much to think about and she was terribly distracted, disrupting her life and making changes so quickly. She would never have left the box out in her room had she been thinking clearly. She tore everything apart, trying to find it, but halfway through the search, she realized it was really gone.

She was about to run off and tell Miss Kit that her ring had been stolen and demand that every room was searched, but if the ring were never found, Alice might change her mind and not want to leave the mansion. Sheela kept the theft to herself; she'd determine on the plane how to eventually let Alice know. After all, she had promised her that damn ring, and maybe she was counting on it.

But Leroy noticed it right off. They had just strapped themselves into the soft gray seats, and the stewardess had started to show the passengers how to inflate the life vests. Sheela reached out for Leroy's hand the moment she felt the speed of the large DC 3 under her, just tearing down that runway with all the confidence of a mighty eagle.

"Where's the ice, Beauty?" he asked her.

"Safe and sound." She grimaced as she felt the ascending lift into the wind.

"Safe and sound where?" he pressed her.

"It's loose. I didn't want to lose it, so I packed it away."

"We'll attend to that first thing tomorrow."

Sheela wondered how she was going to make Leroy forget about the ring. His eyebrows had knitted so close together when she told him she had packed it that he almost looked about to cry.

In the aisle across from her, Alice had her face pressed against the window, staring out at the clouds as if she were seeing angels nestled in the sweet soft blue of endless sky.

Leroy held Sheela's hand the entire flight, except when he brought out the fifth of Johnnie Walker that they drank straight from tiny cups.

"I saved you from a life of perversion," he said. "You do know that, don't you?"

"What are you talking about, Leroy?" she asked

as the scotch burned her throat and she coughed.

"Your Jack Stanton is a queer." He chuckled. "He collects a lot of little fairy things. Keeps women around just so people will think he's normal."

Sheela stared at him with a pained expression. "How awful," she said.

"Yeah. He's a real three-dollar bill, Beauty."

Sheela giggled. "I meant the scotch. I hate the way it tastes. Burns like hell."

Leroy laughed. "Black Label. Only the best for my little bride."

Queasy from the air in the cabin, with so much pain in her ears, Sheela thought she might die before she ever got to San Francisco. Leroy handed her a piece of gum.

"How old are you, Beauty? Am I really robbing the cradle?"

"Eighteen," she lied. She had turned seventeen two months before her high school graduation and wouldn't be eighteen for another four months.

Leroy leaned back and looked past her at the big old white sky angels floating by like fat, complacent bubbles. Sheela tried to sleep. She found talking difficult because her ears felt full of wet sponges. Leroy kept handing her tiny cups of Johnnie Walker, which numbed her senses enough to make the flight bearable.

They stopped somewhere in Texas and picked up more passengers, but Sheela didn't open her eyes again until she heard the pilot's voice over the loudspeaker talking about the Rocky Mountains. She pressed her nose to the scratchy window and stared out.

Every now and then, she would look over at Alice, who kept looking back at her and pointing to the mountains. The sun fell on them like some radiant mystical gift, and the enormous, jagged splendor of rock and earth beheld the mighty sun as though to cherish the light. It was as if the endless mountains reached up to heaven in a jubilant song of gratitude.

"Quite a sight, eh, Beauty?" Leroy said.

# Chapter Fifteen

The stranger stepped aside in the aisle to let her pass. Leroy was busy reaching for some overhead bag and Sheela was unaware that he was not directly behind her.

"Are you from Chicago?" she asked the stranger without thinking. His shirt was as dark as his suit, and he wore a fedora. He made her think of someplace with cold winters.

"No," he said.

Sheela had just seen a movie with George Raft, and he reminded her of the film. He even looked like George Raft with his dark and wooly clothes.

"I'm from New Jersey." His face softened somewhat.

Sheela mused that he might have been handsome if not for his badly pockmarked skin.

"I'm from Florida," she said over her shoulder. She had to keep turning around to look behind her for Leroy.

The man carefully folded his coat over his arm.

"Excuse me," she said and ducked into an empty

seat to wait up for Leroy and Alice to catch up with her.

The stranger's aftershave tickled her nose as he moved down the aisle. Sheela would remember the scent much later: strong, like Old Spice. She would also remember that his eyes were unusually dark, and he carried a leather bag the color of caramel candy.

Leroy had booked a suite at a large but elegant hotel on Geary Street that wouldn't turn away Negroes. Alice gasped when the taxi pulled up to the rich forest-green awning and the beautifully paneled doors opened to a lobby surrounded by ornate dark woods and enormous chandeliers. Tasteful arrangements of flowers subtly placed on Queen Ann writing tables, and muted oil paintings of demure and anonymous faces, gave silent approval to their most gracious surroundings.

The sight of the man with the pockmarked skin in the hotel lobby surprised Sheela. *He must be staying here as well,* she thought. He had just pressed for the elevator, and she saw him stand back and glance toward her. He nodded casually in her direction. He carried the same caramel-colored bag. Sheela watched him disappear behind the beautiful brass doors while Leroy signed the register.

On her second night in San Francisco, Sheela dreamed that she chased the man with the caramel-colored bag all the way up a hill to an old, haunted house. When she finally caught up with him, she demanded to know what was in the bag.

"Don't worry," he said and snapped it open.

Sheela gasped. Inside the bag was a baby in a pink blanket, clearly a girl. When she turned to thank the man for showing her the baby, he was wearing wire-rimmed glasses and his skin was as smooth as velvet.

"What are you doing?" she asked.

"Holding the moon in my hand," he said. "Care to dance?"

Just as she walked into his arms, she awoke. The dawning sun glowed across the room and landed on Leroy's light green suit and those odd black sandals he wore with white socks. The half-empty bottle of Johnnie Walker caught the morning light and appeared conspicuously peculiar. The odor of Leroy's cigars stuck to her skin, and she longed to shower, but Leroy climbed on top of her and scratched her face with his bristles. Her thoughts returned to the dream as she mechanically stuck her tongue in his ear.

Sheela loved San Francisco. "God," she told Alice. "I wish Jack Stanton owned one of those houses overlooking the bay so we could live here, instead of way up north in Connecticut."

"San Francisco is too far from Florida," Alice said with a huff. "I'd never see my daddy again."

The hilly streets enchanted Sheela, even though walking in the city left her breathless. San Francisco made her think about her mama even more than usual, made her wonder if this pretty city with all the hilly slopes and rocky cliffs on the Pacific was anything at all like Dublin.

Alice must have been too excited to ask why she wasn't wearing the ring, and Leroy was hardly around. He hadn't even brought up getting married or purchasing a guard to keep the ring from slipping. He disappeared for most of the day, and then he'd leave her messages at the hotel and tell her what bar to meet him in later.

The third night in town, they went to the Redwood Bar for drinks before dinner. They were sitting at a comfortable round table. The room, much like the hotel itself, made her feel privileged, with candlelight everywhere and the carpet beneath her feet thickly ingrained with tranquil colors. The sweeping redwood bar was consumed by an array of lively people who appeared to be enjoying the anonymity of momentary tourism.

Leroy was holding her hand with both of his. Sheela wasn't sure why she turned her attention back to the bar, or why she remembered the man on the plane. She didn't think he recognized her, but she spotted him immediately. He was sitting in profile, facing the door. She could see how badly his skin was marked, even from her table. He was wearing the same dark suit he had worn on the plane.

Leroy seemed distracted. He surveyed the bar as if he were looking for someone.

Sheela was about to tell him how much she loved San Francisco when he suddenly jumped out of his seat.

"Excuse me, Beauty. I've got to see a man about a horse."

Sheela watched as he walked the length of the bar and stopped very briefly to speak to the man from the plane. They obviously knew one another but pretended they didn't. The man with the fedora took out a cigarette, and Leroy lit it; just as quickly, he walked away, but not before sliding an envelope into the man's breast pocket. Sheela wondered why they were being so surreptitious.

"Know him?" she asked when Leroy returned to his seat.

Leroy looked around the room. "Know who?"

"The man with the pockmarked skin."

Leroy pulled his lower lip all the way back in his teeth.

"He's my benefactor." He released his lips and said, "Like you."

That evening, Leroy took her to dinner on a houseboat. The room was filled with people who appeared to all know each other.

"This a private party?" she asked.

Leroy nodded. He walked her around and introduced her as his fiancée. "Smile," he whispered under his breath. "Pretend I'm your Prince Charming, Beauty."

"She makes me the happiest man alive," he said into a crowd of men. Leroy practically had tears in his eyes when he said it.

The men slapped him on the back. They stared at Sheela and winked at Leroy, then handed him a cigar.

"You lucky devil," they said.

Sheela felt as if she was in one of her dreams and that she'd wake up any minute. She hardly knew the guy, and there he was, acting like they were sweet on one another. She wanted to tell everyone that Leroy was just a good deal, but she kept her mouth shut.

"I've got an important meeting," Leroy said. "Keep yourself busy." He disappeared for close to an hour with a man he'd introduced as Anthony.

Sheela surveyed the room. She felt more and more out of place. Some of the women attempted to engage her in idle chatter, but mostly, Sheela was bored to death. The remnants of conversations she picked up from the men appeared even more uninteresting.

"Lights out on the moon," she heard one of them say, as they broke out into loud guffaws.

*What's so funny about that?* she wondered.

# Chapter Sixteen

Sheela was sleeping soundly. Leroy got up and found his way to the john in the dark. The cold tiled floor made his feet cramp, so he sat on the bowl and rubbed his toes. The mirror threw back his reflection with stark indifference; he looked bedraggled under the glare of the light, and his eyes drooped pathetically, like some old hound dog about to be shot.

He reached for a small suitcase and counted out the numbers in the tiny combination that released the lock. Inside was a 45-automatic, and some small jars of paint. Small blue and green jars. He undid the lids and moved his finger around the oily substance. Lightly, he painted two blue lines down his left cheek. He lifted the gun and held it up over his head.

"Ohh, ohh, ohh, ohh, ohh, ohh, ohh, ohh," he ululated softly, as he put his other hand over his mouth and slapped it against his lips. He grinned at his reflection.

"Cherokee Chief Leroy.Ohh, ohh, ohh, ohh,

ohh, ohh, ohh, ohh." He continued to slap his lip with his hand.

He put the gun back in the case. "Ain't no one gonna cage this bird, fellows. 'Cause I'm crazy in love, and my big old Indian heart is gonna get pierced so bad that I'm gonna flip my fucking lid, boys." He laughed. He laughed so hard he started to urinate. He turned and pointed his penis toward the bowl. He continued to laugh so hard that his shoulders were jumping up and down and his stomach hurt. Blue paint stained his penis, and that made him laugh harder. He bit his lip to keep himself quiet.

"Cherokee Chief Leroy says fuck you, wop bastard. Can't skin this Indian in the loony bin. Want to come get me there, you oily little rat?"

Those two wop thugs, Anthony and Richie, had been green with envy. The girl was a real looker. She was so pretty it made a man catch his breath.

"Lucky bastard, that Stanton," he said, as he winked at himself in the mirror. "I love her so much," he had told Anthony and Richie. Tears welled up in his eyes, and he told them again, "I love her so much. Never been this happy."

He sat on the bowl and laughed some more. The girl in the bed coughed, and he heard her turn. He washed the paint off his face and found his way back in the dark. He put his arms around the girl and called her his lucky charm.

Sheela freed herself from his embrace and hugged her face to the pillow. Leroy rubbed his scratchy face against her bareback and reached for her hand.

"Shit. Where's the fucking ice, Beauty?"

It was time now, time to take the fucking ring back. Get his refund. He didn't need a fucking prop anymore. The fucking stage was set. He had set it up good. It looked like he really did love her, his pretty little whore, really did want to marry her. *Ha! I'm such a smart fuck.*

The girl rolled over and mumbled something about taking the ring in for a guard.

"Shit," said Leroy. "Shit. I was going to take the fucking ring in for a guard. Shit."

"Had to leave it. Pick it up today, maybe. It needed something," she mumbled.

"Needed something?"

"Yeah."

"Fucking got one over on me, huh? Fucking got one over on me."

"What did you say, Leroy?" The girl opened one eye and stared at him. "You want your ring back? Is that it?"

Leroy sighed so deeply, all the dust in the room traveled right up his nostril, and he sneezed.

"Nah. It's nothing, Beauty. Go back to sleep. Keep the damn thing. Why not, you're saving my ass. Ouch, still, cost me a bundle, this line of bull. Aw, hell, my life is worth it, right, sweetheart?"

Leroy sat on the edge of the bed and put his head in his hands. He sighed deeply.

*Money out the window... out the motherfucking window.*

# Chapter Seventeen

On the fourth day, Kit called Sheela's room. "Get the hell out of San Francisco."

Sheela was surprised at the agitation she heard in Kit's voice, but she teased her anyway.

"Did you get wind of an earthquake?"

Kit ignored the remark and continued. She spoke quickly. "The bastard's check was rubber."

Stunned, she said, "I don't understand."

"I don't know what his game is, but it gets worse."

A cold spot in her stomach bloomed into nausea.

"Bull told me there's a contract out on Leroy. Get out of there. I can't have your blood on my conscience. I made a reservation for you on United Airlines flight 6, one of those skyline planes. It leaves at 9 P.M. tonight. Be on it!"

"Good God, should I warn him?"

"No!" Kit almost screamed it, and Sheela held the phone out from her ear.

"But they'll kill him," she whispered.

"Bull knows I'm getting you out of there," Kit

said. "They'll find you and blow your brains out if you start singing to that fool."

Sheela looked around, as if someone might be listening over her shoulder. "What about Alice?" she asked quickly.

"Listen, kid, I think you're nuts to take that little Negro girl with you all over the country, but she's got a reservation under your name as well. Both of you are going direct to Idlewilde. But if Stanton won't let you keep her, she's not coming back here. I've found someone."

"Are the tickets paid for, Kit?"

"Yeah, a farewell gift. I feel I got you into this. Now get the hell out of there."

"Yeah, right away."

"Good luck, Sheela. Be careful."

Oddly nostalgic, Sheela wanted to run back to the mansion. She had a horrible vision about discovering Leroy lying in a pool of blood and finding herself looking down the barrel of someone's pistol.

"I should never have left the mansion," she said as she started throwing her things into a suitcase.

The man from the plane materialized in her thoughts and just as quickly vanished. She was too confused about Leroy's bad check to wonder if the man on the plane was significant in any way. Perhaps he had been hired to take out Leroy. Her thoughts were muddled as she called Alice's room and told her to pack her bags.

"What? Where we going?"

"No questions now. Answers later. We're leaving

immediately. Don't dilly dally."

Sheela prayed Leroy would not change his schedule and appear back at the hotel before she and Alice had left for the airport. Meeting his eyes wasn't something she wanted to do. Though their flight wasn't scheduled for hours, she needed to get out of the hotel and sit in a place filled with people. She did not tell anyone at the front desk that she was leaving. Luckily, there was too much commotion in the lobby for anyone to notice Sheela and Alice carrying their luggage.

The minute she walked off the elevator, an ambulance at the hotel's side entrance, and someone on a stretcher lifted into it, caught her eye. A crowd of people had gathered, and there was a lot of excitement.

"What's going on?" she asked into the crowd. Her heart sat at the back of her throat.

"A man is dead," someone said.

"What man?" Sheela cried and tugged at his arm. But he shrugged his shoulders and said he didn't know.

"What man? What man is dead?" she cried again as she ran through the crowd.

"Why you so interested in some dead stranger?" Alice asked as she followed behind her.

"Some guy was murdered right in the lobby," a man in a soldier's uniform told them.

"What?" Sheela screeched.

"Yeah," the soldier said. "He was shot while he was sitting right over there reading a magazine.

"Lord have mercy." Alice's eyes were wide as a

three-lane boulevard.

The soldier shook his head a few times back and forth. "No one noticed for a full three minutes."

"Who was he?" Sheela asked, practically holding her breath.

"I don't know. A guy with pockmarks, I heard someone say."

# Chapter Eighteen

Sheela didn't want to wait around until 9 P.M. She managed to exchange the tickets out of San Francisco to an earlier flight.

"What's up?" Alice asked. "Why you acting like you're being chased by hornets?"

She told Alice that Leroy had given Kit a bad check, but she didn't tell her that there was a contract out on Leroy. Sheela was afraid that Alice would want to return to the comfort of the mansion and beg Kit to take her back.

"I'm excited now about flying into New York, aren't you?" Sheela said from the window seat.

"*Hmph.*" Alice closed her eyes and fell off to sleep beside her, snoring softly.

Sheela put her head back on the small white pillow to find sleep as well, but it wouldn't come. She thought about something Leroy had said to her that first night at the hotel while he stood at the open door holding a toothbrush.

"Do you know that death is an aphrodisiac, Beauty?"

Sheela had looked at him and laughed.

"No kidding. Doomed men are sexy. Let's not forget Valentino. That's why I'll never be a sexy man." Then he closed the door, and she heard him swishing the water around his mouth and spitting it out.

Sleep impossible, Sheela's thoughts drifted back and forth between Leroy and the dead man. She couldn't get past seeing the pockmarked man on the plane just four days ago and that he'd smelled like Old Spice.

She sat up, her mouth dry, and her head ached. She pulled the small bottle of scotch out of her bag and poured it into a paper cup.

Alice wished she liked the taste of liquor, but beer was the only alcoholic beverage she could get down her throat without feeling that awful burn. She'd managed to sleep for an hour, but her heart was ticking overtime, like a hummingbird spotting a clematis vine inside her chest. She wondered what her father must be thinking. She had sent him all kinds of postcards from San Francisco, not to mention most of the money Sheela had given her. Now she was going to be settled somewhere in the state of Connecticut. She hoped he was proud of her, flying all over the country with the white girl she had written him about. She couldn't wait to write to him again, just so she could tell him proudly that she was almost completely unafraid of being up in the clouds; no, not hardly afraid at all anymore. She had spent some of the money on a beautiful suit almost the color of the sky, and doused her ears with French cologne and painted her nails the color of fresh raspberries. She surely was becoming sophisticated. Her daddy might not even recognize her.

Every now and then, she'd lift her eyes and stare at those creamy, white mashed potato clouds floating by, and something near delirium would make her feel as giddy, as if she'd drunk all of Sheela's whiskey.

After a thirty-minute stopover in Atlanta, Manhattan ultimately appeared like the crescendo at the end of a quiet symphony. Alice struggled to see past Sheela and capture what lay below the tip of the wing.

Sheela pressed her face to the glass, captivated by something both intensely alienating and yet magnificently exciting. The spiraling city seemed to reach up and offer the cold indifference of its brilliance to anyone brave enough to challenge the mighty force of its magic.

Sheela held onto Alice's hand all through the airport. She didn't know if her vertiginous excitement was a result of a pace that upset her natural state of gravity or if the scotch had teased her sense of balance. Luckily, when she called Stanton, he was at the Connecticut estate.

"I'll send a car service to pick you up," he said. He sounded delighted to hear from her. "I've been anxiously awaiting your call, dear," he added.

Once the long sleek car arrived, Sheela stretched herself out in the back seat and relaxed into a comforting distraction of anonymous road signs. The first snow of winter lay on the ground, seeming to dance about the land like the dead set free. Sheela took Alice's hand again.

"Look! Snow."

Alice peered out the car window. "Lord have mercy. Beer foam all over."

Jack Stanton was waiting when the car drove up. His estate appeared like a welcome source of stability. If he was surprised to see Alice, he didn't show it.

"Alice tends to me, Uncle Jack," she said simply.

"Good. Every lady should be tended to."

Jack had his butler show Alice to a cottage next to the house, then he took Sheela upstairs.

"This will be your room, dear."

Sheela was surprised to have a room to herself but also relieved. The room, a large perfect square, had windows as tall as doors. Rich yellow silk draped luxuriously over the glass. The walls were a very pale green. An immensely carved armoire stood in a corner. A delicate striped white-and-blue chair lay in wait near a dark wooden desk with a top that curved around at the edges and made her want to follow it around with her fingers.

The four-poster bed was a high climb to a sumptuous rich comforter with a design of green and yellow vines. The wood burning in the large stone fireplace was a new scent, as new as the taste of cold air.

Jack watched as Sheela looked around the room. She finally turned to him with a wide-eyed grin.

"It's the most beautiful room I've ever seen," she said.

There were no fat smiling cherubs on the wall, nor any long floral chaises, but the room was so enchanting, she wanted to put her name above the door and stay forever.

"You haven't seen anything yet," he told her. "I'll show you the entire house as soon as you've had some time to relax."

Sheela lay down on the high four-poster bed underneath its soft lace and full pillows. She pulled up the comforter and hugged it around her, enjoying the warmth of the fire from the other side of the room and the smell of the wood as it burned, but the chill in the air remained, and she shivered. She had never felt this type of cold, not even in San Francisco when the wind came from behind and tried to trip her. Like some brutal force of nature, the Connecticut winds carried an ominous threat and shook her senses clear, demanding its presence be felt as effectually as the slap of birth.

She slept nearly twelve hours, and when she awoke, the sunlight seemed incredulous after the cold bleak sky of the prior day. The icy wind that had hurled itself so unmercifully about the earth was now still. The morning brought a white ground, redeemed by a gentle sun. Sheela went to the tall windows and looked out. As far as the eye could see, land lay covered in a complexity of forms more synonymous with the hand of an artist than with the breath of nature. *It's so beautiful*, she thought. The sun warmed her skin while the ice outside dripped

into a pool of water, and the air inside her chest
blew out into the room like smoke.

# Chapter Nineteen

Two days after Sheela arrived in Connecticut, Dakota called her.

"Leroy flipped his lid. He showed up at Kit's with a .45 automatic."

"What?" Sheela quickly sat down.

"He shot Bull in the leg and then went running up the stairs looking for you."

"Why was he looking for me?"

"Said you double-crossed him."

"I double-crossed *him*? He gave Kit a rubber check."

Sheela felt as if she were spinning like one of those wooden tops her little brother used to play with.

Dakota continued. "Leroy shaved off all his hair. He came over here dressed like an Indian. He looked ridiculous. When he didn't find you here, he started telling everyone that he was going up to Connecticut to take you away from Stanton."

"Jesus."

"You sure are lucky you weren't here when he

showed up with that gun."

"I'll say. How did he know where I was?"

"He knew you'd taken Stanton's deal. Christ, who wouldn't? When the cops picked him up on the New England thruway, the only place he had hair was running across the center of his head, and he was naked from the waist up. I hear it's freezing up there."

"It's pretty cold."

"He got out of his car when the cops stopped him for speeding and started running down the highway waving a gun."

"Did they shoot him?"

"No, they locked him up in the loony bin. He had war paint on his face. He flipped. He kept saying you broke his heart. Love sure is cruel." She chuckled.

"Jesus."

Dakota paused. "Look, I told you Leroy was in deep with the Mafia."

Sheela's heart raced forward, reminding her of someone she didn't want to see standing behind her.

Dakota went on. "Your Leroy St. James was in a mess with some crime bosses. Anthony Rizzo had some police chief in Chicago killed, and the FBI went on a real vendetta. Bull told us Leroy was working with them."

"He was working with Anthony Rizzo, that guy I met in San Francisco?"

"No, the FBI. He was informing for *them*."

"Why would Leroy help the FBI?"

"Your Leroy was facing time in a penitentiary for falsifying evidence in extortion charges against some Mafia boss. Apparently, he worked a deal."

Sheela breathed in the cold morning air. She leaned back into the soft protection of the wing chair that stood by the window of her room. Somehow the whole stupid mess was starting to make sense.

"The bastard is pretty slick," Dakota whispered, and Sheela heard the admiration quiver in Dakota's breath. "Pretty slick. You following me? I think he was playing both sides. Now he's running from a contract. Well, who can get to him in a loony bin? Pretty damn slick. You watch that snake slink right out of this country."

"I've got to go," Sheela said.

She almost felt the lashes around Leroy's pretty eyes tickle her skin. She brushed her hands over the spot and felt the lashes lie against her fingers like the legs of a fly, one too distracted to flee the very hand that could crush it before it was altogether forgotten and serendipitously freed from danger.

# Chapter Twenty

Jack referred to the house as his "tiny chateau," though it was a large old farmhouse that dated back to the early 1800s. The house had four bedrooms upstairs and a library, parlor, dining room and large kitchen downstairs. Not far from the house were several small cottages for the servants and hired help. Jack told Sheela that he had owned the property for twenty years and attracted to the challenges of restoration.

"This table predates the house," he said as he led her through the rooms. "You'll notice that the legs are mahogany, and the top is Italian marble. It's eighteenth century. These rather large imposing chairs are English wing chairs, also from the eighteenth century. The couch is a marvelous reproduction of an Empire settee."

"The couch doesn't look very comfortable, Jack. Is it?"

"Well, no, dear, but it's not about comfort, you see?"

Sheela nodded, even though she considered

couches to be about comfort.

"Have you seen where my rose bushes are planted?" he asked her suddenly.

Sheela shook her head and followed Jack to a window in the foyer. He drew back on the richly entwined velvet pull. As he stood there grinning at her, she noticed that there were moments when he appeared handsome, like some small, delicate prince in one of his paintings. Perhaps, the one of Napoleon on a horse, the large oil that graced the dining room wall and made her feel like skipping dinner.

"They will come to fruition there." He pointed to the long stone walk that curved out toward the front gate. "And they will follow the drive all the way to the road. I cannot wait until June just to see my roses."

He pulled on the drape and enclosed the room again in dim light.

"Come, Sheela."

He took her hand and led her out of the foyer and into the parlor.

"I prefer romantic art," he told her as he squeezed several of her fingers and continued to show her about the house. "Look. Look at my Degas," he said breathlessly as he brought her to a lovely canvas of dancing ballerinas practicing for a recital. "How does the painting make you feel, dear?"

Sheela walked up close to the painting and stared into the eyes of the spinning girls.

"No." He grabbed her hand and held her back.

"Look at art from the appropriate distance and do not stare or search. Just look and let yourself experience what's on the canvas."

They sat before the painting and he held her hand in his.

"Well, my dear?"

"Oh, I feel the girls would rather be somewhere else. They don't seem to be enjoying what they're doing."

Jack laughed. "What am I to do with you? You cannot sing, and you appear to have no eye for the aesthetic."

He brought her to another painting of a woman with reddish hair piled high on top of her head. She stared out from the canvas as if she were laughing at those who so studiously stared back at her. Jack had showcased the painting by putting it in the middle of his parlor so it could also be seen from the front hall.

"My Renoir," he told her proudly.

Sheela smiled. "She looks lost. Perhaps a little embarrassed because she can't find her way to the powder room and she needs lipstick."

Jack threw back his head and filled the room with a high-pitched laugh.

"You appreciate the humor. Good. But what do you *feel* when you look at the encapsulated vision of this man's interpretation of what he sees?"

Sheela wondered what it was that Jack wanted her to say.

"Sad. I feel a great sadness."

"Aha!" said Jack. "A great sadness?"

"Yes, Uncle Jack. She doesn't belong to herself anymore. She belongs entirely to the artist. She's just an object. And now she belongs to you. But she's gone from the earth. No longer real."

"No, not gone. Captured in canvas. Eternal."

"Don't you feel sorry for her, Uncle Jack? I mean, one man's interpretation is not who she really was, or ever was, for that matter. Now she only exists in art as he saw her."

"What has greater value, dear? Art or life?"

"Life, Uncle Jack."

She stared at his small frame. He touched his dark blue silk ascot and rolled his eyes to the ceiling. He appeared more effeminate than she had remembered him.

"Really? I will consider that the next time I spend so much money on my tiny treasures. Come."

He grabbed her hand again and quickly took her into the second library. Someone had built a fire in the large brick fireplace, but the room did not reflect Jack Stanton. Over the mantle was a landscape painting.

"Durand," he told her, "a much-admired American painter."

The room was a great deal less floral and lacy than the rest of the house and there was an odd smell in the room... an oily smell, as if just painted, but clearly the walls were a faded beige and had not been touched in years. An old brown globe stood between the desk and the window. Sheela went to the globe and spun it around, glancing at a case full of guns on the far wall and small objects scattered about that he did not give her time to examine. Stanton looked around uncomfortably. She wanted to ask him what the oily smell was, but he was in a hurry to leave.

"I call this my "male room.""

"Mail room?" she asked.

"Well, it is more masculine than the rest of the house. Don't you think?"

"Oh, male? Well, yes, I guess."

"One of my sons loved it. So I... Ah! It doesn't matter. Come."

Sheela heard something creak, and when she turned to follow the noise, Jack had opened what might have been a closet.

"You see? An old secret passage. Come, come, Sheela. I want to show you my treasures. Let's not waste time here."

Behind the door was a staircase that went right up to Jack's bedroom, a room she had not yet been in. After he had settled her in that first afternoon, she had not seen him again for close to three days. The servants reluctantly brought food to Alice's cottage, and Sheela took most of her meals there. She'd spent her time with Alice, the two of them giggling over the possibility that Jack might never return. But out of nowhere, Jack appeared before her and announced that he wanted to give her a tour of the house.

Jack's bedroom was a shocking transition from the "male room." A large bed took up most of the space, covered in white satin and surrounded by lace pillows. A faint blush-colored fireplace curved out into the room. Beautiful red oriental cabinets stood against the wall, and a rather obese bronze Buddha sat in the corner of the room with the aromatic scent of incense burning from a bowl beneath his belly.

"Come here, Sheela," he said with a strange smile, that bordered on lascivious.

Sheela stumbled over the pale blue carpet and peered over Jack's shoulder. He held up an elaborate hand-painted egg.

"Magnificent," he said passionately. "My Limoges porcelain eggs."

"Limoges porcelain eggs?"

Jack laughed. "Fabergé, my dear. A limited collection."

"Oh."

Sheela stared into the misty dark eyes that traveled over the complex and delicate object, as if it had come from his womb. She reached out and touched Jack's hand.

"Exquisite, Uncle Jack," she whispered. Her eyes crinkled, and she forced back the giggle that tickled her belly. *He is the silliest man I have ever known.*

"It makes me feel so fragile, so delicate, so transitory," she said.

"Yes," whispered Jack Stanton. "Yes! Now you've got it, Sheela."

# Chapter Twenty-One

The second bedroom upstairs in Jack Stanton's "tiny chateau" belonged to Sharon Marin. Sheela did not see Sharon until she'd been at the chateau for close to two weeks. Sheela noticed that the door to Sharon's room was always closed, but she heard scratchy music from a phonograph player from behind the closed door.

Sheela sat before the vanity table in Stanton's bedroom while Jack played with her hair. Sharon suddenly passed by.

"Sharon!" Jack gleefully called out. "Come look at this exquisite child I have found among the reptiles."

It surprised Sheela that another of Jack's human treasures inhabited the mysterious room with the closed door and soft music. She'd imagined that Sharon was a guest, perhaps even a relative.

"Who are you?" Sheela asked.

The girl smiled and held out her hand. "Sharon Marin. I live across the hall from you."

"Oh." Sheela stared at her. "How long have you

been here?"

Jack chuckled. "Sharon came to me when she was nineteen years old." He winked at Sharon. "I believe she's turning thirty next month."

"Really?" Sheela, confused, wondered if too many nights with Sharon had made him too tired for her. He had not come to her bed even once. She felt relieved that Jack had someone else to amuse him.

Jack held Sheela by the chin as he stood behind her. "Look at these cheekbones." He ran his fingers over her face as he tilted it back. "Look, look at the eyes. Night-sky-blue, I'm going to call them."

Sharon gazed at Sheela's reflection in the glass mirror.

"Pretty." She smiled.

Sheela stared back at one of the loveliest faces she had ever seen. Sharon was wearing a sweater the color of wheat, and wide pants hung from her tiny waist and touched her ankles. Her hair was the color of cherries, and her skin was so flawless it appeared like milk, with just a gentle blush across the surface. Her eyes were nearly as green as a priceless emerald. Silver bracelets dangled from her wrist and made a jingling noise as she reached out to touch Sheela's hair.

"Very pretty," she repeated.

Jack was filled with excitement.

"I have booked a room at the Waldorf, and we are going shopping this weekend. Lord & Taylor, Bonwits, Saks. Let's have Christmas. The child needs a proper wardrobe, don't you think?"

Sharon looked at the glass reflection of Sheela and winked.

"You're in for a treat," she whispered and left the room as quietly as she had entered it.

Jack commuted to New York City daily and did not necessarily return in the evenings. He never informed Sheela of his schedule. He just appeared before her and announced his presence. Sometimes he'd ask her to join him for dinner, and then disappear again, and she would not see him for days. She assumed that being a millionaire kept Jack on his toes.

The upcoming trip to New York City had been another of Jack's sudden surprises. Since Sheela had arrived, Jack had avoided sleeping with her, making Sheela feel more like an adopted child than a new mistress. She wondered if she had failed to do something that a mistress was supposed to do to get a man's attention. She was curious that Sharon left the house on weekends in a small sports car and usually did not return until Sunday evening. Sharon inhabited the house like an older daughter with her own private itinerary and a father who seemed only moderately interested in her whereabouts.

Everyone in the house took meals in their rooms, and Jack only joined Sheela for dinner if they went out to a local restaurant. If Sheela had not seen Sharon that afternoon in Stanton's doorway, she might not have discovered her presence for months.

Sheela spent most of her time in Alice's cottage. They found some old warm clothes in the closet and explored Stanton's estate sloshing through the snow in large rubber boots.

"Seems I got to walk a damn mile to get anything to eat around here," Alice said, as she wrapped a wool scarf so tightly around her face that only her eyes were visible.

"He's taking me into Manhattan for a shopping spree," Sheela said, ignoring the sad fact that the servants often refused to take food out to the guest cottages and Alice had to walk to the chateau's kitchen for food three times a day.

"Shoot, girl, I'd love to go into Manhattan. Think I can come?"

"Not this trip. But we'll go together soon. We'll stay at a fancy hotel and go to all the night-clubs."

Alice picked up a ball of cold white snow and tossed it at Sheela.

"Living here is not like living at the mansion," she said teasingly. "He's got so many damn servants that I can't even tend to you."

"Ever see that girl?" Sheela asked her.

"What girl?"

"She's got sort of red hair, and she's real pretty."

"Nope. You the only person seems I ever see up close, except Dominick, his driver, and Laurette. You know Laurette?"

Sheela shook her head. "No."

"She bakes all that fine pastry. She's from France. I learned to say *bonjour.*"

Sheela felt guilty for making Alice leave the

mansion and follow her east. She felt the same reckless boredom being cooped up in Stanton's house, and she wondered if she'd ever get a chance to ask Sharon to take her somewhere.

"Bonjour?"

Alice giggled. "Yep, bonjour!"

"I'm going nuts in that house. You know, he's never even knocked on my bedroom door, not that I want him to."

Alice laughed and threw more snow at Sheela. "You pulling my leg, ain't you, girl?"

Sheela giggled. "I think he's queer, just like Leroy said."

Alice giggled with her and fell in the soft white snow.

"Queer? Queer? Oh, no. You crazy girl. Ain't no queer millionaires."

Together they sat in the cold dry powder while the sun made them feel toasty, as if they sat before a fire.

"We're going to Manhattan, Alice. We'll find ourselves some men. Some tall, dark and handsome men."

"Mmm. Mmm. Mmm." Alice tossed some snow up in the air. "Sounds good to me."

Talking about tall, dark, and handsome men, Sheela had a sudden image of Leroy St. James and his wide, broad shoulders. She remembered the dream she'd had right after falling asleep in the library the first week she'd arrived at Stanton's.

"Want to hear my dream?" Sheela asked.

Alice shook her head. "Nope."

"It was about Leroy St. James."

"Now I know I don't want to hear it."

"He kept trying to speak to me, but I couldn't understand a word he said. I put my ear close to his mouth, but it was still gibberish."

Alice put her hands over her ears and turned her head in the opposite direction.

"I just turned and walked away. I wasn't going to stand there and listen to a man speaking gibberish. But he screamed at me."

"I ain't listening to a word you're sayin', Sheela."

Sheela pulled Alice's hands down to her side.

"I knew he was screaming even though I couldn't really hear him."

"Shoot, that don't make no sense at all."

"Dreams never do."

"So why bother repeating them?"

Sheela ignored her and continued. "His screams were muffled, as though coming from inside a seashell. I wondered if I were crazy, wondered if I were the one doing the screaming." Sheela walked close to Alice and looked right into her eyes. "I was frightened, so I started running away, but Leroy only screamed louder. When I looked behind me to tell him to shut up, I saw my father standing in front of me. He had blood in his eyes and an old, cracked crucifix in his hand."

Alice tossed a snowball at Sheela. "That's the dumbest dream I ever heard. Shoot, girl, you need to get out more."

# Chapter Twenty-Two

Sheela was nothing short of elated when the long sleek Cadillac turned off the West Side highway and took to the streets, streets that had only moments before stood off at a safe distance. The traffic was a loud confrontation of honks and motor engines. People hurried about as if with great purpose about arriving at a destination. It was a city preoccupied with its own tension.

Stanton couldn't wait to show Sheela Tiffany's. After buying several trinkets there, they made their way to Saks.

"Put these in the dressing room," Jack said as he handed a stack of dresses and coats to a salesgirl.

Sheela gasped. "They're beautiful."

"Try them all on, dear," Jack said as he sat in a chair quickly brought over by a gregarious sales manager.

The salesgirls brought him ashtrays for his cigar and paraded Sheela in front of him with ebullient flattery. Jack stared in admiration while Sheela modeled evening dresses and coats with fur sleeves and collars. He smiled at Sheela like a proud father.

"What a beautiful girl," they told him.

"A rare, rare beauty." He beamed. "Wrap it all up and bring me my bill."

After their shopping spree, Jack took her to lunch at the Twenty-One Club.

"I have a very special gift for you, Sheela," he said. "I had it brought to my room, and I'll surprise you with it this evening."

"Can't wait, Uncle Jack."

"This will be a special celebration for us," he said.

"What are we celebrating, Uncle Jack?"

"Life, dear."

"Everyone looks like a celebrity here. I love Manhattan," she said with an excited squeeze of Jack's hand.

Jack smiled. "Yes, it's a magical city."

"It's exciting, Jack. I want to live here."

"I'll be your little genie in a bottle then." He leaned in close to her. "And satisfy your every whim. I'll get you an apartment here."

Sheela looked at him curiously.

"And so, you will satisfy mine?"

"Your what, Uncle Jack?"

"My whims, dear." He smiled slyly.

They had separate rooms, adjoining but separate. He had told her to wear the new lavender dress with the square low-cut front and to come to his suite at eight P.M. sharp.

There appeared to be no one there when she

entered. He had on a radio that he insisted the hotel provide. Sheela heard a female voice singing a soft ballad. She walked to the window and looked out. The city below had a pulse, and it thrilled her to be so close to it. She heard water running, and Stanton called out to her.

"Dear, is that you? Come here to your Uncle Jack."

Sheela felt an anxious tug at her chest. The bathroom door was ajar, and she felt the steamy heat of a hot bath. She made a nasty face in the direction of Jack's voice; she had not expected her first sexual encounter with Jack Stanton to take place in a bathroom and wondered if there was a way out of it.

When she walked through the door, she found him in the tub surrounded by pink and white bubbles. He wore a large grin and had one leg stretched straight up in the air.

"Did I miss any hair?" he asked her.

Sheela walked carefully around to the front of the tub and stared at the back of Jack Stanton's leg. Tiny soap bubbles had found a home on the flat part of his foot. His face peered at her in earnest anticipation. Her stomach bounced, and she commanded control of her reflex to laugh.

"Right behind your knee," she said helpfully.

"Ah. Damn hard place behind the knee. Do you find that, too?" Jack slid his razor behind his leg and carefully shaved the hair. "I've left my robe in the other room. Will you get it for me, dear? It's in the top drawer. The purple one."

Sheela left the bathroom quickly and caught her smile in the glass above the dresser. She allowed her stomach to bounce up and down quietly, and she held her hand up over her mouth before she lost complete control and let out a loud howl. Jack had several pairs of neatly folded silk pajamas in his top drawer and a purple silk robe. When she brought the robe to him, he was standing behind a towel.

"Thank you, dear. I'll be out in a bit," he said and motioned her out with his hand.

Sheela settled into the chair by the window and listened to a smoky female voice singing about her broken heart. Tears fell from the corners of Sheela's eyes as she giggled quietly. From the bathroom, she heard Stanton's booming alto voice as he sang along with the music.

Sheela put her head back, squashing the urge to laugh; unable to stop her impulse to let loose, she reached for a cigarette. She dragged deeply and kept her eyes on the bathroom door. By the time Stanton appeared with the towel around his head and his purple robe tied in front of him, she had willed herself serious.

Stanton was wearing lavender mule slippers with two-inch heels and soft, round puffy bows. Sheela quickly dragged on her cigarette as she watched Jack walk around the room as though there was nothing unusual about his appearance.

Sheela bit down on the filter and prayed for composure. She tried not to watch Stanton as he engaged her in idle conversation, his unmistakably feminine robe flowing around his ankles.

Stanton went to the closet and carefully laid a dark suit across the bed.

"Should I wear a bow tie tonight?" he asked.

Sheela smiled broadly. "Oh, yes. I love bow ties."

"Really?"

Sheela blew the smoke in front of her.

"Tonight, we are going to the Copacabana," he said.

"The Copacabana?"

"I knew you'd like that."

Sheela watched as Stanton walked back over to the closet and bit on the tip of his tongue. He had no difficulty walking in the slippers, and they made an amusing click-clack noise as he moved.

"I am going to give you your surprise now. I want you to wear it tonight. Close your eyes."

Sheela left the cigarette in the ashtray and leaned her head back. She listened to Stanton moving around the room and the *click-clap-slap* of the heel of his feet as they hit the open slippers. She tightened her jaw to keep her giggles from exploding. Finally, he settled in front of her.

"All right, dear. Open!"

He was much too small for the black sable coat, and it covered him like a blanket, despite the two-inch heels.

"Oh, Uncle Jack," she cried. "Is it mine?"

"Yours," he said as he slipped out of the luscious fur and put it around her.

Sheela put her arms through the silky sleeves and walked around the room, twirling in front of every mirror she passed and hugging the warm dark coat as close to her skin as she could get it.

Stanton stood in the center of the room in his two-inch white slippers with the round puffy bows.

"It is the most magnificent coat I've ever seen," she said, throwing herself onto the bed.

Jack held his arms across his chest, his right leg pointed slightly toward the wall; the weight on his left leg pushed his hip up; his robe hung open from the waist.

It was only after she sat up at the foot of the bed that she realized Jack Stanton was wearing an old pair of her panties.

A knock at the door surprised Sheela just when she expected she and Jack would be leaving.

"Oh, that must be Margo," he said excitedly.

By this time, Jack had dressed in his dark gray suit and blue bow tie. His thin brown hair combed straight back, his skin appeared to glow. Sheela knew he had not removed her panties, and she smiled to herself, wondering how he would manage in the men's room.

"Who's Margo?" she asked him, but he had already run to the door and opened it.

A woman stood in the doorway, so glamorous that Sheela immediately assumed she was a showgirl. Jack embraced her as if she were an old friend. Margo handed him a gift-wrapped box as she entered the room.

"For you, Jack."

Margo let the mink she was wearing fall from her shoulders. Jack reached out and caught it before it hit the floor. Margo smiled at Sheela and extended her hand. Sheela was surprised to realize that Margo was Kit's age.

"Margo Sweeny." She looked into Sheela's eyes. "You outdid yourself this time, Jack. She's gorgeous. Love that jet-black hair."

Jack laughed and tore the colorful paper from the box. He held up a lovely white silk sleeping gown with narrow tiny straps.

"Oh, my dear," Jack exhaled a full minute as he held the gown to his face. "Oh, my dear. It's spectacular."

He kissed Margo and gave her a long hug. As he gently laid the gown across his pillow, Sheela glimpsed that it was not new and had undoubtedly been worn before.

# Chapter Twenty-Three

"Jack and I go back a long way. At least twenty years," Margo said as they sat on either side of Jack Stanton at the Copa.

Both women had a hand on Jack's arm, and Stanton flirted with each respectively. Men from other tables shot admiring glances at Stanton, and he basked in their envious glances, coveting their fantasies with all the respect of a confession priest. *Oh, what money can buy.* He smiled to himself.

"I met Jack when I was working for Ziegfield. Jack was a stage-door Johnny."

Jack told Sheela that he used to send flowers backstage, but it had taken him three full months to get her attention.

"You could be a showgirl." Margo looked at Sheela carefully. "Billy Rose would love you."

Sheela smiled appreciatively. "What do you think, Uncle Jack? Should I go work for Billy Rose?"

"Ha! Better not let him hear you sing." Jack roared with laughter.

Margo winked at Sheela and shook her head. "Don't listen to him. If you swim, you're in. You could join his Aquacade."

Sheela looked at the girls on the stage of the Copa with a certain amount of envy. She tried to imagine living on her own in New York City, working in some fancy nightclub. She wondered what Margo Sweeny did for a living now that she was well past forty.

In the ladies' lounge, Margo leaned over and asked her how she liked living with Stanton. Sheela brushed some color on her lips and wondered just how much she should reveal.

"It's fine. But … I probably shouldn't tell you but, well, we've never ah, you know?"

"Made it together?" Margo raised one eyebrow.

Sheela nodded slowly.

"Oh, he won't bother you very often. He's not that much into sex. Personally, I think he's a fairy."

Sheela laughed. "Then why does he like woman's underwear?"

"Maybe he feels that if he smells like a woman, he'll attract men. Who knows? You know men, they can be very strange."

"Do you think eventually he'll want to ah...?"

"Make it with you?" Margo shrugged her shoulders. "Well, yeah, I guess he's 'bi,' but let me tell you a little secret; you won't feel a thing."

"What do you mean?"

"Well, he's a real lady."

Sheela was confused. "A lady?"

Margo held up her pinkie finger.

"He could almost be. Don't think he really gets aroused with a woman. Ah, never mind. You'll understand soon enough."

Sheela looked at Margo's smile in the mirror. She liked Margo and hoped there would be some way of seeing her again when the evening was over. As if Margo read her thoughts, she reached into her purse and wrote her phone number on the inside of a pack of matches.

"Call me," she said. "My girls do well."

"You mean, you're a...?"

"Madam? Well, yeah, of course."

Sheela thanked her and took the number.

"I won't need a connection unless he throws me out. I'm not even working for the money."

Margo laughed loudly at that. "Yes, you are. Don't kid yourself."

Sheela didn't think that taking money from a man without having to give up anything for it was work, but she didn't probe Margo about what she'd meant. Sheela knew Jack would expect something from her eventually; she just didn't know what it would be, and it made her uneasy that it could be something strange and bizarre.

"Do you know about the other girl who lives with us?" Sheela asked quickly. She thought perhaps Stanton was just waiting to get her involved in a threesome.

"Sharon?"

Sheela nodded, and Margo leaned into her ear.

"Sharon Marin is a collectible, just as I was twenty years ago, just as you are now. Only difference is, she's in his will. She must be doing something right."

"Oh," Sheela said softly. "Will he want me to ah...?"

Margo laughed again. "Sleep with her? No way! If you were a man, well then, maybe."

"Sharon just lives there doing nothing?"

"Oh, don't think Sharon doesn't work for Stanton. She earns every buck he gives her. My bet is that she's got a boyfriend he's hot for. You'll find out soon enough."

Sheela looked at her quizzically.

"If you don't figure out what he wants from you, he'll get rid of you. It's not complicated, just kinky. He'd rather wear your underwear than get in them. Understand?"

Margo winked at her, and Sheela felt that some diabolical shift in the universe had just revealed the secrets of easy money.

# Chapter Twenty-Four

He'd been in Creedmoor sixty days, insisting that he was Chief Cherokee Lightfoot. He sat in the corner of his room all day with his legs and arms crossed. Sometimes he closed his eyes, and sometimes he darted them about. When they forced him into the recreation room, he jumped up and moved swiftly, keeping his eyes in an unblinking stare.

"Mr. St. James—" the doctors would implore.

"White man! White man!"

"Mr. St. James, please try and listen to me—"

"Ahhh! Me hate white man. White man enemy. Ahhhhh!"

They had him sedated. But he was able to hide the pills under his tongue and flush them down the toilet later.

"Stupid bastards," he said as he laid his head on the pillow. He thought about his cabin in Ellenville and all the money he'd paid that bastard, Bergman, to get him a phony passport.

*The bastard wanted the cabin, too.* He smiled to

himself. *Crafty little Jewish bastard.* He looked around the small white room. "A lousy metal bed and a frigging kitchen chair," he whispered and shot his middle finger into the air.

He thought about sneaking out the gate and jumping into Bergman's car. He'd be out of the country in just two weeks. They had planned it quietly on the phone. His new name would be Robert Lopez. "Had to make me a spic?" he had complained to Bergman. "Couldn't make me a fucking American?"

He thought about that pretty kid, pretty Sheela, sucking on him good. He tried pulling on himself, but the goddamn smell of the room kept him soft, damn room smelled like damp diapers and old musty closets.

"Fucking loony bin," he whispered. "How long till I get a piece of ass?" He pulled on himself again.

"Turn out the fucking lights," he screamed. "Indian want squaw!" He tore off his pajamas until he was naked.

"Me want Indian Pussy!"

He shut his eyes tight and brought up an image in his mind. Yeah, some big-breasted round woman straddling his waist with thick Indian black braids that tickled his nipples.

"Ah, yeah."

Finally, he felt the nice large growth under his hand.

"Well, ain't you cute, Indian?" some voice from behind the mesh at his window called out in a hoarse whisper.

"What the fuck?"

Leroy didn't stop pulling on himself. He was too close. Too close to getting it on. He squinted through the wire and saw the outline of a face. He stood back.

"Who the fuck are you?" he asked, yanking on his penis until he almost felt a woman's squeeze around him. "Ahhh. Go away, you fuck," he moaned.

"Nice going, Indian," the voice cackled.

"Ahhh. Ahhh. Get the fuck away, you crazy fuck." Leroy moaned again, about to let go. His eyes were closing and opening on the window.

*Let the crazy fuck watch me.* "You want some?" he whispered. "Come on in here, you crazy fuck. You can finish me."

Leroy's eyes were half-open on the mesh. Something pointed at him, something as long and hard as what was going off in his hand.

"What the—?"

The force of the bullet knocked him to the floor. His head snapped back against the door, and his eyes stayed open.

Death had swallowed him so ferociously that his last thought remained transfixed in the second of his passing, transcended in the air, unfinished and unuttered.

# Chapter Twenty-Five

Sheela had only slept with Jack Stanton three times in five years. Each encounter was around a significant occurrence. The first time was right after their trip to New York City, right after he had surprised her with the black sable.

"Sounds like the phone is ringing off the hook, Uncle Jack," Sheela said, watching one of the servants' rush to answer it.

"A Kit Malone, sir."

Jack exchanged a look with Sheela. "Thank you, Edward, I'll take the call."

It was not unusual for Kit to call Jack in Connecticut, so Sheela took to the stairs. She turned when she heard Jack call her name.

"Yes, Uncle Jack?"

"Leroy St. James has been murdered," he said quietly.

Sheela slunk back down the stairs and fell onto the couch. She watched as Jack continued his conversation with Kit. Surprisingly, the news had not come as a complete surprise.

"Did you know that Leroy St. James worked for the Mafia, dear?" Stanton asked. After hanging up the phone he sat beside her.

"No," she lied.

"Well, he did, and according to Kit, they got him," Stanton said. "Too bad. Such a young man, very brilliant. Horrible taste in clothes, though. Just ghastly."

Sheela felt a dark foreboding, a sadness, as if Leroy's ghost were trapped somewhere in the shadows of the earth and he hadn't even had enough time to know he was dead. She thought about the diamond he had given her and wished she still had it, just because it suddenly felt terribly inappropriate not to have it.

"What will they do with all his alligator ties?" She looked at Stanton and tried to smile.

"An odd chap, wasn't he?" Stanton took her hand.

Sheela stared at Stanton for a long time.

"Yes. An odd chap," she whispered.

Margo Sweeny had been right about Stanton. Sheela didn't feel a thing when she suddenly found him on top of her. It was the same evening she'd heard about Leroy's murder.

"Jack?" She was startled to see him, lying quietly between the sheets when she came out of her bathroom.

He took a puff of one of those fat cigars she hated and returned it to the ashtray on the bedside table. He was naked when he pulled back the sheet and patted the space beside him.

He didn't kiss her... just seemed to leap on top of her. He puffed out wisps of air and smiled benevolently down into her eyes, as if she were a private, pleasurable fantasy underneath him that he sanctioned like a prayer and willfully paid homage to.

"Oh, Jack," she whispered, knowing she was expected to react as if it mattered.

A short feminine moan escaped from his lips and she assumed he'd ejaculated though she hadn't even thought he was hard. Sheela stared at the ceiling and waited for him to finish whatever it was he was doing.

He jumped from her body and ran to his private bathroom, where Sheela was sure he was soaking his testicles in a tub of warm soapy water, with a fragrance of lavender bubbles.

# Chapter Twenty-Six

Leda moved out of her aunt's motel the summer following her graduation from high school. She found herself an apartment over on Edgewater Drive, as far away from the Sea Spray Inn as she could get. Sheela sent her close to fifty dollars a week, and that money sure came in handy when Susannah Miller asked her to share a place near St. Joseph's Sound. She didn't tell her aunt about the money from Sheela, but she told Susannah her sister was living with some millionaire up north, and soon enough, the whole town seemed to know that Sheela was just about as high on the hog as anyone could get. She didn't exactly tell Susannah Miller in confidence, but she didn't expect that people from one end of Clearwater to the other would start questioning her so much about Sheela.

"Why I hear that pretty sister of yours has gone and caught herself a millionaire," they said to her.

"Well, you know Sheela," she had answered them. "Taste so fine that only a fancy man can afford it."

Then one fine morning, Calvin Woods chased after her on her way to her new job over at Woolworth & Co. He ran just as fast as he could to get in step with her. When he tapped her on the shoulder, Leda turned to find him looking sadder than that little Cocker Spaniel that sat in front of the barbershop all day on Peach Street, wondering where on earth his owner had disappeared.

"Calvin Woods, you just scared me to death!"

"Hear from Sheela? How is she?"

"She's just fine, Calvin. She's real happy."

"She married?"

"No."

"I hear she's rich now."

"Sort of."

"Tell her hello for me, will you?"

He moved on down the street so quickly on those long legs of his that she barely had enough time to say goodbye. Before he stopped her, Leda had been thinking about that odd little man in the photograph her sister had sent her. In the picture, Sheela was sitting in a nightclub, and this little guy with barely any hair had his arm around her. Sheela looked so glamorous that Leda hardly recognized her.

Leda wanted to call out at Calvin and tell him not to look so sad, that Sheela was only interested in that guy from Connecticut because he was a millionaire, and that one day she'd want to come back and marry him and have his babies. But then she remembered that Calvin was already married, and that Sheela had said she'd rather drown in the ocean than ever set eyes on Clearwater again.

Leda liked her job at Woolworth & Co. Her boss was so handsome, he made her stumble when she walked and stutter over her words when she tried to talk to him. He didn't seem to notice that she turned five shades of red when she closed out on the cash register and had to bring him the money at the end of the day.

"Good work, Miss Fournier. You work hard, and you know your stock." He smiled that boyish smile and kept his eyes on the table.

"Thank you, Mr. Langram." She lingered near him, and the silence teased the self-consciousness that remained between them until she turned on her heels and left the room. "Goodnight, Mr. Langram," she whispered.

"Ah, goodnight, Miss Fournier," he called after her.

Her walk back to the apartment on Edgewater Drive was brisk, and her hands filled her pockets in tight, angry little fists. *Goodnight, Mr. Langram. Thank you, Mr. Langram. Is that all I will ever get to say to him?* She wanted to cry out in the night air. "Oh, follow me home Bill Langram. Let me turn around and find you behind me."

Slowly she turned. She was so close to believing that he would really be there and run up to her as swiftly as Calvin Woods had done, asking if he could hold her hand.

"You may, Bill Langram. Oh, yes, you may," she said to the wind that came off the bay, bringing with it the scent of seawater and orange blossoms.

She did not expect to turn the corner of Edgewater Drive and find her aunt waiting for her in the old black Ford convertible. She quickly pushed the image of Bill Langram's face out of her mind. It was too sacred to share, even in secret, with this great witch of a woman.

Leda wanted to pretend she didn't notice her aunt sitting there, but the damn woman sat on the horn until Leda turned and got into the car. She glared at her aunt.

"Do you have to bring so much attention to yourself?" Leda whispered fiercely.

"Your Uncle Chester is dead."

Leda let her mouth fall and wondered how many husbands one woman could lose in a lifetime.

"I want Sheela's address in Connecticut."

"I don't have it," she lied.

"Don't have it? You don't have it?" Rena leaned over and put her face up so close to Leda's that she could smell the old sour breath wrapped around those large rabbit teeth.

"You get it real fast, or I will tell that handsome boss of yours that you're whoring on your off hours. Just like your whoring sister."

Leda glared at the fierce blue of her aunt's eyes, lit by some supernatural fire.

"You and that mother of yours always thought you were better than me. Fine Irish lace that crazy woman used to call your whoring sister. Fine Irish lace? Ha! Get me that address, or no decent man in the state of Florida will have you, you hear me? I have information to share with that fancy millionaire she's with."

Rena reached out and pushed Leda from the car. "Uncle Chester's funeral is tomorrow. You show your respect."

Leda slammed the car door and watched it rattle down the road, filling the evening air with its noise. She tried to remember the soft tan bend of Bill Langram's arms and the straight brown hair that rested near the top of his ear, but she couldn't find him anymore in the dark space behind her eyes.

Inside the apartment she shared with Susannah Miller, she took a piece of paper and wrote down Sheela's address in Connecticut.

*I guess she wants to tell her about Uncle Chester's death.* But then recalled that their aunt didn't even tell them about their father's death. It wasn't until the little trunk with his belongings showed up at the door that Rena broke down and cried. "My dear beloved brother has gone to God," was all she said.

Then, as if the moments of life were unfolding in unexpected bursts of circumstance, Leda heard a knock on the door. She didn't want to answer it, didn't want to see that short square frame standing in the moonlight. She was sure the old woman had come back to torment her. She started to cry, furious enough to tell her to go to hell.

"Go on and tell everyone in Clearwater that I'm the biggest whore on earth. Go on, old woman. Go on and sell my sister to that beefy little man up north, just like you sold her to Eugene Howe, you nasty old bitch."

The knocking continued. Leda stared at the door.

"Why didn't you leave us with the nuns? Why the hell didn't you leave us with Sister Vincetta?" she screamed.

"Miss Fournier?" he said softly.

"Oh, my God."

When Leda opened the door, the young man took in her tears, and whatever detached indifference he was attempting peeled away like the skin of an apple.

"Ah, I noticed that your lights were on. Ah... oh, you left this behind." He held out a small brown package.

Leda reached out and took the package.

"Fudge."

"I love fudge." He smiled at her.

They stood in the open doorway for a long time; so long that he had to shift his weight.

"Why are you crying?" he asked her at last.

"Sheela never liked fudge," she said, and tried to laugh.

"Sheela?"

"My sister. One of her boyfriends was shot by the Mafia and... ah."

She didn't know why she went and blurted it out like that. It was the last thing she wanted Bill Langram to know. Sheela had told her not to tell anyone. Leda had begged her sister to just come on home; things were too dangerous in those northern cities. But Sheela just laughed at that.

"Uhmmm," Bill Langram said, and crossed his

arms over his chest.

When she looked up at him, Leda noticed that the creases on his forehead looked like wiggles.

"Sheela always hated fudge," she said again.

He closed the door behind him and stepped into the room. "Is that so?" he said. He put his hands in front of him and smiled at her. "Is that so?"

"Yes. All the rest of us... we loved fudge. Especially my older brother, Wade. But Sheela... she never liked fudge."

Then, quite unexpectedly, Leda burst into tears. It was hardly a moment before she felt the strong, sweet touch of his arms reach around to the small of her back.

"Oh, God, I'm so scared for my sister... and Mama... Mama would be scared, too."

Leda broke into large choking sobs that made her stomach feel like it had just taken a punch. She knew she had soiled the white of his shirt with her mascara, but he only held on to her tighter.

"I miss my sister..," she sobbed. "Is she going to be all right with those people? Oh my, is my sister going to be all right?"

His firm warm hug closed in around her even more until the squeeze found her bones and she tasted his skin on her lips. She continued to weep like a small baby, remarkably soothed by the enclosure of human warmth. It was one of those moments in life when one extraordinary person shelters you in the sweet soft bend of their arms and the darkness fades to light.

# Chapter Twenty-Seven

Jack Stanton took Sheela and Sharon to New York City every time there was a new act at the Copa, a cocktail party to attend or a fundraising dinner for some Republican politician. Sheela always looked forward to it because she loved the city. Jack would show up at elegant restaurants with both girls on his arm and wink at the men around him, while they fixated on the girls' bosoms. Other girls, usually from Margo Sweeny's employ, often joined Sheela and Sharon, and of course, it was not unusual for Jack to offer "the pick of the litter" to a new business associate.

There were quite different parties held at the main house in Connecticut where Jack's wife played the hostess and Stanton, the dutiful husband. Sheela had seen Jennifer Stanton from a distance when she and Alice were out by the pond and Mrs. Stanton was walking on the other side with one of her sons. She briefly looked up and glared at Sheela.

Another time, Jennifer Stanton came up behind

her, out of nowhere, and so quickly, it had startled her.

"What are you doing on my property?" Jennifer asked harshly.

"I live here," Sheela said defiantly. She was rather surprised that Jennifer Stanton was petite, like Jack, and looked as perfectly beautiful and as expressionless as a porcelain doll.

Jennifer stepped back.

"No. You live there." She pointed to the "tiny chateau." "And I live *here.* Didn't Jack tell you that you're restricted?"

"No."

"I'll remind him. Now get back. Don't come within more than fifteen feet of that house or I'll put up a damn fence."

Sheela never saw Jennifer Stanton again after that, not for the full five years she lived on the property. Jack had never invited any of "his girls" to the main house. He did, however, borrow Alice once to help him at his oldest son's engagement party.

"Two hundred people were at that party," Alice said with a scowl. "And that Jennifer Stanton is a bitch."

Sheela laughed. "She looks colder than ice cream and nowhere near as delicious."

"She yelled at me for serving her stupid hors d'oeuvres from a torn doily on the serving tray."

"Who cares?" Sheela giggled.

"The rip was so small I had to bend down close

to see it," Alice complained. "I ain't ever doing another party for that fool woman, Sheela. You tell your Jack Stanton that."

"Did they act like a married couple?" Sheela asked.

Alice snickered. "Yeah, they were holding hands, mostly when the guests first started arriving, but then they pretty much ignored each other. She's got herself another man, you know."

That wasn't surprising. Sheela assumed that any woman in her right mind would certainly need another man. Jack was practically a woman.

"That bitch was devoting herself to a Mr. George Woodhill. He had a face like a cold piece of granite if you ask me."

An image of Jennifer Stanton and George Woodhill following each other around suddenly popped into Sheela's mind, stuffing their mouths with tiny hors d'oeuvres, then moving apart, one from the other, tossing tidbits of brief conversation into the crowd and sweeping through the room as if they followed the steps to a dance that would invariably lead them back where they had begun, standing with shoulders touching and mouths moving in inaudible secrecy.

Jack employed two of his sons. One held the title of President of Stanton & Sons, and the other was General Manager. Jack had made himself Chief Executive Officer, and it was clear that his sons did little more than travel from one city to the next to make decisions on various land deals, decisions that Jack invariably altered and often, ignored.

His middle son was mildly retarded and lived in the big house with his mother. The youngest boy, Daniel, came often to his father's "tiny chateau" and would lock himself away in Jack's "male room." Once, Alice and Sheela tried to see into the room from the outside, but Daniel had closed the drapes.

"What does Daniel do alone in the 'male room'?" she once asked Jack. "He's in there for hours."

Stanton had laughed. "Nothing. He does nothing," he told her.

"Oh."

"Strange boy. Don't pay any attention to him," he said. "He'll grow out of it."

"Grow out of what?"

"Oh, his strangeness," Jack said.

Sheela was to learn of Daniel's obsession with the "male room" the evening she found out that her Aunt Rena had threatened to blackmail Stanton.

"The woman is mad. Threatening statutory rape charges." He held up her Aunt Rena's letter. "How old are you?" He glared at her.

"I'll be eighteen next month."

"Why didn't you tell me you were only seventeen?"

"You never asked, Jack."

"That snide old woman wants ten thousand dollars for you, or she'll go to the papers with this." Stanton walked to his desk in the parlor and wrote out a check. "She'll get five, and not a penny more. And you had better be worth every silver nickel, my sweet little tart, or I'll sell you back to Kit Malone."

Sheela hurried into the "male room." She ran to

the first place she could think of with a phone. She wanted to call that mean, wicked woman and tell her she was as ugly as a worm, and just maybe, those husbands of hers hadn't died all that naturally.

Sheela still had Leda's letter in her pocket. She'd been carrying it around for two days, angry as a hornet with her sister. Leda had written and tried to warn her that their aunt was up to something because she had asked for Sheela's address in Connecticut. She said in her letter that when she tried to get out of giving it up, the old woman threatened to tell the entire town of Clearwater that Leda was a whore. Well, she couldn't let that happen now that she was practically engaged. She couldn't let Bill Langram hear that kind of gossip. She wrote that the old woman was on her fifth husband now.

*Married him just two weeks after Uncle Chester's funeral, must have had him on the sly. He's a big old red-faced man named Pete O'Brien and he makes unbearably long squeaks with his nose. Please don't be angry with me, sister. I tried not to give her your address. I stalled just as long as I could. Please understand that I tried my best.*

*I love you, Sheela. I pray for you all the time.*

Sheela took her sister's letter out of her pocket, rolled it into a ball, and tossed it into the basket under the desk.

"Damn her for telling," she whispered.

She had been so angry when she first entered the room, she hadn't taken notice that the lights in the "male room" were on. Now the sudden brightness startled her, and she stepped back, almost blinded by another lamp clipped onto the bookcase, giving off an unusual resplendence.

Daniel Stanton stood up. He had been in a corner of the room, sitting on the floor where she couldn't have seen him.

"What do you want?" he asked her abruptly.

"I want to use the phone."

She had never seen Daniel Stanton up close. She stared at him curiously. He was a boy about her age and Jack must have looked like him as a young man. The boy was not very tall, and his frame was so slight that he could have been mistaken for a girl. His hair was beautiful... wavy, thick brown hair that fell onto his forehead.

"There must be other phones in this house," he said.

"I'm sure there are, but I wanted to use this one."

"Can't. This is my room. Now get out."

"You don't live here," she said and sat down in the chair that faced the desk.

"I suppose you're one of Father's feminine collectibles?"

"That lamp hurts my eyes. Please turn it off."

"If you won't leave, I'll throw you out."

Sheela walked to the lamp and tried to turn it off, but she couldn't find the switch for it.

The boy followed behind and yelled at her.

"I said I'm going to throw you out."

Sheela laughed and walked back to the chair.

"You just try it."

He glared at her. Sheela stared back until it hurt her eyes and she had to turn her head away.

"What's that?" she asked pointing to a painted butterfly on a small canvass.

"Nothing," he said.

Sheela walked over and picked up the painting. The butterfly's wings were beautiful golden tones, and wispy trees reached out and touched the tip of its back; so delicately done it made her sigh. She held it in her hand and read, in the lower left corner, a tiny signature.

"Give me that," he said angrily and reached for it.

"No." She moved her hand away too quickly for Daniel to get the painting away from her.

He stared into her eyes, and she stared back.

"What's your name?" he finally scowled.

"Sheela."

He relaxed his face.

"Do you like it?"

She looked at the painting carefully.

"It's lovely."

She went to place it back on the table when she noticed something familiar on the desk, near a cup of pencils. It was a tiny egg standing on a small gold circle. Sheela thought it odd that Stanton would allow one of his painted eggs out of the case.

"One of your father's collectibles?" she asked incredulously.

"Hardly. Look closer."

Sheela brought the tiny egg to the lamp; the boy

had scripted his name in small black letters at the bottom of the egg's base.

"Yes," she whispered. "Clearly, its signed Daniel Stanton, like the painting. You did the egg, too?"

Daniel nodded and turned away.

Sheela held the egg under the light. A painted forest, deep with tall, lean trees, revealed the delicate eyes of a startled reindeer peering through the branches.

Carefully, she replaced it and walked around the room. Almost everywhere she looked, she noticed another brilliant painting or softly muted painted egg. She wondered if Stanton was aware that Daniel was using the library as his private art studio.

"You're an artist?"

"Not really. It's just a hobby."

"You're good," she said. "You're so talented."

"You think so?"

"But why here? This room? Why not get a studio?"

Daniel's expression turned angry, and he went back to his corner and sat on the floor.

"Mother is allergic to the paint, and why not here? Nowhere else. Father certainly won't pay for a studio."

Sheela walked over and stood behind him. Something caught her eye high above the bookcase.

"What's that?" she asked him.

Daniel turned and looked up and blushed. "A portrait."

"Of who?"

He didn't answer her. He picked up the tiny egg

he had been painting and reached for one of the small brushes from a bowl on the floor.

"I want to see it," she said. "She looks familiar."

"Then you'll have to climb on a chair and get it yourself."

Sheela stood on Stanton's desk and carefully lifted the painting from the top shelf. It was a portrait, small and so detailed of Sharon Marin.

"The eyes are just like Sharon's," she said. "I've never seen anything like it. It's so real."

Daniel stood up behind her.

"You think so?"

"Why don't you give it to her?"

His face beet red, he grabbed the painting out of her hands. "You tell her about this, and I'll really bop you one."

"You're lucky she never comes in here."

Sheela dismissed what she had come in the room to do and sat down beside Daniel on the floor. She watched him while he painted his little egg. She observed how his mouth remained in a circle and how his eyes traveled over the egg the way a mother might stare at her child. She remained very still while he chose his colors and wistfully touched the small bristles into jars of paint. The egg had seemed old and plain when she'd first seen it, but when Daniel finished painting the egg, it was undoubtedly unique.

"How incredible," Sheela uttered. "What kind of dog is it?"

"A spaniel," he said.

"Is it your dog?"

"It was. Her name was Princess."

Daniel had painted a lonely little house in a clearing on the egg behind the dog. He gave the evening sky a moon that shone down on a dark stream. Inside the house, a lamp glowed, giving the simple scene inviting warmth.

"Does the house exist?"

"Well, actually it does," he told her. "Father has a hunting cabin in the Catskills, and if you climb up over the hill behind it, this is what you see. I much prefer this simple farmhouse hugged by the mountains to his rustic old smelly cabin. He's such a dichotomy, isn't he?"

Daniel winked at her and put the brush between his teeth as he held the egg to the light.

"David tells me that we dream in the womb and are born to enter into the illusion we've created."

"David?"

"My brother."

"What does he mean by that?" she asked.

"I wish I knew," he said softly.

"You are a very expensive little trinket," Stanton announced as he walked into her bedroom later that evening. He was carrying a magazine and had on a terrycloth robe with a gold crest on the pocket.

"Aren't I worth it, Uncle Jack?"

"Youth is beauty," he smiled. "Shakespeare had it wrong. Youth is beauty, and truth is insignificant."

Sheela thought about Daniel the moment Jack mentioned beauty. He had made her cry when he told her about his brother. They had been sitting for an hour without speaking a word to each other, and then unexpectedly, Daniel raised his eyes and looked at her.

"My brother died in this room," he'd said simply. "It was an accident. Those guns." He motioned with his head very briefly to the gun case. "Father loves guns. Why not?They're so phallic, don't you think?"

Sheela was surprised and stared at him curiously. Daniel frowned more deeply.

"Odd," he continued. "My brother was the artist. I could never paint. Then he died, and I started to paint. Just like that. I paint in the room my brother haunts. Probably couldn't paint outside of it."

Sheela watched his eyes become hard.

"David and I were twins, not identical, but people always knew we were twins. Father forced David to shoot rifles, to hunt living things. David hated it. Father kept taking him to target practice anyway... kept making him prove his manhood."

"Really?" Sheela whispered.

Daniel laughed so much she thought he would ruin the painting he had started, but he seemed to be in perfect control of his hands.

"Odd, isn't it? Now that my brother is dead, I paint and Father wears dresses. He never used to, you know?"

Sheela sat back and stared at Daniel. She was surprised that he knew about his father's behavior.

Daniel looked pensive again. "David was different. David was like Father in many ways."

"You mean he...?"

Daniel cut her off. "Think what you like."

"I didn't—" She intended to say she hadn't meant anything by it, but he cut her off again.

"Here. Careful, though. It's not quite dry."

He handed her the egg with Princess. She didn't ask for it. He simply held it out to her.

"You're giving it to me?"

He nodded his head. "It's a magic egg."

Sheela smiled. "I don't believe in magic."

"Well, you should," he said. "Everything worth having … worth saving … always has a bit of magic, doesn't it?"

"Thank you, Daniel."

"Wait!" he said.

She watched as he also gave her the egg with the startled reindeer and the butterfly painting.

"David likes you." He kissed her on the cheek and quickly left the room.

Jack Stanton turned over the magazine and placed it on the night table with the butterfly painting. He looked at it for quite some time before he picked it up. He placed it in the palm of his hand and walked over to the light.

"What is this?" he whispered.

"Isn't it beautiful?" she said. "And look at this." Sheela walked to her desk and showed him the painted egg. She placed it in Stanton's hand. "Look how delicate it is."

Stanton seemed surprised. "Are these yours, my dear?"

"No. They're Daniel's. He makes them. Look at this beautiful egg with the painted reindeer."

Sheela walked to the fireplace and showed Jack the painting. "He's talented. Why aren't you bragging about him? He uses the 'male room' as his studio. Did you know that?"

Stanton put the tiny butterfly painting back on the table. Then he put the tiny egg in his pocket.

"I know everything, dear."

"Isn't he good?"

"The boy has some crude ability."

"Crude?" she said incredulously.

Stanton took a cigar from the pocket of his robe.

"Yes, crude."

Sheela watched as Stanton lit his cigar and placed some logs in the fireplace.

"I'm going to build a fire," he said slowly. "Why don't you disrobe and lie on the bed?"

Sheela looked at him. The last place she wanted to be was under Stanton's body.

"Do as I ask you, please."

Sheela lifted off her nightgown and lay back on the bed. She watched Stanton build the fire. Then she watched as he took the little butterfly painting and lifted it over the flames.

"The wings are not right. Look, one is higher than the other," he said.

"Daniel said we're all imperfect, and that's what makes us beautiful, like the butterfly."

"Ha! Well, the imperfections disturb me." He placed the tiny butterfly painting on a burning log.

Sheela watched as Jack reached for the beautiful

egg, the one with the fragile reindeer.

"Some crude ability, I suppose."

She gasped as he started to toss it into the fire.

"No, don't!"

He threw the egg on the bed.

"Toss it," he said.

"Please, Jack."

"Toss it."

"No, Jack. Please. Daniel said we're all fragile as deer, surrounded by a forest of predators."

"Oh, really? So my son has become a philosopher, and not a very good one, I might add."

Sheela stood, trying to protect something that she saw in the eyes of the reindeer that she didn't quite understand. "Your son said we destroy what we cannot accept, like fragility. We see it as weakness."

Jack had an odd smile. "My son said that?"

"Yes. He said the reindeer has his brother's eyes."

Jack stared at her as if he were confused, couldn't follow her.

"His brother's eyes? David was the real artist. Daniel never had his sense of beauty. They were not identical twins, you know? David had the physical perfections of an Olympian God, the talent of Renoir, Manet, Picasso! I'm not just saying that because he was my son."

Jack sat beside her on the bed and stared at the fire. He reached out and dimmed the light.

"David had problems, though, so many

problems."

"What problems, Jack?"

"His mother said he was different. I tried to fix what was wrong with him. Anything less than a man isn't worthy of the power God has given him."

Sheela's mouth fell open, and she stared at him in disbelief.

"I failed. Ah, no matter. Look, I brought you a present," he said. "Look at this." He handed her a magazine and lay down next to her.

Sheela opened the magazine and flipped through pictures of naked men. Jack reached over and took the magazine back from her. She watched his face as he turned the pages.

"For you, dear, big brawny men. Look, a magazine of cocks, big, big ones. Ah, ha. For you, dear. How do you like that? Ah, look how large this one is, so thick and hard. Do you like that one best?" He laughed nervously. The veins on his forehead moved as he placed his hands over the naked men; saliva ran from his lips.

Abruptly, he raised his eyes. "Toss that damn thing into the fire. Damn it. Toss it!" he yelled.

Sheela stared at the tiny egg in her hands. The startled reindeer seemed to plead for its life. She brought it to her lips.

"Forgive me," she said, tossing it into the air and watching as the flames surrounded it.

Stanton forced her back on the bed so quickly that she could barely catch her breath. He was on her instantly, letting his robe fall open, puffing out his tiny wisps of air and making odd sounds in the back of his throat.

"Oh, long and luscious, so hard and thick. Oh, my dear," he exclaimed as he squeezed his eyes and held his breath. A brief feminine moan escaped from his lips, and it was over. Almost in the same moment of relieving himself, he rolled off her and went back to the cigar he had left burning in the ashtray.

"What a pleasurable little trinket you are." He smiled and closed his robe. "Very pleasurable. Worth that five thousand, I'd say."

She watched as he picked up his magazine and left the room. She breathed a sigh of relief as she noticed that Daniel's beautifully painted egg with Princess, and the warm little house, had survived.

# Chapter Twenty-Eight

Mickey Fusco was a handsome man. His suits were tailor-made, and he liked brown wing-tipped shoes and long, loose cashmere coats. His 14-karat-gold cufflinks held a diamond chip, and his suits were all dark double-breasted gabardine pin–stripes that never showed a wrinkle. His dark and wavy hair, he wore combed back off his forehead. His eyes were noticeably black, and his lips looked so warm women could taste his kiss. Mickey Fusco was a big man. Yet his hands were slender. On two of his fingers, he wore rings: one small sapphire on his left index finger and on his right pinkie, a diamond set in a square of onyx. His nails were as neatly trimmed as the hair that fell onto the back of his neck.

Mickey Fusco insisted on silk underwear: white silk underwear that embraced his strong olive-skinned thighs and hugged the perfect round curve of his buttocks, seductively shielding the unusually thick penis that drove Jack Stanton into fits of frenzied masturbation. Jack insisted that it was the act of watching his beautiful Sharon Marin spread her lovely legs to receive this great massive man, but Sharon knew better. Sharon knew that if she could get Mickey Fusco to lie on his back, or better yet, to walk around the room stark naked, unabashedly aroused, and pass the very hole from which Jack peered, her open legs would be ignored and Jack would devour the naked and quite beautiful man who called her his "Doll," his "Sweetheart," and his "Bunny Bunny."

"Get him to masturbate," Jack would beg her. "Or let me lie under the bed while he penetrates you, dear. Ah, please."

"No, Jack. He must never know you're watching us. Promise?"

And Jack would sigh and promise.

Sheela found out what went on out at the lake house when Daniel drove her there and the two of them sat in the car across from the house. They watched Sharon and Mickey drive up.

"My father's in there, too," Daniel told her.

"What? How do you know? I don't see Jack's car."

"This has been going on for years. The bastard. I don't know exactly what they're doing in there, but I have an idea."

The next afternoon, Daniel took her back to the quaint Tudor house on the lake. He showed her the room with the tiny peepholes hidden behind a sweet Renoir sketch of two girls sitting under a tree. The holes revealed a bedroom and were covered by wallpaper that had to be lifted back.

"None of us are permitted to use the lake house. Father gave it to Sharon."

"Why the holes in the wall?"

Daniel frowned so intensely it seemed to age him, the lines in his forehead so deep they formed ridges.

"I think Dad is a voyeur. Wouldn't you say?" He scowled. "You're lucky he hasn't asked you to bring any men up here. But if he does, well, now you know."

Sheela ran around to the bedroom and tried to find the holes, but they were difficult to spot. The wallpaper was very bright and ran a busy flower pattern around the room. Directly inside one of the flowers was a series of holes as large as the tip of a pen. The holes appeared to be perfectly cut in even circles. It would be difficult to notice them without running a hand over the paper.

Quite spontaneously, Sheela began to dance. Almost immediately, she heard Daniel on the other side of the wall tapping out the melody to "Lady of Spain."

"How much of me can you see?" she called to him

"East, west, north and south of you," he hollered.

Sheela put her eye to the holes.

"Ouch. There you are."

"Let's plug the damn things up," Daniel chided.

"Come on. Let's go into the city and have some fun," she called through the wall. "This gives me the creeps."

"Better yet, let's give the holes a rip. Wouldn't it be just super to have Father caught standing on this dumb chair watching Sharon and that ape do it?"

Sheela managed to talk Daniel out of knocking out more of the holes and into taking the 8:10 train out of Darien. They wound up going to every swing joint on Fifty-second Street between Fifth and Sixth Avenues and got so drunk they had to use Stanton's Manhattan apartment to sleep it off. The apartment was on West 57th Street in one of the most beautiful buildings Sheela had ever seen. Doormen with neat blue uniforms stood watch over a brass lobby with tall stained-glass windows and chandeliers that majestically draped the ornately beveled ceiling, throwing a gentle Gothic hue about the marble floor.

"I didn't know Jack had an apartment in New York," she told Daniel.

"Yeah. It belonged to my brother, Jerry, until he got married."

"Anyone use it now?" she asked.

"Nope. It just sits here collecting dust. Maybe Father uses it every now and then. Who knows with him?"

# Chapter Twenty-Nine

Mickey Fusco had been dating Sharon Marin going on two years. He wanted to marry her, but she told him she came from an aristocratic family that wouldn't think well of her marriage to an Italian.

"My uncle is the infamous millionaire, Jack Stanton. Ever hear of him?"

"Sure," Mickey said and shrugged his shoulders.

"He raised me, and he's always been like an overprotective father. He wouldn't approve of me marrying a guy who's the muscle behind Fats Ferarro and still runs numbers for his cousin Sal."

"Ah, Sharon, two years is a long time to date a girl I could lose to some blue-blooded asshole with family assets."

"Who needs marriage?" she insisted.

"I want kids."

"I don't."

Well, hell, he didn't really want children either, but he didn't want that dumb bastard of an uncle of hers marrying her off to some jerk with a Park

Avenue address. He'd kill her if she went and soiled herself with some other man.

"The thought of you drinking some other man's saliva," he told her, "drives me nuts."

"What are you talking about, Mickey?"

"I ever catch you going crazy under some other guy, I'll fucking strangle you with my bare hands."

"Don't be a jerk, Mickey."

Well, they might just as well have been married. They used the lake house her uncle gave her as if they lived there. He'd been driving up from Brooklyn almost every Friday night for the last two years, and they'd rendezvous on Pine Tree Drive. He wanted to meet Jack Stanton, but Sharon kept putting it off. The guy had quite a reputation for being a ladies' man, and Mickey was curious about him. Besides, meeting a legitimate millionaire up close would have been kind of interesting for Mickey. He was sure there were plenty of millionaires in his own family, but no one talked about it. Money was always something his family got illegally, so they just spent it garishly and avoided telling anyone where it came from.

"I'm going to crash Stanton's house and steal you away," he insisted.

That got her real angry. "Don't you ever come near Stanton's house, or I'll put sand in the engine of that sweet little convertible I gave you for Christmas last year."

"Oh, yeah? Then I guess I'll have to take the bastard out and you with him," he teased.

Of course, he did meet Stanton once, quite by

accident. He got to the lake house early one Friday and found Jack Stanton mixing himself a martini at the bar. Jack became visibly upset, and his face turned an odd shade of purple.

"Oh, ah. Are you one of Sharon's friends?"

Mickey was glad he wore his new sport suit and had a nice new shine thrown on his shoes.

"Uh, yes. Mickey. Mickey Fusco. Yeah, I'm one of Sharon's friends."

He noticed the old guy's hands were shaking as he held his glass. Didn't look like much of a ladies' man to Mickey.

"Well. I, ah, only came over to see my niece. I'll catch her some other time."

"No, no. Don't leave on my account. I wasn't expected until later."

"No, really. I don't wish to intrude."

"At least finish your drink."

"No, no really. I must be going."

Jack finished his drink quickly and walked into the room behind the bedroom just as Sharon drove up.

Mickey never saw Jack leave the house, and he never heard a car, but Sharon always liked to keep the music up nice and loud, so he likely missed it.

"Are you sure your uncle has gone?" he asked her, while he straddled her hips later that evening.

Sharon laughed. "He's in the next room watching you fuck me," she whispered.

Mickey jumped off her and stared back at the wall, but the wallpaper pattern was such a maze of flowers that Jack's small dark eye was easily undetectable.

Sharon laughed louder. "You idiot."

"Scared me there for a minute. But I never heard him leave."

"Why don't you turn and let me see that cute ass of yours?" Sharon said sweetly.

Mickey turned around. He tightened the muscles in his rear end and held up his arms to show her the muscles on his back.

"That's it, sweetie. Now why don't you turn around and show me your sugar?"

"No." Mickey smiled. "You've got to make me." And he slowly gyrated his rear end in a long, slow circle while his unusually thick penis reached up toward the little hidden peepholes. Mickey Fusco's penis bounced up and down while he moved his ass around to Ella Fitzgerald's rendition of "If You Can't Sing It, You'll Have to Swing It."

Mickey's thick, erect bouncing penis peered defiantly back at Jack on his chair, who was turning five different shades of red and shooting off in his hand with all the fervor of a sexually stimulated chimpanzee.

# Chapter Thirty

Alice didn't work a day in two years, except that night she had to work the son's engagement party at the big house. Sheela had kept her word, though. Every Friday, like clockwork, she knocked on Alice's door with twenty-five dollars in her pocket. Alice wanted to tell her father how strange these white folks were, but if she did, he might tell her that if she didn't lickety-split right back home to Jacksonville, he'd send her brother, Jim, right up there to get her. Anyway, it wasn't half bad collecting that money and driving into Darien with Sheela to buy herself some pretty clothes every now and then.

But even that didn't feel as good as knowing her father was putting the boys through school and keeping the house up nice, the way it was when her mama was alive.

Still, it was easier giving up that money than listening to Sheela carry on the way she did. Crying and pleading for two whole days, begging her not to leave and holding onto her like a baby being ripped from its mama's arms. Sheela even offered her more money to stay on at the estate.

"I ain't working for this money. Ain't doing a damn thing for it," she told her. "And besides, me and Wilfred going to get married."

Sheela told her to bring Wilfred up there to Connecticut and she'd pay them both twenty-five dollars a week. Alice laughed at that and told her Wilfred had a good job as a porter in one of those fancy buildings in New York City and he wouldn't take money from no white girl for doing nothing. "Black man knows better than that. Going to lose his hide for taking easy money from white people."

"Please, Alice," Sheela whined.

"No. I got to take care of my man now and that little boy of his. We got to have a place of our own."

She told Sheela that it hadn't been much fun sitting around in that cottage all day doing nothing. Only fun she ever had was going into Jack Stanton's kitchen at the main house and helping that woman make cakes, the one that had come all the way from France and could barely speak any English. Sometimes she got invited into a poker game with Stanton's driver, but mostly life was pretty boring on the Connecticut estate.

Sheela never did take her in to New York City like she promised, and if she hadn't gotten up the courage to call some second cousin of hers living in Harlem, she might still be sitting in Connecticut getting fat on Laurette's pastry.

That's where she met Wilfred Thomas Decker.

Right there on 125th Street while she was buying red tomatoes. She told him he was buying all the rotten ones right off the cart, and then he smiled at her and said, "Then teach me how to pick 'em, girl."

She loved Harlem. "It was smoking," she told him. All those jazzy, moody wide-open avenues, with tall tin cans, and those houses that were so close together that when she slept over at Cousin Cleary's she could hear people coughing in their sleep right through the walls.

On their first date, Wilfred bought her dinner in one of those noisy little restaurants down four steps from the street.

"This here's the best food I've had since I come east." She smiled and wiped her lips.

He laughed and looked at her kindly. That's what it was about Wilfred, kindness sat on his face like it was never going to leave. Her father had a face like that... one of those faces that never go sullen on you.

She came into town every weekend after meeting Wilfred and stayed with her cousin, Clarise Cleary, over on Lenox Avenue. Wilfred came knocking on the door with flowers and grins so broad he might have been hiding secrets. He took her dancing and told her he was from Chesterton, South Carolina, and he had a son named Willie who needed a mama. He said his wife died when the boy was only eighteen months old. That was the only time he lost his grin, but his kindness stayed there, transformed a bit by sadness but holding forth in his eyes like something defiantly good-natured.

She hadn't seen Sheela since her wedding and that was close to three years ago. She and Wilfred had gotten married in Wilfred's hometown where his folks were looking after little Willie. Sheela had flown down to Chesterton for the wedding with that boy of Stanton's. Sheela had cried so loud during the ceremony that Alice had to turn and stare her down; and there she was, holding onto some of Wilfred's aunts. She had them crying so loudly that their sobs could be heard over the wedding March. Only two white faces in the church, Sheela and that strange little Daniel Stanton.

At the end of the reception, Sheela handed her an envelope with one thousand dollars in it. Then Sheela turned and hugged Wilfred so tightly that she saw his eyes bulge out.

"Take care of her, Wilfred," Sheela cried.

"Where'd that white girl get that kind of money?" he asked her later.

"She's playing the hand the Lord dealt her, and she's all aces," she said.

Alice thought about the little boy she was going to raise as her son. "But the Lord done give me the King and Jack of hearts. Don't need no wild aces now." She winked at him.

Wilfred took her in his arms; she felt his body all warm around her like a sweet dream landing in her sleep.

They brought Willie back to New York City and moved into a larger apartment on 135th Street. Wilfred took the subway every day down to Sixty-first Street where he worked as a porter. A lot of rich people lived there, and sometimes he'd bring home some of the stuff they would throw away—lamps, silver, even chairs. Willie was still too young to be left alone, but Alice would get herself a job soon as the boy was in school. They were always counting pennies, but it never spoiled their happiness. She missed being able to send her father all that money Sheela had given her, but her daddy was so pleased she was married to a hard-working boy like Wilfred, he said he didn't even notice that all that extra money wasn't there anymore.

She could have given her daddy the ring to hock, but it didn't seem right. She gave it back to Sheela the day she packed her bags and left with Wilfred.

"Here, I been saving this for you."

Sheela had the most incredulous look on her face; she almost looked unfamiliar.

"I told you not to trust those women. You left it out. That fool Leroy's ring. You were going to lose it for sure if I didn't grab it."

"Why didn't you tell me you had it?"

"Hell, girl. You give it to me. Now I'm giving it back."

"Why?"

"I got me a ring." Alice held the small diamond in the air. "You going to need that fool's ring more than me. Anyway, it don't feel right, me keeping it."

Sheela refused to take it, and Alice had to chase her all the way outside and put it in her pocket.

"You hold onto this, girl. It's yours."

"Oh, all right, all right, I'll hold onto it long as you're being so obstinate. I'm always going to wear it now that it's from you. It's a friendship ring. From Alice Henry to Sheela Fournier. That's what it is, and that's what it will always be."

Sheela slipped the ring on her finger. She hugged Alice and said she'd be visiting her soon.

But, somehow, Alice lost touch with Sheela. Never wanted to. Just did. Alice got busy with the baby and before she knew it little Willie was old enough to leave with Cousin Cleary and she was out looking for a job. The last time she heard from Sheela was in 1942. Sheela had called to tell her she was living in New York City and had just gotten a job as a showgirl at a place called The Diamond Horseshoe. But now she couldn't find Sheela's new phone number anywhere, and she wanted to pay her respects.

Was a terrible thing about Stanton's youngest son. It was all over the papers. Never had a chance. And that girl, Sharon Marin, disfigured by acid like that. Both dead. Terrible. *Lord have mercy. Them white folks got a pact with the devil. Lord have mercy.*

# Chapter Thirty-One

Daniel kept staring at the lake house. He always wanted to stop by before hopping a train into the City. Sheela was increasingly frustrated with his obsession with Sharon. She turned up the radio and glared at him.

"You're just watching the lights go on and off, Daniel. We'll miss the train."

"Why the hell does she do it?" he whispered. "Why?"

"Have you ever even spoken to Sharon? I mean, she never speaks to me. Maybe three times in five years," Sheela said.

Daniel turned to her.

"She's an angel. Angels don't speak. They walk on air and read your mind."

"She's so much older than you, Daniel. Don't you know she's over thirty? That's old."

"My brother, David, told me that Sharon and I were married in another life. We're old souls and perfectly suited."

"How do you know what David says, Daniel?"

"I can speak to him," he said simply.

"Then tell him to talk some sense into you," she said, trying to get him to laugh at himself, but Daniel hardly ever smiled, not even when he had too much to drink.

"You know, David is in love with you and begs you to leave Father and move to New York." He turned and stared deeply into her eyes. "Please, Sheela. Go get married. Marry someone like David."

"I thought David was like Jack, you know, queer?"

"David is like me. But I'm spoken for."

Sheela took his hand and brought it to her lips. She pressed her mouth down on his skin and brought his fingers close to her eyes.

"Something so lonely about you, Daniel Stanton," she whispered.

"Loneliness is a bond," he told her. "It speaks a language all its own, you know."

She kissed his hand again. "What language?"

"The silent one, the one you don't hear… the one you feel. The bond is recognizable between people who ache."

"C'mon," she laughed. "Let's go get looped."

Daniel graduated from Bridgeport University in 1940 and went to work for his father as a land manager. Sheela saw less of him after that because he traveled often, but she met a lot of amusing people in the city on her own, mostly women who liked scouting out movie stars in night clubs and dancing to Swing. Sheela hopped a train into Manhattan every Saturday night to spend time with all her new girlfriends.-

She was out at the Cotton Club with two girls from Ohio one night, Patty Cakes and Connie Sinclair. Out of nowhere, a man named Harry stopped at their table. He eyed the girls, one by one, but settled on Sheela.

"Can you dance, sweetheart?"

Sheela grinned. "Can Billie Holiday sing?"

Harry pulled over a chair.

"Harry Stein. I work for Billy Rose. Promotions. I make sure The Horseshoe is the hottest spot in town." He extended his hand.

"This here is the Cotton Club, and it's pretty hot." Sheela laughed and winked at the girls.

"Wise guy, uh? I'm just checking out the competition. Ever been over to the Paramount?"

"Sure. Everyone's been to The Diamond Horseshoe. Can't go to the same place every night, though. Right, girls?"

"That's right, Sheela," quipped little Patty Cakes as she reached for a Chesterfield.

"Light me, will you, honey?"

Patty put her hands around Harry's while he held the match and stared at Sheela.

"I noticed you before when you came in. You're tall, ain't you?"

"Is the Pope Catholic?"

"You always answer a question with a question?" Harry stared at her breasts as they bounced up and kissed at the crease.

Sheela took the Chesterfield away from Patty and blew her smoke into Harry's smile.

"Seems I'm a lot taller than you."

Harry laughed so loud he could be heard above the crowd. Several people swiveled their heads around and peered over at Sheela's table. Sheela winked back at a small bald man who was sitting with one of the hottest stars in Hollywood, Hedy Lamar.

"Hedy's got bad legs," Connie whispered to Harry.

"Not many people care when you have a kisser like that." Sheela laughed.

"Better to have the kisser *and* the gams. What's your name?" Harry leaned in closer.

"Are you writing a book?"

"Ever think about being a showgirl?"

Sheela grinned. "Sure. What's the pay?"

"Billy is auditioning girls for The Diamond Horseshoe tomorrow. "You're a sure thing. Here's the time and the place."

Harry reached for a napkin and scribbled something on it. Then he handed it to Sheela.

"What do I have to do?" she asked him. "Dance?"

Harry shook his head. "Just walk. The way you did when you came out of the powder room, sweetheart... like you own the place."

# Chapter Thirty-Two

Mickey Fusco loved the Five Spot and the Blue Note Club. Wouldn't be caught dead uptown at the Quarter or the Horseshoe; too many stiffs from sales conventions packed into a room of Jersey drivers. His friend, Eddie Pucci, finally talked him into hitting the Latin Quarter, though.

"Just for a couple of drinks, Mickey," Pucci said. "We oughta check out these uptown clubs. Ain't nothing wrong with the glitter of dames in diamonds."

Mickey could never get Sharon to join him at any of his favorite places downtown. She said she hated crowds and smoky rooms. That's why it surprised him to see her at a big round table at the Quarter with Jack Stanton and five men in business suits. Mickey watched her from in-between the crowd at the bar. She was bouncing her breasts in front of some short old man with a fat cigar and thick lips. Jack Stanton was sitting back in his chair with his arm around a tall blonde. A dark-haired girl was sandwiched between two other men who kept leaning over her chair and staring down the front of her dress.

Mickey watched as Sharon got up to leave with the short old man who stopped briefly to shake Stanton's hand. Then the old man leaned in to tell Stanton something that made Stanton laugh and slap the other man on the back.

Mickey took a deep breath and curled the fingers of his right hand into a fist.

He asked around the club that night and found out that Sharon Marin was Jack Stanton's favorite whore and she'd been "chosen" to please Stanton's business associate from Palm Beach. The other girls were the losers that night, but the girls were used to it because Sharon was usually the favorite "pick of the litter."

"How often does the bitch come here?" he asked the bartender.

"You can count on Wednesday nights. Sometimes Thursdays. What's it to you?"

Mickey clenched his jaw and shoved some bills into the bartender's pocket. The skin seemed to burn off his body, and his heart raced so fast he thought it was going to explode and blow the place to bits. He put his fist through the glass door of the Latin Quarter, and he kicked in the side of someone's new Buick before three bystanders came by and tossed him out in front of traffic.

Sheela didn't know why she bothered letting Patty and Connie talk her into showing up at the audition. There must have been at least a hundred girls there. She was just about to leave when Harry walked into the room and spotted her.

"Kid! Hey, kid. Come on in here," he shouted over the crowd and waved his hands toward the door. "Come on, kid. I don't have all day."

He brought her into a small theatre and put her on a stage with several other girls. Sheela wasn't sure what Billy Rose looked like, but she surmised that he was the short intense man in the back of the room doing a lot of talking. Suddenly, she heard a piano playing "A Pretty Girl Is Like A Melody," and she found herself walking around the stage. Billy Rose stopped talking and moved into the third row. There was a tall, delicate man on the floor below the stage, who kept walking around and moving his hands slowly up and down to the music; he had a slight bend to his knees and a simple bounce to his hips. Sheela imitated him to perfection. Soon, she was out in front of the line with five or six girls trying to follow behind her. There was something enjoyable about the tune and being able to walk inside the melody and she was gliding around as though nothing but Champagne bubbles were under her feet. She threw Billy a flirtatious smile as she passed. Out of the corner of her eye she saw him point in her direction.

Sheela was hired at ninety-five dollars a week to work the chorus line at The Diamond Horseshoe, a popular club in the basement of the Paramount Hotel on Fifty-second Street. She had saved twenty-five thousand dollars in the last five years, and she was more than ready to leave Jack Stanton's Connecticut estate and settle in Manhattan. She planned to tell Jack that weekend that she was moving to Manhattan, but he showed up unannounced at the apartment on Fifty-seventh Street the very night she was hired at The Diamond Horseshoe. His clothes were unusually disheveled, and he appeared distraught.

"You look awful, Uncle Jack. What happened?"

"Nothing, really."

"Jack, I'd like to move into Manhattan," she told him.

Surprisingly, he offered to give her the apartment and did not seem the least upset by her departure. He fixed himself a drink and sat beside her on the couch. "Do you have a boyfriend?" he asked.

"No, Jack."

"Pity. Tell me what kind of men do you like?"

"Rich," she answered.

"Big, muscular men?" he pressed her. "With big, luscious cocks to suck like lollies? Oh, dear. Come sit by me."

Jack kept talking about what her boyfriends should look like naked, how well-endowed they should be, while Sheela listened distractedly and puffed on a cigarette.

"No end to the long, hard cock of a well-appointed young chap." Jack chuckled.

He worked himself into such a frenzy that he leaped upon her and in a matter of seconds had released his passion in a puff of feminine moans and yelps that culminated in an ejaculation that landed somewhere between the pillows on the couch and his own hand.

After Jack had washed his testicles in the bathroom, he returned to the living room.

"I want you to find the most handsome man in Manhattan, well-endowed, of course, and if you do, I will put you in my will. You'll be set for life."

Sheela looked at him skeptically and remembered the peephole at the lake house.

"You mean, like Sharon?" she asked slowly.

"Oh, no. No, no, no, no. She is gone. I cannot... Ah. Well. Sharon is no longer with us."

"What do you mean, Jack?"

"Well, I cannot tolerate the damage. I cannot bear the, ah—"

He changed the subject abruptly and left the apartment quickly, without telling her anything, only making her promise to find a boyfriend with an exceptionally large penis, and if she did, he would put her in his will for one million dollars.

Sheela called Daniel immediately after she heard the elevator doors close behind Jack. Daniel had been crying and was difficult to understand.

"What's happened?" she asked him.

"That ape found out she was Father's whore. He found her at the Latin Quarter with one of Father's business associates."

Daniel was weeping so badly that Sheela had to keep asking him to repeat himself.

"That fucking ape started stalking her, came back to the Quarter another night and waited for her. He tossed acid in her face as she left the club, and while she stood there screaming, the bastard backed his car into her and ran over her legs."

"Jesus!"

"Father threw her out. Said she was like broken china. Useless."

"I'm so sorry, Daniel," she told him. "I'm so very sorry."

The next morning, Sheela found her own apartment on West Seventy-seventh Street off West End Avenue. She called Daniel to tell him she had left the Connecticut estate forever and would never speak to Jack again, but Daniel never returned her call.

The night Sheela opened at The Diamond Horseshoe, Daniel checked Sharon Marin out of New York Hospital and drove up toward Connecticut. He was going to take her to the Tudor house on the lake. But somewhere out near the Goodwives River, he told her he had loved her forever and it didn't matter now what she looked like. Sharon smiled at him and touched her face, now badly disfigured and scarred. She had been blinded in her left eye, and her right leg had been amputated below the knee.

As the car sped along toward the bridge at Rings End Landing, she reached for his hand.

"I'll marry you in heaven, only in heaven," she whispered.

His heart pounded and a smile broke out across his face.

"Promise?" he asked.

"I promise," she said and brought his hand to her lips.

Daniel turned to her.

"Do it for us," she pleaded. "Daniel," she began to cry, "I can't live like this."

He nodded and pressed his foot all the way down on the gas until the speedometer popped up to eighty. The salt from his tears lingered on his tongue and tasted a bit like rain. He never removed his eyes from hers.

"I love you," she whispered.

The car hit the bridge in under ten seconds and crashed over the side, quickly sinking into the quiet waters of the Goodwives River. It was a tragic but blindly euphoric race toward heaven.

# Chapter Thirty-Three

The small turn-of-the-century railroad apartment houses sat in the shade of the famous skyline, right off the waters of the East River, oddly shadowed by the geometric grandeur of New York City. The Brooklyn streets were wide and lined with trees that stood tall, proudly shielding the houses from passing cars. Young boys played stickball or pulled each other on wooden sleds and tossed compliments at girls who sat on concrete stoops and whispered secrets.

Polish and Hungarian immigrants dominated Greenpoint, Brooklyn, in the early part of the twentieth century. Theirs was a close-knit community, people who eagerly offered each other solace in times of suffering and laughter, if the hand of the Lord had blessed them. They drank rich German coffee in china cups and cold Russian vodka over ice. In the summer, they played cards out in the street on little folding tables that they would place under the trees. In the winter they sat in tiny parlors, under a crucifix, and told stories about the "old country."

On Sundays, the Catholic church on Java Street opened its doors to the carefully dressed community and shared the passion of its Latin Mass with those who came to worship Jesus in broken English and with pockets full of quarters to toss in the collection box.

The streetcar on Manhattan Avenue could take them all the way to Prospect Park, and the busy open boulevard known as Greenpoint Avenue bustled with shoppers who bought Kielbasa and Pierogi. The scent of fresh homemade bread dominated the air as white bags of Hungarian pastry, bursting with apricot and cherry fillings, teased the children home.

Americanization had only seeped into Greenpoint from radio shows and local movie houses. New York City had been earnestly internalized as that far away country across a simple river where only the brave and the wealthy dared tread.

Janos "John" Kuvik and his second wife, Mary, had bought a small red apartment building at 107 Freeman Street in 1919. All the houses on Freeman Street were green, yellow, or red and lined the quiet street like strands of gemstones. John Kuvik planted a weeping beech tree right in front of 107 and created a garden out of the once-barren backyard. The tree grew tall and beautiful and seemed to mark the house with its own insignia. John was proud of his weeping beech tree, the only one of its kind in Greenpoint, perhaps in all of Brooklyn.

Each morning in spring and summer, John would go into the kitchen and look out on his flowers. America was not as prolifically colorful as Europe, and that had disappointed him.

"They do not love gardens here. Where, where are all the gardens?" he would ask strangers bewilderedly. "In Europe, gardens are as necessary as water."

But no one ever answered the perplexed Hungarian who had left his beautiful Budapest for a better life in America, only to land tearfully and ambivalently in a flowerless paradise.

Long before he met Mary, John had had three daughters with his first wife, Berta. For many years, they had lived not far from the little house on Freeman Street.

Only a month after their last daughter married, Berta died from a two-year illness, a disease that had affected her lungs; "lung cancer" they had called it. By the time John Kuvik married Mary Mushansky, Berta had been dead for five years. John was considerably older than Mary, but she didn't seem to mind. She had lost her first husband in a freak accident at a factory in Long Island City and had a little daughter to take care of. Mary had received a good deal of insurance money from her husband's employer after the factory was found liable for his death. She gave John all the insurance money to help him buy the house on Freeman Street.

"We will rent out five apartments," John told her proudly, "and we will live on the second floor in our very own apartment."

This arrangement brought John and Mary a nice second income. Within three years, they had two children, Margaret, and Julius. When Mary's first daughter grew up and married, followed by her second daughter, Margaret, John rented the apartments to their husbands for a very reasonable price, and this arrangement made Mary delirious to have her family so close.

"Oh, my daughters will be just down the hall and up the stairs." She cried buckets full of delirious tears.

John worked as a night watchman for Brooklyn Savings on Thursday through Monday evenings, but his real work became caring for his little house on Freeman Street. He always made sure the tenants were comfortable. He lit the furnace at the first hint of cold, and he always cleared the stoop of garbage. John rubbed the large oak doors and the proud wooden banister with oil every Saturday and swept the stairs every evening before he left for work. In the spring and the summer, he labored in his garden and offered the tenants cut flowers for their windows.

John Kuvik was a quiet man, and nothing made him happier than working with his hands. He loved being alone to repair an old piece of furniture or to build something new, like a birdhouse or wooden boat for his son. It wasn't that he didn't love his wife or his children. It was just that being alone was like prayer to John Kuvik. Milika always understood that. Milika was the German shepherd that had just showed up in John's life one day and followed him home. Mary would not allow the dog in the house, but the bank let John keep her as an added measure of protection. So Milika lived in the basement of Brooklyn Savings, and John Kuvik spent every evening with his dog, whether he worked or not. He always went to feed and walk her. When he could get away with it, he would take her down to the basement workshop back at Freeman Street, and Milika would sit and watch him work. He'd take her into the garden, and she'd lie in the sun and pick her head up every now and then to rest her eyes on John.

His first wife would have loved the dog. There had been so much passion in his heart for Berta. She had been frail and sensitive, and her eyes were large and dark, her features so angular that she appeared aristocratic. John had found her exceptionally beautiful. They had courted in Budapest and married there, and his heart had raced ahead of itself every time she smiled at him.

His marriage to Mary was a compromise, as some marriages are. He was not entirely unhappy, but Mary was sullen, much more so than Berta had ever been and Mary was far more devoted to Jesus. She didn't laugh and tease him the way Berta had. Once their babies, Margaret, and Julius, were born, he and Mary were sleeping in the living room, and passion was something he felt for the sun as it set over the skyline but not for his wife; not as she lay beside him covered in cotton from her ankles to her chin, with her hair in a net and her most loving thoughts on the crucifix that hung over the bed.

John loved his daughters, but it was his son who most resembled him. Julius was his only boy, lanky as his father and just as much of a dreamer. But John's dreams were realized in solitude. Enjoyed in solitude. His son's dreams were ephemeral. John found joy in the garden with Milika. Not Julius. It seemed that Julius only found joy in the fine cut of his suits and the taste of a Cuban cigar.

"What do you want from life, son?" he asked Julius.

Julius would smile. "Lots of dough, Pop. Lots of dough."

Julius had changed his given name from "Kuvik" to Clark. John couldn't understand why it was so difficult to say "Kuvik," but Julius insisted on changing his name. Well, so be it. He was no longer Janos. He had not been Janos for years. Not since Berta died. Everyone called him John now. So, his son wanted to change his name. Big deal. Why not? After all, Julius had been born right there in Brooklyn, so why not? Yet Brooklyn was not enough for Julius anymore. He was always in Manhattan.

"What's so special about Manhattan, Julius?"

"I don't know, Pop. Maybe the streets are lined with gold," he told him.

Lately, the boy just came home to sleep—sleep and enjoy his mother's cooking, but then he was out of the door, running down those steps so fast John hoped he wouldn't trip. Karla Wolensky, that nice Catholic girl he said he was going to marry, stopped seeing him. Just like that. Couldn't get Julius to talk about it. Now he was seeing some showgirl!

Ah, well, the boy was only twenty-two. John recognized from an early age that his son was a romantic, and one had to be patient with romantics. Give them time to come to their senses. The boy was smart and just needed maturity. After all, he himself had once been accused of having his head in the stars. Perhaps he still did. Milika understood that. Berta had understood that as well. He put his arms around the German shepherd and kissed her long snout. Her tail spun in circles so fast he felt the air around it.

"What does my son do in Manhattan, hey, Milika? How has he gotten so rich?"

The dog covered John's face in licks, as if to distract him. As if to say, "Don't worry, John Kuvik. Julius is a very smart boy. A very smart boy."

# Chapter Thirty-Four

Julius had trained as a textile designer. His father had given him the money for a two-year specialized college in downtown Brooklyn. He was hired in his last year of school to work for a textile firm called Markowitz-Rose at 502 Broadway in Manhattan. Julius loved the city. He'd grown up with the skyline dominating his peripheral vision and appearing across the river at sunset like the magical Land of Oz. But before he met Sid, he didn't know what fine wine tasted like or the feel of cashmere brushing up against his arm on Fifth Avenue. Before he met Sid, Julius didn't know that he could open the gates of heaven and find angels in mink.

Sid Bernstein also worked at Markowitz-Rose. He was in every Friday to do the books. He wore a big pinkie ring on his finger and smelled as good as a woman. He and Julius got friendly the night Sid discovered his interest in fine art.

"It was just a minor in college, Sid. I like museums."

Sid asked him all kinds of questions about realism and cubism, and the Renaissance painters, and what he knew of each.

"Bright, handsome boy like you should be dealing art and antiques, Julius."

"Are you serious?"

"Sure, kid."

"Any money in it?"

Sid laughed. "At least a couple of thousand a month. Maybe more."

Julius spilled a bit of his drink on his tie and stared at Sid.

"You're a natural, kid. You know your stuff."

Julius kept his day job at Markowitz-Rose and worked for Sid Bernstein on the side. Within six months, Julius had bought himself three new suits. Inside a year, his closet looked like the men's department at Saks, and he was spending his evenings in the Carlyle Room buying drinks for clients and smoking Cuban cigars.

It was easy money. Sid set it all up, and all Julius had to do was meet the seller, authenticate the work, and collect a broker's fee for finding a buyer. Julius would take the fee back to Sid, and Sid would give him a small percentage. The fees were high, sometimes as much as fifty thousand dollars, to sell the paintings. They were also receiving a substantial percentage on the antiques they were reselling.

Many of the paintings were by well-known artists like Delacroix and Picasso. The antiques could be anything from an eighteenth-century side table to a late eighteenth-century doll. Sid would stall the original seller while the antiques or paintings were sold to an anonymous third party at a reduced rate. The difficulty in finding the buyer appeared to reduce the value of the art, but then, after the broker's fee was received, Sid resold the piece for its actual value. Sid kept the original broker's fee as well as a percentage on the difference of the second sale.

Both men left the firm of Markowitz-Rose in early 1945, and Julius became a full-time partner with Sid Bernstein and some anonymous man whom Sid referred to as "Dick." Dick was the real talent behind the success of the company they called Masterworks. Dick who had all the contacts in the art world. Dick who did the initial buying and reselling, but never personally met any of the clients. That was Julius's job. Julius was the liaison, and it was Julius who passed the art and antiques on to Sid, who, in turn, handed them over to Dick. Julius didn't give much thought to this anonymous man called Dick——not when he was now collecting twenty percent of the total take.

Sid rented a small office on lower Fifth Avenue and spent his evenings with his girlfriend at fancy midtown clubs. He was always asking Julius to join him, but it seemed that Julius had some steady girl in Greenpoint he was going to marry. Then one day Julius came into the office looking like he had just gotten drafted.

"What truck ran over you, kid?"

"I've just been dumped."

Julius knew that his new lifestyle was threatening to Karla. "You're no longer the boy I grew up with," she told him.

Julius wanted to marry her more than anything in the world, even though he felt they were drifting apart. She had been his only real girlfriend, and he had known her forever. He had loved her since the age of thirteen. But he could not get her to accept the lifestyle he was leading in the city.

"I hate eating out in restaurants," she said. "I hate Manhattan. It's ugly and frightening."

Soon after he heard Karla was keeping company with William Wozniak, and everyone was talking about how much Julius had changed since he got out of school. But Julius didn't feel he had changed at all. They were the ones who had changed. They treated him like a foreigner in his own neighborhood. They stared at his fancy clothes as though he had just landed from Mars. Still, he'd never give it up. Not even for Karla. Having money was the truth behind all those lies that it can't buy everything.

Sid took him aside.

"Hey, now that you're unattached, maybe you can join me some night. I know a dame you might like."

"What dame?"

"She's a nice kid. Gorgeous. A showgirl. I think you'd like her."

Julius really doubted it. He had never much of a ladies' man. Wouldn't know what to say to any dame Sid liked, but just the thought of that creep Wozniak making eyes at Karla made him feel he could use a distraction.

"Sure, why the hell not. A showgirl? Sure, why the hell not?"

# Chapter Thirty-Five

Jack Stanton had been heavily invested in the stock market. He believed in the future of America and thought that anyone with a little bit of money was a fool not to buy up stocks in companies like General Motors and US Steel. "Put your money in automobiles, Sheela. Automobiles, oil, steel. You'll never get rich with a savings account."

Sheela took Stanton's advice and invested the twenty-five thousand dollars she had saved over the years in General Motors and US Steel. She continued to buy stocks every month after that, whether the market was up or down. Didn't matter. She just kept buying stocks.

Margo Sweeny offered Sheela an arrangement once she moved into the city and told Margo she had retired herself as one of Stanton's collectibles.

"Good move." Margo winked. "Retired pieces are worth more."

She and Sheela worked out a deal where Margo would send her johns to The Diamond Horseshoe to meet Sheela. That's where most of Sheela's money would come from. Her salary as a showgirl was not enough for her to keep buying up Blue Chip stocks. And protecting her future was the most important thing to Sheela, especially when told that the stocks would pay her a dividend she might one day be able to live on.

The difference between Margo Sweeny and Kit Malone was that Sheela didn't owe Margo more than twenty percent. For Sheela, Margo was her contact for johns, prostitution was a business, and men were a means to an end. Some were regular customers who kept coming back to The Diamond Horseshoe—innocuous fireflies drawn into the night—and some were bad pennies thrown back to piss on another woman's belly or to slap some other whore's behind. It wasn't about sin or judgment for Sheela, nor was it about disappointing Jesus. It was about getting rich and being able to forget one day where it all came from. It was about knowing that money could erase the unsavory gulp of semen, and she'd deal with Jesus when she got to heaven's gate and had to face her mama's disappointment. Scotch burned it all away anyway. Scotch dulled the distance between the bed and all the cracks in the ceiling she could count between the grateful grunts of a satisfied customer.

A gathering delirium gripped Manhattan in 1945. Everyone believed World War II was coming to an end. America had faith in Churchill and Roosevelt and expected that the boys overseas would be home as early as June of that year. Sheela's little brother had been in the Navy since he was eighteen years old. He had even earned himself medals fighting the Japanese. She had prayed for Jesus to spare him, to keep him safe, and Jesus had obliged. She got a letter saying he was coming back home on leave to marry the girl he'd written her about, the pretty one with hair just like Rita Hayworth's. Sheela planned to send him a thousand dollars for a wedding present.

"I can't wait to meet your bride," she told him anxiously.

"You're next, Sis," he had written her, "next to get hitched."

But Sheela didn't think she'd ever marry. She wasn't even sure anymore if she wanted to. It wasn't anything she spent much time thinking about, yet that silly dream kept returning, the one about the baby. She'd had the dream twice in one week: She was back in San Francisco again, staring at the moon, and Leroy St. James was handing her a little pink infant from the caramel-colored briefcase.

Sheela was swept up in her own delirium and looking for love wasn't part of it. She walked to the bank every week and deposited amounts that were sometimes as high as two thousand dollars. Money flowed at The Diamond Horseshoe, and a good deal of it was flowing her way. She was even dating Tommy Manville, one of the richest men in America. But a date with Tommy wasn't even worth a week's work or a call to the broker that told her what General Motors was selling for and how much of it she could buy with a few hundred bucks or a couple thousand.

She liked being a showgirl. Men loved to take front tables and make bets on whether they could get a date for later that evening. All kinds of men sent her notes backstage. Rich men—famous men—and naturally, traveling salesmen. She was almost as popular as Nevada Smith and Stuttering Sam. A lot of the girls dated some of the regulars at the club. But Sheela didn't take dates. She took appointments. The only man worth dating was Tommy. He was a well-known playboy who had been married several times. Well, maybe she'd become another one of his wives if she felt like it. The press was always taking pictures of them together. Even Winchell wrote her up. Winchell liked her. Said she wasn't much of a showgirl, couldn't walk or talk, but he found her sensational. Sheela would just toss her head back and laugh. Didn't seem to be any end to laughter in the spring of 1945. Certainly, there was no end to the men who got more of a bang buying sex than taking it for nothing, and there was certainly no end to the pleasure of walking to the bank and building a fortress.

# Chapter Thirty-Six

Tall men have the most alluring way of making you take notice, especially when their shoulders are so broad you could lose sight of everything else but the sky over you; tall men with a waist so high off the ground that clothes might have been tailored for them alone and heroes fashioned in their countenance. *Why he's as tall as Calvin Woods*, she was thinking as she watched him walk through the crowded dance floor, excusing himself with a hint of amusement, as if he wished it were he twirling about the room to the big band sound of Count Basie. She could tell from a distance he was kind, just watching the way he held his head.

Sheela wasn't working that evening. She was out with Patty Cakes and the man Patty had been seeing for the last six months. Sheela didn't really like Sid Bernstein, but Patty Cakes thought he was the "living end," so Sheela usually got hoodwinked into joining them at one of the clubs on the West Side. They were often out until dawn eating eggs at some all-night diner on Ninth Avenue, trying to sober up.

Sheela usually slept until noon every day, and then she'd get up and drink coffee like it was tap water and lay her cash out on the dining room table in little stacks of twenties, tens, fives and one-hundred-dollar bills. She'd count the stacks separately, total the money and put rubber bands around the stacks and take them to the bank for deposit. At the end of every month, she bought her stock in General Motors and US Steel.

They had wound up at the Paradise Club. After thirty minutes of idle chitchat, Sid suddenly stood up. He spilled his drink all over the table and yelled across the room so loudly it made Sheela jump.

"Hey, Julius! Over here!"

Sheela quickly moved her chair back while Patty Cakes squealed and called Sid an oaf. Sheela took the small square napkin and handed it to Patty, who tried to soak up the whiskey. Sid, oblivious to the spilled drink, reached his hand out in front of Sheela and gestured adamantly.

"Join us, Julius. Here. Take this chair. I'll squeeze in next to my girl."

Patty Cakes kept blotting the table while she slid over. Sheela finally looked up and noticed that the tall man she had watched walk across the dance floor was now fitting himself beside her.

"Julius, this here is my girl, Patty Steven from Steubenville, Ohio, but we just call her Patty Cakes. Isn't that right, hon? And this is Sheela from... ah, where you from, Sheela?"

Julius smiled at Sheela and nodded. She noticed the space between his two front teeth and his glasses, which were almost the color of his hair, which was just a shade deeper than sand.

"Jacksonville."

He took her hand and shook it as if they had just closed a deal.

"I'm from Greenpoint."

"Say 'Brooklyn,' Julius, for Christ's sake. No one is going to know where the hell Greenpoint is." Sid slapped him on the back and asked him if he had one of those great cigars. Julius nodded and reached into his breast pocket.

Sid bit off the end of the cigar while Patty called the waiter over, and they ordered a round for the table.

Julius was quiet for most of the evening, but he seemed to love the music and it looked to Sheela like he wanted to dance. Count Basie started playing "The One O'clock Boogie" when Sheela noticed that Julius was tapping his fingers on the table and moving his legs. She had barely said anything either. She and Julius were both sitting slightly forward in their chairs listening to Sid talk about some "catch" with a Reuben.

As Julius continued to tap his fingers and nod at Sid, Sheela noticed that his suit looked warm—knobby wool that she wanted to touch—and the space between his teeth made her feel oddly nostalgic for something she could not name.

Suddenly, Julius stood and held out his hand.

"Care to dance?"

"For Sentimental Reasons" filled the room, as did the sound of chairs sliding out from behind the tables. Sheela had to throw her chin all the way up to find his smile.

He led her onto the dance floor as if he were presenting her to the King of England. He put his arm around her waist and moved his long legs so smoothly that Sheela didn't have to exert any effort at all to follow his lead. The muscles in her body seemed to let go all at once, and her feet barely touched the floor.

The timbre and tone of the horn lifted and swelled in her ear. "For sentimental reasons," she hummed.

The soft, freshly shaven cheek brushed her brow and leaned ever so gently against her hair as he hummed back.

"I like the way you dance," she told him.

"Not bad for a guy with flat feet?"

"Flat feet?"

"Kept me out of the Army."

Before he walked her back to the table, he stopped and turned her to him.

"Free on Saturday?" he asked suddenly.

Sheela shrugged. "Only in the afternoon."

"Oh, the afternoon will be just fine."

Sheela wondered why she had agreed to see him. He wasn't a ladies' man like Tommy Manville, and he certainly wasn't a john. Maybe it was because he had treated her like the girl next door, like a girl who keeps her virginity as sacred as her belief in God.

She lay in her bed that evening and wondered why keeping a date with Julius Clark made her feel she was that girl again, and love was a yearning so deep it hurt to dream about it.

The sky was a bright blue, one of those exceptionally brisk days in early April, but it felt cold enough to snow. He sat in her living room with his high knees and shoes the color of that wonderful brittle candy that always comes in a tin. He was waiting for her to finish dressing while his eyes traveled across the room.

"Do you play?" Julius got up and touched the piano keys lightly.

"No."

"Who plays?"

"No one."

"Then why do you have a piano?"

She was about to tell him it was an impulse buy to cover up the crack in the wall, but instead, she told him her mama used to play and her papa had just come home one day and sold it in order to invest in a distillery, so she kept a piano in her mama's memory. She thought it was a funny story and that Julius would laugh, but he didn't. He took her hand and looked sadly into her eyes and said he was sorry.

"Sorry for what?" she asked as she placed a cigarette between her lips. Julius leaned in and lit it.

"Sorry for your mama," he whispered.

Sheela puffed long streams of smoke into the open air and realized her jaw clenched every time she stopped puffing, and her hands were shaking.

"How about a scotch?" she asked and got up

quickly.

Julius laughed. "It's one o'clock in the afternoon!"

Sheela took another long puff and stared at him. He was grinning back at her like a schoolboy with a frog in his pocket.

"Do you like animals?" He smiled.

Sheela puffed again. "Animals?"

"Ever seen an orangutan?"

"A what?"

"Or a cockatoo? How 'bout a sea lion?"

"Are you pulling my leg?" Sheela put her hands on her hips and gave him a studied look.

"Come on, Sheela." Julius took the cigarette from her and squashed it down on a plate.

"Let's have some fun."

He stood up and went for his coat and tied a long scarf around his neck.

"Dress warm. And put on a pair of comfortable shoes."

"Where are you taking me, Julius?"

"To a magical place," he whispered.

She had never been to Central Park. It was only a few blocks from her apartment on Seventy-seventh Street, but she had never walked there. There just never seemed to be any reason to. She had never ventured any farther south than Thirty-fourth Street nor any farther east than Broadway. If she looked out her bedroom window, she could make out the tops of buildings all the way over on Central Park West, but that was as close to the park as she had gotten.

They found a bench that faced the lake and sat in the April sun. The tall stately buildings bordering the park looked like the fortresses of kings as they towered over the trees.

"See that building over there? The one with the twin towers? That's the San Remo."

Sheela sat beside him. She looked up at the building's majestic towers.

"All the buildings on Central Park West have names," he told her.

They hadn't spoken much, but they were both thinking that Manhattan had never looked more beautiful than from where they were sitting on that quiet afternoon.

Quite unexpectedly, Julius reached over and took her hand.

"I love buildings," he sighed passionately. "And boats. I love boats," he added, with the same amount of whimsical desire in his tone.

Sheela looked at his profile and thought he looked too sweet to be called handsome, and that made him even more appealing.

"I love the water, but I haven't been on many boats," she told him.

He turned and looked right into her eyes.

"I'll take you on one," he said. "Looked at a real beauty the other day. I think I'm going to buy it. Maybe I'll name it the 'Sheela Jay' after you and me."

She noticed saying that had made him blush, and he stood up quickly.

"Come on, Sheela. I want you to meet some of my friends."

They walked through the park hand in hand, stopping every now and then to light a cigarette against the wind. Once they reached the entrance to the zoo, he took her right to the monkey cage and the orangutan named "Terry."

"Cute enough to marry, isn't he?"

Sheela laughed and put her arm in the warm tweedy crevice of his sleeve. They walked the paths and watched the polar bears, and the sea lions playing in the sun and wondered about how caged birds flew and lions adjusted to rooms no larger than a decent-sized bathroom. She loved that Julius had skin like velvet, and his voice was low—so low he made her listen with her eyes on his mouth.

"Do you like dogs, Sheela?"

"Yes, I—"

She wanted to tell him about Kit Malone's Sweetie Pie but didn't want to talk about the mansion. It didn't matter, though. He cut her off.

"My pop has a great dog. Milika. We all love her, all except for Mom. It's not that Mom hates dogs. She hates the hair in the house."

Sheela laughed. Not because he had said anything particularly funny but because she felt giddy. Giddy enough to put her hands around his waist and squeeze tight.

"Let's get a dog." She laughed again.

He squeezed her back and said he'd like that.

They stayed out until the evening brought a sky full of stars and Julius had climbed up on the concrete wall that closed the park to traffic.

"Stand across the street, Sheela, and look back at me," he said.

He held up his arm and cupped his hand under the moon. The gesture made it look as if he held the small round glow of the moon in his hand.

"I give you heaven's light," he called to her.

His sweetness filled her. His face was as round as the moon itself. The space between his teeth was so endearing, it made her want to weep. She wanted nothing more than the knobby wool of his arm to rest her fingers against as he walked her home.

It begins that way, tenderness so reminiscent of love that it burrows its fragility in the contours of memory and waits for the proper heart to free it.

# Chapter Thirty-Seven

Sheela climbed the stairs at 107 Freeman Street clutching her new puppy in a mink muff. His tiny golden ears fell across his fur and blended like honey sliding over a piece of toast. In her other hand, she held an asparagus fern plant by a silver hook, the shiny silver wrapping paper crinkled as she walked, and the rich spider leaves fell about her arms and tickled her skin like the soft whiskers around her new puppy's mouth.

She was meeting his family for the first time. She had chosen to wear a loose blue-and-white Jersey dress with large square buttons and a sailor-boy collar. She had asked him at least one hundred times if she looked good enough to meet his mama, and one hundred times he had nodded his head and smiled, "she'll love you."

Julius carried two bottles of Champagne and three bottles of scotch under his arms. As he took the stairs two at a time, the bottles clinked against one another and Sheela was afraid they might break and spill all over the clean blue carpet under her feet. But he made it to the top of the landing and embraced his mother.

"This is Sheela, Mom," he said, grinning broadly.

Jay-Jay let out a high-pitched yelp from inside the muff, and Mary jumped back. She held her hands to her heart.

"Good Jesus!" she hollered.

"Oh, sorry, Mom. I hope you don't mind. This is the puppy I bought Sheela. Jay-Jay. He's a Cocker Spaniel, only a couple of months old," Julius said nervously as he took the dog out of the muff.

Mary made a face and eyed the honey-colored creature.

"Jay-Jay? After my son Julius John?" She laughed, and her face relaxed. "They look alike. Same color hair. Dirty blond."

Mary looked up at the tall woman who had just thrown her arms around her shoulders and had lifted her at least two inches off the floor.

Julius quickly took the dog and went inside the small railroad apartment where Margaret and her husband, Joseph, were anxiously waiting to meet Sheela.

Margaret rubbed her hands together as Joseph straightened his tie. Julius grinned as Sheela walked into the room. He saw Joseph's jaw drop and felt the elbow in his side as Joseph leaned over and blew a long, low wolf whistle into his ear.

"What a looker!" Joseph whispered as he poked Julius in the ribs again.

Though there were two doors into the

apartment, it was only the kitchen door that was ever used. The kitchen was clearly the most important room in the house, and Mary and the children had spent most of their time there. The utilities were all along one wall, and the dining room table was along the opposite wall. At the far end of the kitchen was the apartment's only bathroom. It had a window over the tub that looked out onto the garden. The tub sat on little claw feet next to the toilet. Above the toilet was a long chain that was pulled to release fresh water and flush out the old. The only sink was in the kitchen.

Sheela hugged Margaret as Julius popped open the Champagne. Mary put her hands to her heart as the cork flew out and the bubbly substance flowed onto the floor.

Margaret kept her hands tight around Sheela's waist and giggled as the puppy tugged at the legs of John's pants and growled.

"Do you think he hates me?" John called to his son.

"Just a show of affection, Pop."

They all gathered around the stove and watched as Mary lifted the lids from the pots and nursed the meal, taking small samples on a spoon, an enviable privilege.

On the wall behind the table was a print of "The Last Supper." The print was almost as long as the room itself. Sheela and Julius were seated right between Jesus and John the Baptist. Jay-Jay was standing up on Sheela's lap with his paws on her shoulder, showing the Disciple, Paul, the pink of his tongue.

Mary turned from the stove and eyed the dog suspiciously.

"The dog? It always sits on your lap like that when you eat?"

"Poor thing cried so much when I closed the door behind him that I just couldn't leave him alone," Sheela said sheepishly, looking uncomfortably at Julius.

"If it bothers you, Mom... I can take Jay-Jay downstairs and let Milika snack on him," Julius quickly added.

"Oh, you," she said, as she sat at the table. She looked at Sheela and reached out for her hand. "You're a beautiful girl."

Sheela smiled at her sadly. She didn't want to be a beautiful girl for their Julius. She wanted to be a good Catholic girl like his Karla had been.

"Thank you," she replied softly.

Mary kept her eyes on the girl. She looked at the long red fingernails and a face she thought existed only on movie screens.

"You call me Mom," she said and looked into the darkest blue eyes she had ever seen. "Your eyes are navy. Navy blue. Very pretty."

Julius poured his mother a glass of Champagne, and they lifted their glasses in a toast to Sheela, soon to be one of their own.

"Come on, Mom. You've got to drink it. It's a toast," Sheela said as she held her glass up and winked at Mary.

Mary held the glass in front of her eyes. She

stared at the golden color as they all cheered her on. Margaret and Joseph sat grinning at her from the end of the table and even her husband seemed amused. He had never seen her take a drink in all the years they had been married, not even at her own wedding.

Mary put her lips together and looked back at all of them defiantly. She lifted the delicate tall glass to her lips, drank the bubbly drink quickly and smiled proudly at her husband.

"I like it. Champagne? It's sweet. I like it." She grinned.

Julius laughed and filled her glass again.

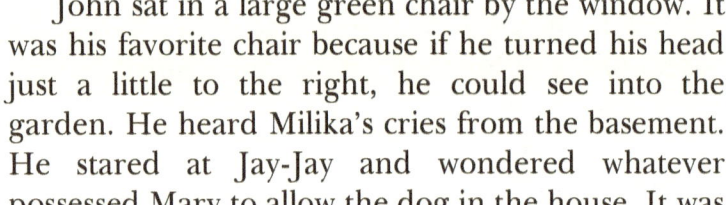

John sat in a large green chair by the window. It was his favorite chair because if he turned his head just a little to the right, he could see into the garden. He heard Milika's cries from the basement. He stared at Jay-Jay and wondered whatever possessed Mary to allow the dog in the house. It was almost as if this girl were casting some sort of spell over her. He'd never seen his wife so lightheaded.

John knew Milika must have picked up the puppy's scent and wanted to meet the little creature. Well, soon enough he would go into the basement and reassure his Milika, tell her that the puppy was too small and inconsequential to be of any concern.

He looked over at his son and this woman who had brought a dog into the house in a mink muff. The girl turned to him as if she read his mind; as if she knew what he was thinking, that his Julius was always too much in the clouds to see the color of the sky. John raised his glass to her.

"To you, Sheela," he said.

The girl tipped her glass and drank. John thought about his Berta and the bones that lay in the cold earth.

"To love." He toasted her again. "To love," he repeated. He brought the bubbly liquid to his lips, letting the cold frothy sweet Champagne run around his mouth before he swallowed it. He avoided his wife's eyes.

"To good-looking women." Joseph raised his glass high and stood up from the table. "Nice plant," he smiled at Sheela as he walked over and ran his fingers across the feathery green leaves.

"Oh, the plant." Mary rushed over and took all the silver paper off and held the plant before her.

"Beautiful. Look everyone, how beautiful it is. Thank you, Sheela. Look, John. A beautiful plant."

Mary put the plant in the window near John's chair. John smiled politely at all the spidery leaves that now took up all his window space.

"Would you like to see the garden later, Sheela?" he asked her.

"Yes, sure I would. Thank you." Sheela smiled politely.

John knew by her answer that she was indifferent to flowers. She never asked him what he grew. He felt relieved that soon he would be able to sneak away. Soon, after an early dinner, he would walk Milika to the river and watch the great golden sun as it set in the sky. He wondered if Mary would

ever care to see the sun set with him again. Since
the first year of their marriage, she had never gone
back to the river with him. The river was so close to
the house he could almost touch it, but Mary said it
was too far, and there should be a reason for where
your feet took you.

The room was so potent with the scent of
carrots, leeks, and turnips that Sheela's unborn
child might have been able to recognize it. The
aroma made her stomach growl. She covered her
stomach with her hands and felt for the life inside
her. She was four months pregnant. They planned
to tell his family that evening. She wanted to tell
them all that the baby was a girl, but Julius thought
she was crazy for knowing. She had been to a gypsy,
and the gypsy told her she'd have a baby girl with a
turned-up nose and a dimple in her chin.

Julius laughed when she came home smiling and
relayed the message. "You don't believe in the tales
of gypsies?" he'd said.

Sheela knew the gypsy saw her future, knew it
by the crooked smile and the confidence that had
settled in her expression as she stared into the
crystal.

"Thirty years," the gypsy had whispered. "Thirty
years. A circle. Danger. Separation. Poof!"

The gypsy stopped talking then and looked
deeply into the round ball.

"Go on."

"No more to tell."

She slipped the five-dollar bill Sheela handed

her into her brassiere and placed a cloth over the ball.

"Don't worry," she said. "Life is not easy for anyone."

Mary noted that her son had not stopped grinning since he walked through the door. He had announced their engagement only a week ago. At first, she and John had thought that it was Karla he was marrying. "Oh, so you've reconciled," John had said happily. But then Julius shook his head and told them his bride-to-be was the showgirl from The Diamond Horseshoe.

"Remember, Mom. I told you I was seeing a girl named Sheela. A girl with a face like an angel."

Mary hid her confusion by talking quickly and telling him to bring the girl to Greenpoint to meet her new family.

"I promise, Mom, I'll bring her as soon as I can. You're going to love her."

Marrying a showgirl didn't seem proper to Mary. Still, she felt his love for this girl, and she believed with all her heart that her son was a good man and deserved to be happy, and this girl, whoever she was, seemed to make her son happy.

"Karla was a fool to give you up, such a successful young man," Mary said. "She didn't understand you."

"I haven't seen Karla for weeks," Julius said quietly. "Did she marry Wozniak?"

"Who knows?" Mary said. "You have done better, my son."

But secretly, she was disappointed.

Mary stared at the diamond on Sheela's finger as it glistened back at her from under the blond fur of the puppy busy licking his mistress on the ear.

"Stop that, Jay-Jay," Sheela whispered.

"Joseph, get the dog some water," Mary said over her shoulder. She then turned back to Sheela and asked where she was from.

"Jacksonville," Sheela said with a slight catch in her voice.

Julius took her hand in his and mentioned sadly that Sheela had been an orphan.

"An orphan?" Mary said with a surprised lilt.

Mary would never have taken this glamorous woman for an orphan.

Julius nodded and held Sheela's hand more tightly.

"Well, not anymore," Mary said as she got up to check on the food. "Now you have a big Hungarian family."

They all laughed and agreed with Mary as they inhaled the air. The chicken sat on the stove in a large pot and tempted the senses with aromatic whiffs that lingered just below the nostrils, stirring up the growls in their stomachs and making them even hungrier.

"Julius, go upstairs and see what's keeping your sister," Mary said as she looked at the wall clock.

Rebeka and her husband, Lou, entered the room on her words, with their ten-year-old son, Sonny, lagging behind.

"Didn't think we were coming, Mom?" Rebeka gave her mother a kiss on the cheek. "When do I ever miss my mom's home cooking?" She all but cackled. "I didn't inherit the trait."

When Sonny saw his uncle Julius, his face lit up, and he dashed to grab the chair next to him, eyeing the stranger shyly.

Sheela noticed that Rebeka was not much taller than her mother and had the same tight curls in her hair. Sheela smiled at the boy, who blushed.

"Hi. You must be Sheela," Rebeka said, taking the chair directly across from her.

"Hi, Rebeka." Sheela reached over the table to shake her hand.

"Cute little guy. A cocker?" Rebeka winked at Jay-Jay.

Sheela nodded and put the puppy down. He ran to the dish of water that Joseph had placed on the floor.

"Grab a chair, Lou," Rebeka said to her husband.

Sheela thought that Lou looked like a large lizard. His hair and his neck seemed to get lost somewhere in his flesh. He had a large birthmark near his lip that sat under the shadow of his nose and appeared to harbor the venomous lash of a tongue from his lips. He sat near his wife and offered Sheela what might have been a nod.

As Mary served the meal, chairs shifted, and they sat almost stiff with anticipation. The puppy could be heard lapping up the water from the dish. He then found a place near Sheela's feet to rest his tiny head. Sheela hoped she hadn't seen him pee in the corner of the kitchen before he found her shoe.

John lowered his head and prayed. "We thank the Lord thy God for the bounty we are about to receive."

"In the name of the Father, the Son and the Holy Ghost. Amen," they whispered as they made the sign of the cross.

Long reaches across the table for bread immediately followed the saying of Grace. The Champagne passed freely as John carved the chicken. The gravy passed down the cluttered oval table along with the mashed potatoes and fresh vegetables. Sheela did not remember a meal ever tasting as good.

"Mom, this is the best meal I've ever had." Sheela licked her lips.

Mary let them fill her glass with more Champagne. "It's only chicken." She smiled at Sheela. "Next, I will make you goulash."

"So, tell me, Sheela, how do you afford such an expensive city?" Rebeka leaned over on one elbow as Mary handed her a plate of white meat.

Lou compared how pale his wife looked next to the dazzling girl. He took in Sheela's red nails and the large breasts that swelled so sweetly beneath her Jersey. *Must be a whore. Poor Julius.*

"Are you Catholic?" Joseph asked Sheela out of nowhere.

"I told you she was Catholic," Mary snapped at him.

"I'm not Catholic," Joseph said. "But close enough. Protestant? Catholic? What's the difference, eh, Mom?" He showed a wide grin as he reached for a piece of bread and winked at his mother-in-law.

Mary made the sign of the cross and kissed the tiny silver icon around her neck as she shook her head from side to side.

"So, Sheela," Rebeka began again, "they must pay you well at The Diamond Horseshoe, eh?"

Sheela looked quickly at Julius. "I'm not at The Diamond Horseshoe anymore. Could I have some more of that white meat, Mom?"

"Oh? Where do you work now?" Rebeka took a large bite of mashed potatoes and peered at Sheela.

Julius lifted his head and smiled broadly at his half-sister, as if the Champagne had made him think of silly things.

"I'm not working at all now, Rebeka," Sheela said sheepishly.

"I was going to wait to tell you, but I think this is the time." Julius cleared his throat and held up his water glass. He clinked his fork against it. He reached for Sheela's hand, the dimples showing up in his cheeks like pockets.

"Attention, everyone! Attention!" Julius kept his broad grin as they all looked up, except for Lou, who continued to chew his food, and Sonny, who reached for his milk.

"We just signed a lease on a big apartment over on Central Park West. In the San Remo."

"That's the news?" Joseph said with a shrug.

"Well, not exactly. There's more." He held Sheela's hand tightly in his lap. "We're having a baby."

Mary put down her fork and her hands went to her heart.

"A baby?" she gasped.

"Yes, Mom, a baby." Julius said carefully.

"Blessed Jesus," Mary whispered and made the sign of the cross. "Before marriage? Blessed Jesus."

John leaned in toward his son and glared at him. "You couldn't wait to marry?" he shouted.

"A grandchild from my son, my Julius?" Mary's eyes were wide.

Sheela nodded nervously. "Our wedding is in two weeks, Mom."

Mary looked at her husband. "Our son's child, John. She doesn't show. No one will be the wiser."

John stared at his son and felt himself soften. *He's in love. I do remember what that's like. Two weeks before my wedding, my Berta in my arms, my shame for not waiting.*

Slowly he sat back. "To my grandchild," he said quietly as he raised his glass and added quickly, "Don't tell the priest about the baby. Not until after the wedding."

Lou stared at Rebeka. "A toast," he heard her say! He watched his wife raise her glass. Even his son lifted his milk in the air. His mother-in-law had tears in her eyes, and Old Man Kuvik even appeared to be crying. He stared back at Julius. *Stupid bastards. You'd think this dumb whore was giving birth to the Holy Mother.*

# Chapter Thirty-Eight

It was right after meeting his family that Sheela told him everything. And if he had left her, his heart would have ached for the rest of his life. The absence of her would have caused him that. But oddly, it didn't break his heart to hear her say she had pleased men for money, and it had made her a rich woman. His eyes filled with tears, and he turned his head away, but his heart didn't ache. Sadness is only a temporary drowning, not like an absence. That kind of pain is forever. And that must have been how Julius saw it.

"It's made me over two hundred thousand dollars," she told him.

She was proud. He tried not to like that about her. Perhaps she expected him to leave quickly once the words were finally out. Oh, he wanted to oblige but his feet wouldn't move. He tried to pick something up and throw it against the wall. But his arms wouldn't move either. Instead, he cried. *What an idiot I am*, he kept thinking. W*hy the hell am I* *crying?*

Sheela didn't touch him. She sat quietly in a big comfortable chair and expected her life to go on without him.

Julius was silent. He didn't look at her. The puppy lay in his lap, but he ignored it.

Sheela went for a cigarette. Julius didn't offer to light it for her, so she walked across the room for matches. He followed the click-clack sound of her slippers. She made a soft, gentle breeze when she walked by, and he smelled her perfume. He thought about grabbing her and knocking her down, but it was only something he thought he should do, the way it was done in the movies. But harming her wasn't an option, though he tried to hate her; if he could accomplish that he could make his exit. But he was immobilized. Frozen to his seat.

He stared at the phone. *Perhaps I should call a lawyer. Make arrangements. Set something up for the baby. I'll tell the family it was all a mistake. I can't marry a whore.*

He tried to take control. He willed himself to rise.

Instead, he continued to cry. He tried to stop. He tightened the muscles in his face so much his jaw hurt. *Why the hell can't I stop crying?*

The puppy had jumped out of his lap to follow Sheela across the room. Sheela lit her cigarette and returned to the chair that faced him.

Julius looked inside himself for rage, but he couldn't find that either. He looked for hatred, but his heart was free of it. Unbearable sadness was all.

Sheela sat and stroked the puppy. Jay-Jay had curled up in a little ball on her lap. She blew the smoke toward Julius, whose face was hidden in his hands. She knew he was weeping for her because she had done something shameful, something nice girls didn't do. She tried to imagine life without him. She felt the coldness in her chest, the empty gaping hole. She reached for her glass. The ice had melted, and the scotch had a diluted burn. She could only taste the water. She wanted to spit it out.

Julius raised his head as if he wanted to speak, but he said nothing.

*I will be fine without him.* She almost said it aloud, to reassure him. But there was also a part of her that wanted to hurt him. She felt pity, but she also felt rage, anger strong enough to throw something at the back of his head if he got up to leave.

Julius felt his body shudder. "Goodbye," he heard himself whisper. He finally pushed himself up and out of the door. He didn't look at her. The door closed quickly behind him.

He found Paddy's Pub on Columbus Avenue, a quiet bar where a lot of businessmen went to drink before going home. It wasn't crowded, and he chose a corner table. He drank slowly. He put his head back on the hard wall and listened to someone singing about the swallows coming back to Capistrano. He tried to sing along. He kept telling strangers to play something by Sarah Vaughn, or Lena Horne, but no one paid any attention to him and the damn swallow song kept playing repeatedly. He stayed until closing anyway, even though he kept complaining about the lousy music. He couldn't understand why the whiskey hadn't made him drunk. He wanted to get inebriated. Piss-eyed. Ossified. Soused. But instead, he felt stoic. Sober enough to drive a car or fly a goddamned airplane.

"Is it all about some pang below my belt?" he asked a blonde drinking alone. "Can I figure it all out by morning?"

The blonde blew cigarette smoke in his face and shrugged her shoulders.

This romance thing was bigger than he had ever imagined. Sheela had invaded his heart, pushed her way into his thoughts and stayed there like some goddamned witch who had control over his soul.

He thought about hailing a cab back to Greenpoint, but his feet took him back to her. *Maybe I'm only going back to tell her again that I'm leaving her,* he thought as he crossed West End Avenue and used his key in the downstairs lock.

He found her asleep in the same chair. He fought the impulse to lay his head in her lap. She looked so alone. He almost started to cry again. Looking at her only put him more in touch with how much he loved her. He wanted to go back and undo any harm that was ever done to her. He thought about her being in the orphanage, losing her mama so young. He wished he'd known her forever, before she'd made any choices without him. He held out his arms and called out her name.

Sheela was surprised to see him. His face had turned so kind. Yet he was distraught and confused. It brought her back so far to feel his sorrow, so goddamned far she could hardly stand it.

"Like touching God," she whispered.

"What?" he asked her softly.

"Something my mama used to say about innocence."

He stared at her.

"I've hurt you?" she said.

He didn't answer her.

She put her hands on her belly.

"Having a baby is like touching God."

Julius felt the tears begin again as he sat on the couch opposite her. He was surprised at himself. He wanted her near.

"Come here," he said softly.

Sheela went into his arms. He lowered his lips to her belly and kissed the unborn child.

"You're under no obligation," she told him. "We don't need you."

Julius returned to her eyes. They were smoky blue and softer than he had ever seen them.

She pressed her fingers into his arm so fiercely her nails dug into his skin. She hugged him. Her hug was tight, as if she would never let go.

"Leave if you have to," she whispered.

He nestled his hands in her hair. "Never," he said.

# Chapter Thirty-Nine

Julius was a nail-biter. He could be as pensive as he was gregarious. When hurt, he became sullen and distant, but he forgave in a heartbeat, and before Sheela knew it, he was imitating James Cagney again and making her laugh.

He was crazy about his angel, and that's what he called her, his angel. He was constant. He would gently put his large hand on her belly. He'd get down on his knees and put his ear against her. He listened for the baby's kick three or four times a day, and he took her to Dr. Shapiro as if he were handling precious crystal, delivering something so fragile and delicate he demanded that cab drivers not exceed twenty miles an hour or brake too quickly. Nor would he allow indifferent pedestrians to walk too close to his angel girl who carried his baby in the soft, dark quiescence of her womb.

He knew everything about her now. She had told him everything, and it hadn't been easy to accept, but then he was over it. He wouldn't think of it again, not ever. She was his now, since the first time he'd kissed her, she'd been his. She never asked to be forgiven, and he never offered forgiveness. It was her past, and it would not invade their future. No one would have understood that, certainly not Sid who had sat bug-eyed and red-faced when Julius invited him to the wedding.

"I didn't mean for you to marry her."

Julius did not want to hear it spoken. His eyes flinched. Something in his expression stopped Sid from telling him to go find a nice little virgin from Brooklyn and forget about the glamour girl with a client list as long as his arm.

Julius clenched his jaw. His hands tightened in his pockets. He stared at Sid. Stared him down until Sid coughed uncomfortably.

"Congratulations," he finally mumbled.

"Will you come to the wedding?"

"Sure, Julius. I'll be there."

Julius let out his breath and leaned in close to Sid. "She's an angel," he whispered. "And she's carrying my baby."

# Chapter Forty

Stuttering Sam and Tall Tex Peterson were there at the hospital the day Juliana Clark was born. They were there with four other showgirls whom Sheela barely knew. They brought tiny woolen booties, rattlers, and little toy Teddies. Tex and Sam pulled a bottle of Piper Heidsieck out of a Saks Fifth Avenue shopping bag and they sipped it out of little medicine cups. Julius was downtown passing around his best cigars and making arrangements to send a limousine to Greenpoint to take his mother and father up to Doctor's Hospital in Manhattan to see the baby.

"Just blew in with the winter wind," Sheela said. "She just blew in with the winter wind. My little girl."

"Where's the little darling?" one of the girls asked a nurse who smiled mischievously and told them Champagne was not allowed in the room.

"Be a dear," Tex drawled, "and bend the rules."

The young nurse was mesmerized by all the glamour: all the mink and sable coats still shimmering with snow and thrown across Sheela's bed and draped over the chairs. Someone handed the nurse a little cup, and she giggled.

"I'll be bringing the baby in now," she told them as she placed the little cup back on the nightstand. "Don't be breathing on the poor little thing, or you'll inebriate the child."

The girls laughed and sat on Sheela's bed. Sam was almost under the sheets with her, and another girl was rubbing Sheela's hands. The world beyond the window was like a white sheet of snow—snow that still fell from the sky and glistened, the way tears do in the light of day.

Sheela wanted her baby. The excitement was so intense that she might have willed the infant to her arms. She was aware of an aching somewhere inside her as though the life removed from her body had been a limb she now lacked. It felt as empty and cold as the snow might feel against the naked body. Perhaps all she needed was to hold her baby. To take the baby's warmth and put her ear to the amazing beating heart of the tiny little miracle that smelled like heaven.

The girls cooed over the infant. Marveled at her priceless perfection and nicknamed her "Fanny."

It was Tex who first noticed the butt on baby Juliana.

"Wow-wee honey, what an adorable ass! We are going to have to call you Fanny, little baby. Cutest little fanny I ever saw."

The girls all agreed, and the name stuck. By the time Mary and John got to the hospital to see the baby, she was known as "baby Fanny." It made Mary grimace to hear her grandchild called so inappropriately, but Julius explained to her that Fanny really was a legitimate name and very popular. "Like Fanny Brice, Mom," he said.

Mary held the tiny infant in her arms. The little fists were closed, and a small sound came from her lips. Mary looked at John and kissed the sweet cheeks of the infant. Sheela was holding Julius's hand. He looked as radiant as his wife. It was a moment Mary wanted to hold and replay for the rest of her life. "God bless you, little Juliana," she said quietly. The baby had fallen off to sleep. Mary kissed her cheek again. "My heart," she said softly, "you now own my heart."

"Are you teaching my daughter Hungarian?" Julius laughed.

Mary didn't answer. She just closed her eyes against the infant skin. "Sweet Jesus.Sweet Jesus. I've lost my heart," she whispered.

# Chapter Forty-One

Julius and Lou bought a bar on Grand Avenue in the Williamsburg section of Brooklyn.

"I don't think that's a good idea," Sheela said. "I think you should form a partnership with your father, buy a building in Manhattan, Julius."

The business with Sid had expanded in yet another even more dubious direction, and Sheela felt that Julius couldn't sever his ties with Sid Bernstein fast enough, but Sheela wasn't convinced that buying a bar was the answer.

"I think Lou and I can turn that little neighborhood pub on Grand Avenue into a gold mine, Sheela."

Sheela disagreed. "There's a building for sale off Park, a brownstone."

Julius ignored her comment. "We're going to take out the pool table and put in a jukebox. Then we're going to modernize the dark, paneled room and turn it into a bright deco oasis. Do you like the name SwingTime?"

Sheela tried to be encouraging, but she still felt

that a bar in Williamsburg was a bad idea, even though it would eventually move him away from Sid Bernstein. A fourth partner had come into the business a month or so after Fanny's birth, and Sid and Julius were doubling what they had made in 1945 by faking masterpieces. Julius took advantage of this double-edged good fortune and stockpiled his cash while putting his own business plans into action.

Sid Bernstein's new partner, Rocco "Sugar" Noffe, was known as the "Patriarch Gangster." They also called him the "Squire of Bay Ridge," the "pretty boy" with a South Hampton summer home and the airs of a prince. If Rocco said he could find an original Chagall, no one doubted him. He had the best copyists in the business under contract, commissioned according to their expertise, and then the fakes sold to the unsuspecting.

Rocco's clientele was mostly the nouveau riche who saw the charming Italian more as a guru of culture, someone who could fill in the gaps of their own ignorance. They had no idea of his identity as the "Patriarch Gangster" or his family's reputed links to organized crime. To this nouveau riche set, he was simply "that charming Mr. Noffe."

Rocco did own a legitimate gallery on 57th Street in Manhattan that specialized in early twentieth-century art. Rocco funded the gallery but rarely showed up there. The 57th Street address, however, gave him the credibility he needed. An older woman whom Rocco had met on a cruise to the Bahamas operated it: Livy Merimar, a fading

Broadway actress who once had a part-time job at the Metropolitan Museum and faked her professionalism so well that no one ever doubted her phony history from Sotheby's.

Rocco profusely denied any connection to "The Family" even though his father was Dominique Noffe, a major player in construction extortion who had been serving time in a federal prison since 1943. Rocco's brother, Stephano "Steps" Noffe, was now the benefactor of his father's turf.

Steps earned his nickname because he had his enemies taken out in steps. His muscle was his bodyguard, "Jimmy the Worm." The Worm followed out the first step by roughing up a guy or leaving a dead rat at his door. The second step was damage to property, which might include a wife or girlfriend. Jimmy the Worm would usually just frighten the broad, throw a dead cat at her, or ram her car off the road. He didn't really like roughing up women, but a job was a job; that's the way the Worm looked at it. Whatever Steps wanted. If Steps wanted the broad taken out, well then, so be it. But it was the third step that earned the Worm his reputation. That's where he was master. He was known for the cleanest hits in the business—one quick bullet behind the ear. The Worm could walk right up behind a man anywhere on earth and take him out without a sound.

Fast.

Grab the neck.

*Pop.*

Then blend in with the dirt and disappear.

Rocco was always in the clubs. He and Steps liked showgirls. Rocco would bring his latest virgin back to one of those fancy East Side buildings, then meet Steps and the Worm at whatever place was offering the best entertainment. Julius and Sheela would always be asked to join them, and Sid was never far behind.

The baby was left in the care of Roselle, a neurotic and heavyset young woman who always appeared to be smiling. She referred to Juliana as "Queen Fanny" and Sheela as "Mum." Roselle was very high-strung and had a nasty habit of screaming at the slightest provocation. Once, she screamed so loudly that a neighbor knocked on the door to see if everything was all right.

"The girl screams every time the baby cries. Every time the alarm clock goes off. Every time she drops a fork or breaks another one of our goddamn plates. What the hell's the matter with her?" Julius complained to Sheela.

Roselle had been hired after six agency rejects, and even though she had broken several of their wedding dishes in the first week and most of their wine glasses in the second, and even though she screamed several times a day whenever the slightest little thing startled her, she treated the baby like royalty, and that was enough for Sheela.

Sid Bernstein had a new girlfriend named Maureen. Julius called her "Steamy Maureen" because she seemed to always be on the make. Little Patty Cakes was pregnant with Sid's child, and he was trying to pawn her off on a cop named Timothy Mooney, who was on somebody's payroll.

Sid and his partners all had their own tables at three or four major clubs. The tables were always held for them whenever they phoned ahead. Men who called each other *pisano,* and talked behind their hands, usually surrounded Steps and Rocco. Even though women hung off their arms like ornaments, the men never looked like they were having a good time. Step's jaw was always tight; so tight his bone could be seen moving under his skin. He would stare out over the room, never at the people he was with. The scotch glass in his hand, he held so tightly that Sheela was afraid the damn thing would break and shatter all over the table. Every time he sat down, he grabbed his crotch and hiked himself up, as though his testicles were so heavy, he had to lift them out of the way, and he constantly had his hand on his fly.

Rocco was a finger snapper. He snapped his fingers at people, kept jumping up and calling people over to him. Then he'd slide his arm around some crony's shoulder and bend in close to the guy's ear. Occasionally, he'd run his hand over someone's lapel and grab him affectionately by the neck. With women, he'd run his fingers across his mustache and then slide them through his hair, showing off his pretty--boy looks with a smile so sweet it made cold women melt.

The Worm was quiet. He'd sit drinking doubles and slip matchbook covers between his teeth.

"There's always wax in Jimmy's ear," Sheela

complained to Julius. "And sweat stains under the arms of his shirt."

Julius laughed. "Don't look at his ears then. No need to look under his arms either. Look at me."

"Stephano makes me nervous," she said.

"Once the bar opens, that's it with Sid. All I want to do is run that bar with Lou. We won't even go out to the clubs anymore." Julius took her hand. "We won't have the time."

Sheela was relieved that Julius planned to dissolve his partnership with Sid as soon as the bar officially opened, but she never changed her mind about it. She still thought it was a bad move, but at the very least, it would put an end to her husband's relationship with Sid and Rocco.

"I know how you feel about Rocco, but he's a class act. He can't help the family he was born into. Besides, you know the mob isn't into fine art." Julius took a sip of his scotch and winked at her.

Sheela eyed him oddly. "They call him the Patriarch Gangster," she reminded him.

Julius shrugged it off. "Stupid rumor," he said. "It's just because his brother and his father are such hoods."

Julius's naiveté frightened Sheela, and as far as she was concerned, Julius couldn't sever his ties with these crooks soon enough. She was grateful that Julius would soon be meeting with Sid to tell him about his new plans but also worried. She wondered what they would do if the bar didn't make money. Sheela was persistent about persuading Julius to buy an apartment building and manage it with his father, but Julius thought it was a dumb idea.

"No telling what the future holds for New York City real estate," he'd tell her. "But there will always be a market for booze."

Sheela wasn't convinced. She knew Lou was expecting to get as rich as Julius, and she wondered what would happen between the two men if the bar was a bust. She had never warmed to Lou. He hadn't even come to the baby's baptism. He and his son hardly spoke to her. The only time either of them ever moved their mouths in front of her was when they were eating.

"You've invested way too much into the place," Sheela said. "All Lou has to give is time."

"Lou doesn't have the money to put up, Sheela. He's a different kind of asset."

"How rich do you think you're going to get running a tavern in a neighborhood that doesn't attract anything other than a bunch of old lushes coming off some assembly line at the end of the day?" Sheela drummed her fingers on the table and stared at him.

Julius leaned over and pinched her cheek. "You don't understand Brooklyn, Sheela."

Sheela sighed. She'd never win this argument. The major risk to Lou was losing a part of his pension. Rebeka was even against it, but Julius had sold his brother-in-law on the idea of ownership. He sat down with pencil and paper and matched Lou's pension against the estimated income from the bar.

"Your pension is only worth around three or

four hundred dollars a month." Julius showed Lou the figures. "You'll bank twice that in the first week."

Lou squinted his face up, making his eyes appear like two tiny slits in his flesh.

"Soon you'll be parking your little cabin cruiser right next to the *Sheela Jay* on Long Island," Julius told him.

Lou insisted he wanted one hundred thousand dollars put into escrow in case the bar failed.

"I need my ass covered, Julius. I don't have your security."

Julius agreed to the escrow, and Lou quit his job at Union Gas five days before the SwingTime officially opened on Grand Avenue.

Julius had put off saying anything to Sid about severing ties until the last minute. He was afraid Sid would be angry and he didn't want to face his anger. God knows, he was grateful to Sid; it was simply time to move on. He'd just tell Sid he wanted to dissolve the partnership. Shit, this wasn't the frigging Mafia; he had nothing to fear. He'd tell him about the bar. Sid would understand.

Sid pushed some papers off to the side of his desk and stared at Julius. He stared at him for a long time before he spoke. Julius kept wondering what he was thinking.

"What's that, kid?"

"I'm going to open a bar, Sid. Things are getting too risky for me with Masterworks, especially since the fakes. The fakes make me nervous, you know. I have a wife and daughter to think about."

Sid continued to stare at him. Julius shifted his weight in the chair and wondered how long the silence would last. Finally, Sid leaned forward.

"Have you told Rocco?"

"Not yet."

Sid leaned back again and reached into his pocket. He tossed a key ring to Julius.

"Here. Take my car. Why don't you drive out to Shore Drive and tell him personally? You owe him that."

Julius missed catching the keys, and they fell to the floor.

"Sure, Sid."

Sid got up and slapped him on the back.

"I think you're making a mistake, but hey, you know your own mind, huh?" He shook Julius's hand and told him he could always come back.

It had been a lot simpler than Julius had imagined.

"You'll take my name off the partnership?"

"Sure, Julius. It's a done deal. We owe you anything?"

"Nothing."

"Like I said, a done deal."

Julius felt relieved driving out to Rocco's. There wouldn't be any connection holding him to Sid anymore, and he knew that would make Sheela happy. He didn't think he'd see either one of them again, not Sid or Rocco, and it didn't seem to matter. He'd always thought of Sid as a friend, but now he recognized that the guy didn't even like him. It was in the silence between them that Julius felt his indifference. Julius had felt like a bug in his presence waiting for the slam.

Sitting in Rocco's living room feeling the same way, it was as if endings revealed truths. Julius felt edgy.

"Is that so? A bar? Great, kid."

Rocco took his hand and looked into his eyes. He was smiling.

"Good luck."

Julius couldn't wait to get the car back to Sid. His stomach was doing turns, and his palms were sweating. He felt he had made enemies by changing his life. It was nothing he could put his finger on, just some uneasiness that kept making his hands shake.

# Chapter Forty-Two

"The Lord giveth and the Lord taketh away." Sheela repeated the phrase as she stared at the telegram from her sister, Leda.

"The Lord giveth and the Lord taketh away," she whispered.

Her older brother had died of syphilis in some rundown Florida hospital, alone and broke. Sheela was afraid that was what life would always be: a circle of death, a vicious repetition. She asked God to prove it otherwise. But God was not negotiating or punishing. God was just being God. It had nothing to do with taking her older brother, Wade, or her mama. Still, she couldn't help but think it. Couldn't help but want something in return for her brother's death. A guarantee. A reprisal. No more, God. No more loss. She wanted to believe she had his word, but in her heart, she knew that God would grant her no favors. That she was on her own.

Wade Fournier Jr. was buried at Saint Mary's, in the same cemetery that held her mama's bones.

Sheela watched the casket lowered into the ground. She wished she'd spent more time with Wade, flown down to see him. She would have gladly given him money if she'd known he needed it. She looked out over the field of stones. She had no idea where in the cemetery Sister Vincetta had laid her mama to rest, and that's where Wade Jr. belonged, close to Hannah.

"I wish we could find Mama's grave," she whispered to Leda.

They knew about the name change, that Sister Vincetta had altered some of the letters of her name so her mama could be buried in Catholic ground. But Sister Vincetta never told the girls where the grave was, and they were unable to reach her when they called the convent. So, Sheela and Leda had their brother laid between strangers. They didn't want to, but they had no other choice.

"Why doesn't he have a tombstone?" Sheela cried.

"I thought you wanted to take care of that." Leda looked at her sister with a confused stare. "That's what I understood, Sheela."

Sheela turned to Julius. "It has to be done," she said. "We have to get my brother a tombstone."

But life happened too quickly for Julius to ever remember anything at all about Wade's tombstone.

The bar in Williamsburg was losing money. Julius insisted he needed more time to establish their clientele. He and Lou were constantly arguing. Lou complained that Julius was always buying booze for the paying customers, just giving it away, trying to bribe people into frequenting the SwingTime by re-filling everyone's glass and not tabbing them.

"Jesus, Julius. You're killing us."

"You've got to put your hand in your pocket if you want a return, Lou," Julius kept trying to convince him.

Sheela became increasingly afraid that Julius would ask her to sell her stocks so he'd have the money to cover his losses. But, as if he knew his wife would never agree to it, he went to his father instead.

"I need to take a loan against the house on Freeman Street, Pop."

John thought for a long time before he answered his son.

"No," he said softly.

"Pop, I'll lose the bar."

"You have a profession. You're a textile designer. You could make a fine living."

"Pop, I can only make a few thousand dollars a year in that job."

"So, you move your family back to Greenpoint. You sell your boat, and you work for your money and live within your means." John was adamant and angry with Julius for not recognizing his options, for putting so much value on all the wrong things. "I cannot risk this house," he told him.

Julius resisted calling Sid Bernstein for as long as he could, but he was losing faith in his ability to keep the bar open another month. He told Sheela that if Sid would take him back into the business, he would only do it to keep his bar afloat, and only for a short while.

"Just for a few deals. I can make what I need inside six months, and Lou will manage the place while I'm working," he said. "He can handle it."

Sheela offered no argument despite her fear. She didn't want Julius asking for the stocks, and she knew he needed money. She had begun to have dreams at night that Leroy St. James kept trying to put his arms around her and take her back to San Francisco.

"Do what you have to, Julius," she told him, and when Sid Bernstein and Rocco Noffe started calling the house again, Sheela pretended that the unsettling anxiety she felt was nothing more than a hangover.

# Chapter Forty-Three

Roselle was finally fired when Fanny was close to three years old. Julius had wanted to let the girl go much sooner, increasingly annoyed with her high-pitched screams and her clumsiness; but both he and Sheela felt that since little Fanny was so attached to the girl, it would be cruel to separate them. So, they tolerated Roselle. They gave Jay-Jay to Rebeka because Roselle was so frightened of the dog that she would not enter the apartment unless poor Jay-Jay was locked in another room. They even tolerated the boyfriends Roselle brought to the apartment to keep her company while she watched Fanny. Sheela came home many evenings to find Roselle's lipstick smeared across her upper lip, like a funny-looking red mustache, and her blouse unbuttoned down to her navel while her gentleman caller blushed and quickly excused himself. The end came when Sheela received a call from Macy's department store.

It must have felt like a small nip, something

from a large fish. Roselle looked down.

"Oh my God," she screamed. "It's eating me! It's eating me!"

"Roselle?" Fanny said.

"Step out of your shoe!" someone screamed.

People ran frantically up the down escalator to try to get off at the top because Roselle's large flailing body prevented anyone from getting past her at the bottom.

"Help, help!" she called. "It's eating me! My foot is going!"

The escalator stopped with a forward lunge, and Roselle went flying out of her shoe. The poor woman was so distraught she was promptly taken to the manager's office, where she proceeded to faint, quite conveniently, the minute she hit the chair.

Sheela's name and phone number were found in her bag, and both Sheela and Julius rushed over to collect Roselle and Fanny. To their horror, Fanny was not in the manager's office. Sheela and Julius turned the store upside down searching for their missing daughter. Eventually, Fanny was found safe and delightfully entertained by a salesgirl on the fifth floor, right at the teddy bear counter near the escalator that had gobbled up Roselle's shoe.

In the week after Roselle's departure, Sheela interviewed close to ten women and began to think she would never find anyone she liked well enough to watch her little girl. When Julius came home in the evenings, she told him the agency was getting annoyed with her because she sent everyone back.

"What's wrong with all of them?" Julius asked.

"One didn't cook. Another one refused to cook. Three of them had thin tight little lips. I don't like thin-lipped people."

"What are you going to do?" he asked her.

"Well, I have one more girl to see in the morning, and if that doesn't work out, I'm going to give that agency hell. I'll work through another one. I'll work with all of them until I find the right girl."

Julius laughed at her and told her she was being "too picky."

Sheela woke early, early enough to see the sun rise. She felt happy and told Julius that she must have had a good dream because she felt that nothing on earth could go wrong that day. She played with the baby and took her for an early morning walk in Central Park. The park was quiet, and lovely, in the first bloom of spring. Sheela noticed how different mornings were from the afternoons. Mornings were weightless. She smiled at her young daughter, with all her sandy-colored hair and the little turned-up nose she loved to kiss. They found a bench that faced a small bridge and sat.

"Are you your mama's angel?" Sheela asked her.

The child giggled. "Will Daddy take me to the lake?" she asked.

Sheela smiled. "Yes, he will," she said. "And you can put your boats in the water, how's that?"

Fanny nodded her head and cuddled in the crook of Sheela's arms.

Julius loved his daughter. Her grandparents doted on the child, too. The old lady was always so happy to see Fanny that it might have been the Pope himself coming up the stairs the way Mary fussed over her. And yet, Fanny always ran to her Poppy and wanted to go out with the old man and that dog of his.

"Hannah would have loved you." Sheela put the child on her lap and hugged her. "Mama, can you see my daughter?" Sheela whispered and looked toward the sky. "She has my eyes and her daddy's hair."

Sheela noticed the time. She realized another girl from the agency would be ringing the bell in just a few minutes. She took one last look at the sky and started back to the apartment. She never would have expected that the beautiful weightless morning was hiding such an astounding secret.

Sheela had just put Fanny in her room and had left her playing house with her favorite doll when the doorbell rang. Sheela opened the door quickly and hardly looked at the young woman standing in the doorway.

"Come in."

The woman did not move. Sheela sighed deeply and wondered if this one was deaf or plain timid. "Please, come in," she said again.

The woman walked slowly into the room and closed the door behind her.

"Have a seat." Sheela tossed the words over her shoulder and sat comfortably in a large armchair. The woman walked ever so slowly toward her. Finally, she sat in front of Sheela and let the tears fall shamelessly down her cheeks.

"Lord have mercy," she said quietly. "Lord have mercy."

Sheela stared at the round, beautiful face. She let her mouth fall open. They looked into each other's eyes until they both broke out in tears and laughter. There was no mistake. She was heavier, much rounder, but somehow more lovely.

"Good God, Alice Henry!" Sheela exclaimed. "I never made the connection. Alice Decker, they told me. They were sending over an Alice Decker!"

"Don't you remember? Wilfred Decker? My husband?"

Sheela shook her head. "Been too long, I guess. I'd forgotten."

"My paper here says Sheela Clark." Alice laughed loud and long. "Good gracious, girl. When you get yourself married?"

"Been married three years, he's tall, blond *and* handsome. Sweet as honey and smart as a whip, too."

"I been looking for you, girl. I been thinking about you forever. How long has it been, nine years or more? You look good, girl. You got a baby? Lord have mercy. And married too? Um, um, um. Lord have mercy."

"Where you been all this time, Alice Henry?"

"Harlem."

"How's Wilfred?"

"Best man on earth, and my son, Willie, he's close to ten years old now. Where your baby, Sheela? Let me see your child."

Sheela brought Alice into Fanny's room, and Alice picked Fanny up and kissed her. The little girl giggled and got off her lap. "Who are you?" she asked.

"An old friend of your mama's."

"I don't like you." The little girl pouted and went over and sat on the floor.

"Fanny! You be nice."

Alice told the child it was plenty all right not to like her. Sheela came and sat beside Alice and took her hand. She was grinning from one side of her face to the other.

"Look," she said. She showed Alice a ring with rubies and diamonds in an oval setting.

"Pretty." Alice smiled.

"This is *our* ring. You can't tell because my husband had it reset, but this is our friendship ring. I always wear it."

"Shoot, that don't look like our ring."

"Well, it is. Julius didn't want me wearing another man's engagement ring, so he had it reset and copied after his mother's ring. I kept telling him it was our ring, but he didn't see it that way. See, the diamond is the same, just cut into smaller stones. He added rubies too. See?" Sheela held the ring under Alice's eyes.

"Don't look nothing like our ring now, but it's pretty."

"I'll give it back to you."

"Shoot, girl. I don't want your damn ring. I'm here for a job."

Sheela noticed that Fanny had taken Alice's

hand, pulling her to the floor to meet her doll, a little GI Joe soldier.

"I thought you don't like me, child."

"You can meet Soldier Boy. He might like you."

Sheela watched as Alice sat around the child like some big old warm wind that tickles your hair and makes you want to stay outside all day. It seemed like a century ago... Kit Malone's whorehouse and crazy Jack Stanton. She remembered a lot of old conversations about never wanting to wipe any white assess or become any white girl's maid. She remembered Kit Malone telling her that colored girls don't mingle and that fool, Leroy, treating Alice like she was less of a human being than he was.

"Will you help me raise my child?" Sheela asked softly.

Alice sat up and put the child back on her lap. "If it don't interfere none with the raising of my own. I know how you can be, Sheela Fournier."

Sheela felt herself blush because she knew it should never be any other way, and yet it was. All around her, black nannies were bringing up little white privileged babies while their own children sat around with aunts and grandmas. Didn't seem right, but she needed her. She needed Alice.

"If you tend to my child, Alice Henry, I'll tend to yours every way I can. He'll always be family. I promise. Just like you, you'll always be family."

Sheela wasn't quite sure what she meant by that, but somehow, she'd figure it out. She'd give Alice all the help she needed with little Willie. She'd start off with a nice little nest egg for the kid, and she'd add to it every year.

Alice smiled so broadly that Sheela could see all the pink of her gums.

"You lucky little baby." Alice laughed as she hugged the child to her breast. "Got yourself two mamas now."

# Chapter Forty-Four

The apartment at the San Remo was referred to in real estate as a "classic six." Aside from a living and dining room, there were two large bedrooms, plus a tiny room behind the kitchen called a "maid's room." The maid's room was just big enough for a twin bed and a small bathroom. Willie slept in the maid's room when his mama watched Fanny late into the night. Sheela put another twin bed in Fanny's room, and that's where Alice slept.

Sometimes, Sheela let Alice take Fanny home to Harlem because Wilfred complained about all the nights without his wife and son.

"You fixing to break up my marriage, Sheela. If I can't take the child to Harlem, you can get yourself another girl."

So, Sheela let Fanny go uptown and sleep in Alice's apartment every now and then, but she made sure Alice was back by the time she woke up. She couldn't stand waking up and not finding Fanny in her own home.

That's where they all were the night of the

murder. Fanny, Willie, and Alice, all safely tucked away in Harlem. She almost wished Alice had been there when they got back home so she could tell her what she had witnessed, but it was really for the best that no one knew about it but her and Julius. Sheela woke up from a nightmare the next morning. She dreamed that a man with a mask pointed a gun at her daughter and threatened to kill her. Then he turned it on poor Willie. She assumed she'd have nightmares for a long time after what she'd seen.

Sheela was the only one who saw it. Or, at least, she thought she was. Steps told her to get inside afterward, and that's exactly what she did. She ran inside for a double scotch and grabbed Julius's arm.

"I've been looking for you," he said to her.

"Let's go home."

Julius knew she hated these parties but made a joke of it anyway.

"Not having fun?"

Sheela looked at him so seriously that he almost dropped his drink.

"What's the matter with you?"

She could see Stephano in the doorway. She smiled. She let go of Julius's arm but kept smiling at Steps until he turned and walked through the glass double doors that went out back toward the patio.

She had recognized the man immediately. His face had just been in all the papers. He looked haggard in person, as though he hadn't shaved or slept for days. Sheela had been on her way into the library in Rocco's large, lavish Shore Drive estate when she saw him. She was going into the library to use the phone to call Alice. She wanted to say goodnight to the baby. She always said goodnight to Fanny no matter where she was.

She knew her way around Rocco's house by now. It had been four years since Julius had renewed his partnership with Sid and Rocco, and the cocktail parties soon became customary. Julius dragged her out to one after another, certainly more times than she cared to remember. She knew just how to find the library when she needed a quiet room. The party was loud and noisy, as most of them were, and she welcomed a peaceful few minutes to talk to her daughter.

They crossed on the stairs. Stephano had a man by the arm and two other men were walking behind him. Sheela was startled to see the face of the man staring back at her. She was sure it was the same man whose face was all over the papers. She remembered reading about him. He had been reported missing. He was some well-known guy, but she couldn't remember just why he was famous. Seeing him made her pause before she continued toward the library. The men on the stairs stopped as well. They all looked at her. The missing man looked about to cry, even to speak. Then they pushed the man down the stairs and out the door, back toward the pool.

His name was Richard Roth Martin, and he'd been missing for a week. The Daily News and The Herald Tribune carried nothing else on the first page because he was a notable "social character," and even though the source of his wealth was speculative, he was usually seen about town with the rich and famous. He was fond of giving money toward restoration of historic buildings and research into psychic phenomena. The rumor was that he and his cousin, Frank, had once been decoys for organized crime, front men who opened the doors of so-called legitimate establishments and then turned them over to crime bosses for illegal purposes.

Then, in 1948, Frank ran for a senate seat in the state of New Jersey and won by a fraction. By 1950, he had turned over a new leaf and was offering up information to the FBI that put a lot of his old friends behind bars. He had given a story to the Daily News, right before Richard turned up missing, that being in politics had brought him to religion and he wanted to do his part to rid the streets of slime. It was Frank Welton who just closed part of Stephano's operation in Newark. Apparently, all the government contracts were going to Canelli Construction. Canelli was paying into Stephano's pocket, and the other payoff went to Louis Dickson, the government employee who analyzed the bids and made the decisions. Now Canelli was under investigation, and Louis Dickson had been indicted for taking bribes. The rumor was that Frank got his information from Richard, who was good at talking out of both sides of his mouth. While Richard kept his hand in organized crime and referred to Cousin Frank as "that bastard" or "that prick," he filled Frank's ear with information for a nice payoff, an invitation to someone's polo party in Buck's County, or an opportunity to shake President Truman's hand at The Sherry Netherland.

Sheela finished her phone call and reached for a cigarette before she realized she hadn't brought any with her. She noticed a pack on a table near the window. Fanny had been crying and refusing to sleep unless Willie stayed in the room with her. Poor Willie wanted to watch that new concoction his Cousin Cleary had in her living room with the moving pictures. Willie finally gave in, though. He always gave into Fanny, and he wound up promising he would stay until the first little snore.

Sheela almost forgot what she had seen on the stairs. It was best not to think about it. It was their business, not hers. She just wanted to sit in that comfortable chair and smoke before going back to the party. She didn't like crowds anymore, and she hated the small talk. Julius was good at it, but she'd almost rather be back in Clearwater than standing up with a drink in her hand in some hood's living room.

That's when she heard the sounds. Not voices really. It sounded more like scuffling and shoving. She could have sworn she heard people breathing. She never understood why she decided to investigate the sound. Looking back, she realized she should have just sat there smoking. Instead, she opened the tall French doors that led out to the patio and walked outside. She knew in an instant that she had made an irretrievable mistake, one of fate, or just one of those moments when the brain fails to control impulse. She would never know. She would never be able to explain it, but she would always be haunted by it. Seeing a man murdered.

They were drowning Richard Martin in the pool. Steps held his head over the water, and the other two men had him by the arms. He was on his stomach, with his head hanging over the shallow end. She heard Steps say, "Motherfucker." He said it three times in all. Next time was when he put his legs over the body like he was riding a horse and grabbed Richard by the hair. "Motherfucker," he said again and shoved his head down under the water and held it there so fiercely Sheela saw Step's lips curl up under his teeth.

She stood very still, afraid to move—afraid they would notice her and drag her off to the pool and drown her as well. She barely heard the party behind her. They were way in the back of the house, but she still thought she heard her husband call her name. She tasted the cold air on her teeth. It was cold for early fall. She watched her breath rise in the air. The whisper of breath seemed to taunt the dying man the way it lingered between them, like a smoky drug; a life preserver he'd never reach. He didn't struggle very much at all. Just once, his head came up. It was only a second before Stephano pushed him under again, but she had enough time to see his face just seconds before death. He was almost frozen in fear. No peace. No desire to meet God, just a death grimace. She wanted to scream. A scream would have brought them all running. But she couldn't let them know she hated their acts of violence, their monstrous pacts of revenge. They were always right, and she had to pretend she agreed with everything they said and every dirty little act they justified. That's what she kept telling Julius. It's a question of loyalty. Whatever they do, you back them. This was family. Rocco had said it too many times to forget. This was family.

Finally, they dragged him up. Turned his body over. He was dead. She was sure of it. "Motherfucker," Steps said again. One of the men wiped his hands on his pants and said, "Get rid of him."

That's when Stephano saw her. She was easy to see standing in the moonlight. She had prayed he wouldn't notice. She prayed he would walk the other way, but not Steps. No, not Steps. He was looking right at her. Walking right toward her.

"Go inside," he told her. "We're just emptying trash."

"What'll we do?" Julius asked her on the way home.

His face was as white as a sheet, sweat falling down his brow, even though the air outside was unseasonably cool.

"What'll we do?" he asked again.

She knew there was nothing they could do.

"They killed a man with all those people there?" Julius whispered nervously.

Sheela nodded and reached for his hand. She

realized her own was shaking.

"Lousy temper on that Stephano. Dumb bastard probably said something to tick Steps off." Julius ran his hand through his hair, then hit the back of the taxi seat with his fists. "Jesus!"

Sheela knew they'd never be able to break any ties with Rocco. Not anymore. She knew Julius was stuck in more ways than one. Not only because the SwingTime was practically in bankruptcy, but also because now they were too far in with the mob to get out.

Lou was furious with Julius because in the four years they'd operated the Swing Time, he hadn't once matched his paycheck from Union Gas. Both men covered each other bartending, but Lou's hot temper drove people out the door. He was often in a foul mood, and the only time he ever talked was to defend his politics against everyone else's. That always led to a heated disagreement, and people thought he was a cantankerous blowhard. Sheela blamed Lou for failing to keep the bar viable while Julius was risking his ass to throw money back into it.

"Look, I made a mistake going in with Lou. Okay? I admit it, but I can't get out of it. I owe him, Sheela. He trusted me."

"Pay him off, Julius, whatever he wants. Just get rid of him. Hire someone with a little personality, for God's sake."

"Look, I'm going to turn the place back into what it was and see if that'll work."

"What are you talking about?" Sheela asked.

Julius tried to be convincing. "I'll get rid of the dance floor and put the pool table back in. I'll put a radio over the bar because the jukebox is hardly ever played, and tear out all the glitter and have the room paneled in dark oak."

Perhaps Julius had the right idea; more of the old clientele returned once the renovation was complete, but business was still slow. The only time they got a real crowd was on Saturday afternoons when a lot of the men sneaked away from their wives for a game of pool. But it had been over a year since the renovation and business was still limping, not soaring.

Sheela was worried about money, now more than ever, but she was also petrified of Steps. She couldn't sleep well after the murder. She kept getting up in the middle of the night and walking through the rooms. Checking on Fanny. Alice told her she was as jumpy as that Roselle girl she'd heard about. Julius had become somber, a mood he seemed unable to break. He kept saying he was walking a tightrope without a net and it left a cold spot in his stomach, but Julius was referring to the bar, not Steps. He avoided talking about the murder. Sheela realized that Julius preferred to deny it ever happened, deny how dangerous his associations were.

Rocco and Steps treated Julius the same as ever, maybe even better, but Sheela was filled with foreboding.

"I feel like someone is walking behind me and I have to keep turning around to look. To make sure

I'm alone," Julius told her and shrugged his shoulders.

Sheela smiled sadly. Perhaps he did realize they were standing in quicksand. "I feel the same," she said.

One week after the murder, the body of Richard Roth Martin was found in the water near the Fulton Terminal in Brooklyn. Sheela bought a copy of the Daily News and followed the story. A ransom note had been sent to his family in Morristown, New Jersey. The ransom was paid, but that bit of news had not been leaked to the press until after his death. It dawned on Sheela why they didn't kill him right away: They wanted it to look like a kidnapping and not a mob hit. The paper said the perpetrators were at large and there were no known suspects.

Six months after the body was found, Julius got a phone call from Sid.

"Keep your mouth shut, kid," Sid told him.

"What?"

"Take the rap for Masterworks, or you'll wind up sucking a bullet. I tell you this as a friend."

"What's going on?" Julius tried to press him for answers, but Sid hung up quickly.

Within four days, Julius was arrested for fraud. The police walked into the San Remo Apartments and took him out in handcuffs. Sheela kept hitting the police on the arm until they had to push her aside. After days of crying and angry unsuccessful calls to Bernstein's office, she hired an attorney to represent her husband and made his bail for fifty thousand dollars. Their attorney, Kenneth Friedman, informed them that both Rocco Noffe and Sid Bernstein had signed an affidavit naming Julius Clark the sole owner of the art and antique business known as Masterworks after they were both brought in for questioning.

Julius realized that Sid had given him a warning, but he wasn't going to take the fall. He refused to pretend that they were the innocent victims, and he was the goddamned criminal. Frightened, Sheela tried to talk him out of it.

"Take whatever sentence they give you, Julius. Serve your time and you're out. If you turn on them, they'll kill us both."

"They're going to kill us both anyway. It's just a matter of time. You're a witness to a murder, and I've got enough information on them to buy my freedom from the cops. They don't even like me. They don't consider me one of their own. I can't let myself be used anymore. I can't let them come to me saying, 'You understand, don't you, Julius? We have to get rid of you. You know too much.'" Julius held up his finger like it was a gun and put it to his head. "Boom," he said softly. He dropped his hand and put his arms around her. "We're screwed any way you turn. We've got to put them behind bars, or they'll squash us."

Sheela didn't know what she thought anymore. She stopped taking the baby outside, and she shopped by phone. The money was slipped under the door, the packages left in the hall. She told Alice never to let anyone in, and she told the doorman to tell anyone who inquired that she was out of town.

Julius devised a plan. They were going to disappear. Change their names and start out new in California. "I'm not taking the rap for those bastards," he told her. "I'm telling Friedman everything."

"What about the murder?" Sheela asked cautiously.

Julius frowned.

"That's our ace. I don't know for sure what to do, but that murder, well, it's our ace."

# Chapter Forty-Five

That first afternoon in Friedman's office, Kenneth showed Julius a copy of a contract that listed him as sole owner of Masterworks.

"It's a forgery, or I didn't know what I was signing. I didn't own the goddamn business."

"How were you paid?" Kenneth asked him.

"Cash. Always cash."

Julius lit a cigarette with shaking hands.

Kenneth leaned forward in his chair and stared at Julius. "Sid Bernstein is saying that he was hired as an accountant for Masterworks and for no other reason, and that you hired him."

"He's a liar!" Julius slammed his fist on Kenneth's desk. "I didn't pay taxes on Masterworks."

"That's another issue. You guys were running an all-cash business. There's no bank account and no paper trail. There were no taxes."

"Look, I never questioned Sid. I just took the fee."

"In cash?"

"Cash. Always."

"Weren't you suspicious?"

Julius shook his head. "No. It was just money to me. I didn't even think about it."

"Right now, it's your word against theirs."

"What about Rocco and the other guy? The one who did the reselling?"

"Rocco claims he was an independent dealer. He says he's legitimate and he got the fakes from you. You were the contact. But Rocco is under investigation if that's any consolation."

Julius slowly exhaled. "What about this guy I never met? Dick."

"Dick who?" Kenneth asked. "Do you know his last name?"

"He was the one with all the contacts."

"You never met him?"

"No. But he was the guy who bought low and sold high. Neither Sid nor I would have known how to pass that stuff. This guy Dick was some Park Avenue hotshot."

"Well, unfortunately," Kenneth looked back and forth from Julius to Sheela and continued, "this Dick you're talking about? I think he's dead."

"Dead?" Sheela felt her stomach fall. "What do you mean, dead?" She felt as though she were being swallowed up alive.

Kenneth leaned back in his chair and looked from one to the other.

"Remember the guy who turned up in the river a few months ago, Richard Roth Martin? Bernstein gave his name to the cops. Said you hired him. I'm sure he's the guy you say you never met."

Senator Frank Welton looked at his watch. It was two in the morning, on the nose. The traffic light was long. Welton reached for the radio dial and switched channels. Smoky clouds hid the moon, and rain threatened the air.

He wanted to run the light, no Lincoln tunnel traffic this time of night. He sat forward and looked up 41st Street. *Not a fucking soul in sight*, he thought as he lightly pushed on the gas.

The sudden face in the rearview mirror startled him. Welton turned.

"What the fuck?" he said.

He put the car in park and swiveled to open the door, his last action, his last mistake.

"Bye, bye, canary."

Someone grabbed him by the throat and put a bullet through his head, right behind the ear. Frank's brain was all over the windshield inside a second.

The Worm made his first fatal mistake that night. The police traced a button found at the crime scene to a shirt purchased by James Navarro. They issued a search warrant and found a missing button on a pale gray shirt that matched the button found on the ground around Frank Welton's car. The bullet retrieved from the victim's head was fired from a .45 automatic pistol. Two guns were found in Jimmy's apartment. One was a .45 automatic.

The police now had enough on Jimmy to arrest him for the murder of Senator Frank Welton.

Julius and Sheela felt the heat and knew they needed to ditch their present address. They moved out of the San Remo and signed a lease for a smaller apartment on Riverside Drive.

One week later a woman was murdered across the hall. She was strangled to death with a nylon stocking in the middle of the afternoon. Someone had gotten past the doorman, the elevator man, and several tenants. Yet no one had seen any strangers on the premises. The woman had been a tall striking brunette just a few years older than Sheela.

"It was meant for me," Sheela said, after hearing the news. She took a long sip of the scotch over ice in her glass.

"They don't make mistakes," Julius assured her.

"They do make mistakes. If it had been Jimmy, I'd be a corpse right now."

"I'm going to the FBI," Julius said slowly. "I really need to do that."

Sheela had half expected him to cave but knowing that didn't make it any easier to hear.

"What are you going to tell them?"

"That I saw Steps murder Richard Roth Martin."

"Are you crazy? I was the one who saw the murder." She looked at Julius's expression and knew he'd never change his mind. "What if someone says you never left the room?"

He went to her and took her hand. "I did leave the room. I went to the bathroom and then into the library to look for you. I knew you were probably in there talking to Fanny, and I wanted to say goodnight to her. But when I didn't see you, I went back inside. I was gone long enough to have seen the murder."

"Do you think that's wise?" she asked. "What if they find out and retaliate?"

Julius looked off. "They'll be put in jail. They won't be able to get to us."

"Sure," she said, suddenly thinking of Leroy St. James. "I hope you're right."

Agent Carter put his hands through his hair and looked at Julius for several minutes. Julius was biting his nails. Finally, Agent Carter sat forward.

"Look, Julius, Rocco and Sid's little art scam has been under investigation since last year."

Julius looked surprised. "What, that long?"

"Ever since Martin dissolved his partnership with Bernstein and let Cousin Frank in on the scam."

"Christ." Julius put his fingers back in his mouth.

"We offered Martin immunity for turning state's evidence."

Julius stood up but not before Agent Carter noticed his cuticles were bleeding.

"No one much cared about me." Julius laughed nervously. "I guess I'm just the punk with a little classroom knowledge."

"Yep, they used you to push the art. You'll probably go off to a federal prison for a couple of years. Not bad."

"Shit." Julius sat back down. "Will they fine me?"

Carter smiled. "Look, Julius, its Noffe and Bernstein we want, and we got 'em."

Carter's gut was telling him that Julius was about to sing a very melodic song. He could always rely on his gut; it had served him well.

Julius turned and looked at Carter. He held his lip in his teeth before he spoke. "Bet you'd also love to see Stephano fry, uh?"

Carter stared at Julius. He spoke rapidly, as if his words were the line and poor Julius was the fish at the end of it.

"Yeah, sure would. We've been pursuing Steps the way Ness went after Capone. We've even got a nice little deal going with Bernstein." Carter leaned into Julius and never left his face. "We've got testimony from Bernstein that'll fry Steps on extortion charges."

Julius sat back and tapped his finger. "A murder rap would really put him away though, wouldn't it?"

Julius lit a cigarette and offered one to Carter. Carter took it; he reached for a book of matches, lit the fire with one finger and held it to the end of his cigarette.

Ross Carter blew a smoke ring out into the room. "Got anything you want to tell me, Julius?"

Julius nodded his head. "Yeah, but I want the fraud charges against me dropped first."

Carter stood up and went to the window. He expected this.

"I'll see what I can do," he said.

"Not good enough." Julius leaned forward and bore his eyes into Carter's; he'd play every hand he had.

Ross Carter met his eyes from across the room.

"You give me what I need, and I'll see to it that you're granted immunity."

"Deal."

"I'm all ears, Julius."

Julius took a drag on his cigarette. He kept his eyes on Carter. "Look, I was at a party that night, on Shore Drive." Julius took another deep drag on the cigarette and let the smoke out. "I know who killed Martin … I saw the murder."

Carter walked back to his desk and tossed his cigarette in an old cup of coffee. Stephano had been under investigation for years, but the FBI never had enough evidence to bring him to trial. Carter laughed.

"Yep, a murder rap is a sure-fire way to put an end to that bastard. So, you saw it, uh?"

"Yeah, I saw it," Julius said.

"We're finally going to see that son-of-a-bitch fry?"

Carter watched Julius tear another piece of skin off his pinkie finger.

"I wonder what made Stephano carry out his own vendetta. That wormy little bodyguard of his usually does the hits."

"Steps must have been really pissed off," Julius said quietly.

"Start talking, Julius," Ross Carter said as he

opened his notebook. "Give me the whole story, everything."

Agent Ross Carter suggested to Julius that he move into a hotel until the trial, just as a precaution.

"I can only give you limited protection, Julius."

"Can you guarantee the safety of my family?" Julius asked.

"Move your family out of town, Julius, just until after the trial."

Julius nodded. "You'll have bodyguards watching me?"

Carter shook his head "I can't guarantee you twenty-four-hour protection, Julius, I'm sorry. But we'll do everything we can to keep you and your family safe."

Stephano Noffe was arrested for the murder of Richard Roth Martin based on Julius's eyewitness testimony and that of sworn witnesses who knew Richard Roth Martin was being held at the Shore Drive estate. Sid Bernstein was arrested for extortion and fraud. Rocco was given a court date to stand trial for fraud and aiding and abetting a kidnapping. Despite protests from the District Attorney's office, they were all released on bail, including James Navarro, alias Jimmy the Worm.

# Chapter Forty-Six

Aside from a brief encounter on Miami Beach, Sheela had not seen Jack Stanton in over ten years. She and Julius were staying at the Americana Hotel on their honeymoon when she ran into Jack at the Peacock Lounge.

"Sheela, my dear. Oh, my dear Sheela."

When she turned toward the familiar high call, she noticed Jack and his entourage of Kit Malone's most beautiful girls. She smiled in his direction and walked Julius over to his table. Jack was astonished at her condition.

"My God, you're pregnant," he exclaimed and put both hands to his cheeks.

Sheela quickly introduced him to Julius. She heard Jack chuckling as she took Julius's arm and walked him away.

"She used to be so beautiful," Jack said to one of the girls.

"I'd say she's still beautiful," said a small blonde woman of about twenty.

"Oh, yes, yes, yes. But she was a goddess when I

knew her. Good God! Pregnant. Good God."

But now she needed him. She didn't know where else to turn. Julius had moved into the New Yorker Hotel on 34th Street and wanted Sheela and Fanny with him, but Sheela didn't feel safe in the city. She asked Jack if she could stay at the Connecticut estate.

"You're not still pregnant, are you, my dear?"

"Jack. I really do need a favor. There's been some trouble, and I could use a place to stay for a while. Fanny and I... my daughter."

"What kind of trouble?"

"I'll tell you everything when I see you. It's Julius, my husband. He's in a bit of trouble, and I need to take my daughter away from any danger. I have to protect my daughter, Jack."

She almost expected him to turn her down. It was a long shot, but she had to try. Jack Stanton didn't owe her a damn thing, and she would not have blamed him if he slammed down the phone on her. But he didn't.

"How old is the child and is she well-behaved?" he asked her.

"She's an angel, Jack. Just going on ten, but an angel."

"Well, why not? We've had a history together, haven't we, dear? Yes, of course. Come whenever you like."

Sheela was relieved to tell Julius over the phone that she had found a safe place to stay, and she would call him the moment she and Fanny arrived at Stanton's.

"That crazy millionaire we met in Miami? The fruitcake?" Julius laughed. He sat down on the hotel bed and rolled over on his side. He laughed until he started choking.

"Are you all right?"

Julius took some long breaths and sat up. "It's come to this," he said.

"What's come to this?"

Julius stretched out his arm and reached for a cigarette.

"My life." He blew the long smoke out in front of him. "You dirty rat." He wanted to give her the old Cagny routine. "Turning to another man. You dirty rat."

"I'd hardly call Jack another man." Sheela smiled, despite herself. "It won't be forever," she said.

Their world together had suddenly turned upside down, and Sheela didn't know what else to do but move. Grab the child and go. Even the money was not as important as making herself and Fanny invisible. She would not even show up at the trial unless she was subpoenaed.

"You think I can make it as an actor?"

She knew he was smoking. She heard him spit the tobacco and blow the smoke through his lips.

Sheela planned to ask Jack Stanton for a loan. She had sold off all her US Steel, and they were getting by on that. She knew she couldn't touch the General Motors. It was all she had, and if she sold it there would be nothing left. She couldn't go through money as if she had no future. She would do anything but sell it off.

"We'll get those bastards," she heard him say.

The bar was up for sale. Lou got his old job back at Union Gas but lost close to five years off his pension. Julius hadn't put one hundred thousand dollars into an escrow account for him as he had promised. He and Sheela needed money and had stockpiled all their cash into safe deposit boxes right after they'd hired Kenneth Friedman to represent them. Lou no longer spoke to Julius. He was so damn angry he took it out on the dog. He told Sheela that the next-door neighbors had poisoned little Jay-Jay, but she didn't believe that the neighbors had anything to do with it. It must have been Lou who did it.

"We should have taken the dog back as soon as we got rid of Roselle," she told Julius. But Rebeka had begged her not to, said she and Sonny were attached to Jay-Jay. Reluctantly, Sheela had agreed to let Jay-Jay stay where he was.

"We found the body on the front stoop. Must have been the neighbors. They fed him something. Then they just left him lying there," Lou had said.

"You prick." Sheela said into the phone. If he had been in front of her, she would have hit him hard, right across the jaw.

"You cruel son-of-a-bitch."

All Lou did was breathe. She could almost smell his nasty breath.

"It wasn't me," he hollered, right before she hung up with a slam.

"You don't think Jimmy killed the dog, do you?"

she asked Julius. "You don't think it's the first warning?"

Julius sighed deeply, a sure sign that he was thinking the same thing and wouldn't admit it.

"I don't know. I doubt it. They would have left poor Jay-Jay at our door, not my mom's."

But Sheela had an uneasy feeling about the whole thing. She wanted to blame Lou, but the cruelty seemed so timely.

"Listen, we're going to get Bernstein and Noffe. We're going to put them behind bars."

"Yeah, we're going to get them," she said, touching the phone as though it was his cheek.

She dreamed that night that she and Julius were dancing, the way they had on the first night they met. They were turning around and around so fast that their silhouettes looked like one. Suddenly she noticed that the light around them was fading. She wanted to tell him that it was all changing and the moon was no longer full, but Julius just kept on dancing.

"It's all gone," she whispered. "The light is all gone."

"No," he said, "there's still darkness."

Sheela was surprised at Jack's condition. He walked with the help of a cane, and his movements were unbearably slow. He had lost a lot of weight and looked like a little sparrow peering and squinting at her from behind small wire glasses.

"Good God. Don't look so shocked. Do I look that bad?"

She gave him a warm hug. "So good to see you, Jack," she said. Fanny stood off to the side and stared at the old man.

"And this is Fanny?"

Fanny smiled and stood behind her mother.

"Charmed, little Fanny." Jack bent down to her. "A little beauty. Blonde? I do like blondes. She's about five, I'd say."

"She's nearly ten, Jack. Look, my husband—"

"Ah yes, that man I saw you with in Miami. He was very masculine. Very dapper if I remember correctly."

"I have so much to tell you," she said.

"All in due time." He took the little girl's hand, and they walked inside.

Sheela was surprised to see how much the house had stayed the same. The large Renoir had been moved somewhere and, in its place, Jack had hung a tapestry. He had changed some furniture around but aside from that, it was very much the way she had remembered it.

"I've sold off the big house," he told her. "Never liked it anyway."

"Your wife?" she asked.

"Palm Beach."

The door to the old library was open a crack, and she saw that Jack had turned it into his bedroom.

"Oh," he said, noticing her surprise. "I had a stroke in 1949. I'm afraid I haven't yet fully recovered. Can't climb the damn stairs anymore," he whispered.

She felt sad, remembering it as Daniel's old studio.

"That room is haunted, you know?"

"Ah, I've always known," he whispered again. "David and Daniel haunt it."

"How's business, Jack. Can you still work?"

He told her that his oldest son was running the business and they had voted him off the board. "They've put me out to pasture," he said, attempting to shrug it off. "Little bastard had the nerve to call me mentally incompetent."

Fanny stood at the foot of the stairs and looked up. The beautiful sweeping banister fascinated her.

"Take any room upstairs you wish, dear," Jack told Fanny as he patted the top of her head.

"All the rooms are empty?" Surprised, Sheela had expected to find at least one woman in the house, even in his weakened condition.

"I can no longer walk in my mules." He chuckled. "What's a girl to do? I must live on the main floor. The kitchen is so close to the library … I hate that. How dreadful."

"You're all alone here?"

"Well, not exactly." Jack turned toward the kitchen and called out to someone named Francis. "This is probably why they think I'm incompetent. Who knows?"

A man of about twenty-five came into the room wearing nothing but a pair of tights. He was unusually tall. At least six foot three, maybe taller. Jack introduced him as "my friend."

"Hello," Sheela said, trying her best to be

sociable.

"He's a marvelous dancer. He uses the garage to practice. I've had it redone just for Francis. It's mirrored and heated now. It's simply perfect. We'll have to show you."

Sheela noticed that the boy was exceptionally pretty and walked on the balls of his feet, like a cat. There was a slight sway to his walk, and he held his hands at his side. He kept his palms facing down, even when he sat. Fanny seemed enchanted by him, as if he were a genie who had just appeared in a puff of smoke.

"What an adorable little girl," Francis squealed, and off they went. He had simply swept through the room, capturing Fanny, and disappearing back toward the kitchen, hardly noticing Sheela at all.

Jack chuckled. "Magnificent thighs, don't you think?"

Sheela nodded.

"He's a divine cook. Do you like goose, dear?"

Sheela couldn't help but wonder if Jack only stared at the beautiful man. Had him dance stark naked while he salivated and pulled on himself. Even with the stroke and its debilitating symptoms, Jack looked like a little mischievous leprechaun, as if at any moment he could toss his cane into the air and skip.

Her old room was the same. The sunlight made a golden yellow pattern on the wall, dust motes swirling in the light. The high bed was still inviting, and the sweet smell in the air was rich with summer rain and fresh-cut grass. The white curtain picked up a breeze and threw itself out toward her, like the welcoming arms of a ghost. Her daughter's laughter could be heard from downstairs. Sheela walked back out into the hall and turned toward Sharon's old room. The door was ajar. The past seemed present, as if the distance still prevailed.

"Old houses," she whispered. "Damn place has breath."

Francis had taken Fanny into the parlor after dinner. She insisted that Francis teach her ballroom dancing. Every now and then, Sheela saw his long silk robe fly by with little Fanny right behind, mimicking his every move.

Once she and Jack were alone in the sitting room, she told him the whole story—how Julius would take a fee for selling the artwork, underselling it, and then turning it around at full value. She told him all about the antiques, and the fake masterpieces, and how the mob was involved. She told him everything—everything except that she had seen Richard Roth Martin murdered.

Jack sat with his hand on his heart the whole time, his eyes wide and staring. Every now and then, he would let out a sigh, "Oh, my dear." When she finished talking, he waved his hands in the air.

"My Renoir! My Picasso! My Lautrec! Could they be fakes?"

"Take the work to Christie's, Jack. Have everything appraised."

"I'll send Francis into the city tomorrow. Each one of my treasures must be authenticated. Oh, dear, I'll die earlier than expected if a fake is discovered. Oh dear. This could have a devastating effect."

Julius called later that evening to tell her that the murder trial was scheduled to start in two weeks. Sheela was relieved. She was sure that Stephano would be found guilty and be put away for life. After the trial, she and Julius would move to another part of the country and change their names. They'd buy another bar. Whatever Julius wanted to do. This time there would be no Lou. There would be no Sid Bernstein or Rocco Noffe.

Sheela slept well for the first time in four months, in the high bed, in the golden yellow room.

# Chapter Forty-Seven

Sheela watched as Fanny sat by the pool with Jack and asked him all kinds of questions about the guns in the big glass cabinet and whether she could shoot them.

"The child is a tomboy," he told Sheela. "I like that. She's a kindred spirit, has the soul of an artist. I'm sure of it. Does she have any talent?"

"She's young, Jack. It's too soon to tell."

"Nonsense." He tapped his cane on the patio floor. "You must enroll her at the American Academy. Get her on the stage. She's very imaginative. Francis says she has rhythm."

"When she's a little older."

"How much do you want for her?"

Sheela was stunned. Jack had agreed to lend her ten thousand dollars, and now she was suddenly afraid that she was expected to return a favor, a big one.

"What are you asking me?"

Jack laughed and reached for his lemonade.

"A million? Two?"

"You can't be serious."

He laughed again.

"I love the child. I want to buy her."

"She's not for sale, Jack."

"Pity. I should have had a daughter. I can see that now. My bastard sons can kiss my ass. Every single one of them."

Sheela leaned back in the sun.

"The loan? I'll pay it back, Jack."

Jack Stanton reached over and took her hand. "I see that money isn't everything to you, is it?"

Sheela looked at him and raised an eyebrow. "Certainly not more than my child, Jack."

"Ah, youth is wasted on pretensions, flighty adoptions of attitude. And then you get old, and it's as though a veil is suddenly lifted." He turned to her. "I am happier now than I have ever been, and it's because of Francis. And yet, if I had known him twenty-five years ago, I would have frightened him away with my damn neuroses. I would have been too goddamn timid to put my hands on him. Ha! What pleasure I denied myself. What grief I caused others. Now, I love everyone quite unabashedly, everyone—you, that little girl of yours, everyone—even people I read about but have never met. Compassion. Humility. Kindness. That's what impresses me now. Do you know what matters in life, Sheela?"

Sheela smiled and told him her daughter mattered.

"Ah, yes, little girls always matter. Little girls and roses, my roses, rainstorms, the whisper of a bird's wing on the wind, the call of dawn. That is what life is about, beauty and love. Do you know that I love Francis? I truly do. I'm head over heels. I love everything and everyone on earth. Oh, except for my goddamn sons. There is a limit to my delirium. I don't love my goddamn sons."

Sheela held his hand very tightly.

"Your son, Daniel?"

"Ah, yes, Daniel." He looked off in the distance. "He haunts me now. He always will, he and David. I could have helped David, accepted him. I could have comforted Daniel after his brother's death... but I couldn't accept or comfort myself, could I?"

"You've changed, Jack."

"Yes. How my cruelty distresses me now. The only blessing that comes with age is wisdom. The only weakness of youth is arrogance."

He sat back and looked out past the trees. Sheela thought he looked so small and fragile in the large lawn chair.

"Ha! What a foolish old man I've become. Soft in the head."

Sheela squeezed his hand.

"Life is so precious to me now, Sheela, so very precious. I haven't long, you know. I won't wait for the ravages of it either, the pitiable end. Do you want to know how I shall die?"

She shook her head from side to side.

"I will tell you anyway. I will die watching my young man dance. I will lie in the cold snow and freeze to death thinking of luscious things. That will be my death, my thoughts on art, beauty, music. Ah, sweet mystery of life, Champagne, and chocolate mousse on my lips. Lamb and goose in my belly. Yes. Then let death come. On my terms."

Sheela watched as he closed his eyes. "It's near, you know." He brought her hand to his lips. "As near as you are."

# Chapter Forty-Eight

Julius blew the smoke in spirals. His feet were crossed at the ankles and one hand was back behind his head. His shirt was white, like China linen. He wore it rolled up high at the sleeves. Summer air came in through the open window and kissed his hair. He gazed at the moon from his hotel window, a sliver of brilliance. His slippers sat neatly under the bed. The soft brown leather slippers Sheela had given him for Christmas. His socks were brown with small blue dots and felt soft against his leg. His trousers were loose, and the crease ran straight and perfect.

He needed ice. The night was warm. He missed his wife. His child. He touched the wedding ring on his finger and spun it around. Soon life would return to normal, and he'd lift his little girl in the air again and catch her the way he used to. Take her on pony rides and let her sit on his lap and drive the car.

He put his cigarette in a square glass ashtray on the nightstand next to the bed. The white paper was red-hot at the end and brown with tobacco at the tip. He left it burning. Wouldn't be gone long, just a walk down the hall for ice.

He slipped his large feet into the soft brown slippers. He chuckled, thinking about his little girl.

"She stops traffic," he told his wife. "A walking doll. A little dream."

He reached down and took one more puff from the Camel. A piece of tobacco sat on his lip. Ash fell on the floor; some of it landed on his slipper and left a smoky gray smudge. He took a deep drag and returned it to the glass ashtray. The wind felt so warm, so tender on his skin. He loved summer. He thought about his father's garden: the colors, the bursts of pink and white, lavender petals in perfect plots of pebbled stone, the hose coiled against the attic stairs, the wall of fence behind the trellis of flowering vines. The pride in his father's eyes.

He opened the door of his room and walked out, down the long hall. He turned and walked another hall, toward the very end where they kept the ice. He was humming a tune that had just been playing on the radio. A waltz. The halls were empty. He heard distant sounds from behind closed doors. He heard the whispers of strangers, the creak of the floor.

"Hello, Julius."

He was barely startled. It was too quick, much too quick.

"What the—?"

The breath in his face came fast and hot. It stank of cheap food and old cigarettes.

"Hey!"

Behind his ear, cold hard steel pushed up against his flesh.

"No, Jesus!"

The sound of the blast was quiet.

*Pop.*

The Worm licked the sweat off his lip and looked around, all was still, nothing was disturbed. And as the body lay slumped in the hotel hallway and blood ran off the wall like paint, the Worm tossed a dead rat in the dead man's pocket... and took to the stairs.

# Chapter Forty-Nine

*Holy Mary, Mother of God, pray for us sinners now and in the hour of our death. Amen.* Mary brought the rosary to her lips and kissed it.

*Holy Mary, Mother of God, pray for us sinners now and in the hour of our death. Amen.*

The silent statue extended her hands and looked gracefully at the grieving woman. The red glass lanterns at her feet were alive with fire.

Mary rocked on her knees in the wooden pew. "Julius, Julius." She wept, crying out deeply from the back of her throat. "My son. Julius, my baby."

Fanny sat beside her, frightened and shattered.

"Where is heaven?" Fanny asked, but there was no satisfactory answer.

John was silent. He sat stiff-lipped and stared at the altar. He did not pray. Tears fell from his eyes that he wiped with the back of his hand.

Sheela sat beside him. Her head went up and down, as if trying to agree with death, accept its consumption of Julius. John wanted to console her, but he could not. *Was this because of her?*

Wilfred had walked in late and stood at the back of the church. He bowed his head as tears ran down his cheeks, lining his rich dark skin. *Julius never meant no harm to no one. Treated me like any man. More than I can say for most white folks.* He raised his head and watched as the little girl slumped her shoulders. "Poor child," he whispered. "Loved her daddy."

It was Wilfred, Alice and Willie who had driven up to Stanton's to tell Sheela that Julius had been killed.

"Worst thing I'm ever going to have to do in my life," Alice kept repeating.

Willie ran right to Fanny and took her outside. Alice and Wilfred each put a hand on Sheela's arm. They watched her take the news, listened to her screams.

The little girl heard it. Willie grabbed her and took her farther back on the lawn, as far away from Sheela's screams as he could get. It was an awful sound. Fanny cried anyway. Cried and asked what was wrong with her mommy. Willie started to cry himself. Couldn't help it.

"Tell Fanny. I can't. I can't," Sheela pleaded with Alice.

"That your child, Sheela. You have to tell her."

"No! Please." And she pulled on Alice's arms and shook her.

So, it was Alice and Wilfred who went out there on the lawn and gently told Fanny that her daddy had gone to heaven. Willie kept crying. Cried so much he had to walk away.

Fanny looked for heaven. They all told her she couldn't get there until God called her. But Fanny believed she could find her daddy in heaven, and so she had to go, too.

"How far away?" she kept asking them. "It's got to be somewhere."

"It's in the sky," they told her.

Fanny looked around the church. Jesus seemed so sorry for taking her daddy. She wanted to ask Jesus how to get to heaven, but her grandmother kept pulling her and hugging her close.

"I want to go to heaven," she told her grandmother, but that just made the old women cry louder. She pulled Fanny so close that she nearly sneezed from the talcum powder smell under her grandmother's arms.

Rebeka and Lou sat silently with their son between them. They stared straight ahead and mumbled along when the priest led them in prayer. Their eyes were dry, their faces sullen.

The Mass came to an end. The body lay in the open casket. Everyone formed a line to say goodbye to Julius. Fanny held on to her grandmother's hand. Her father lay stiff and quiet. She stared at his body. "Isn't he supposed to be in heaven?" she asked, challenging them, as if they had lied to her.

"Shush," said her grandmother.

John held Sheela up and helped her walk past Julius. Sheela touched the corpse and kissed it. She wept so loudly that Fanny saw monsters in the shadows of the church, monsters who fed on screams and grief.

"What are you going to do with all his good clothes?" Joseph approached Sheela and touched her arm.

Sheela stared back at him, as if she hadn't understood.

They were standing just outside the church. Wilfred sucked in his breath as he listened to Joseph. He wanted to hit him hard, hard enough to draw blood.

"What the hell's the matter with them?" Wilfred whispered to his wife. "The man is not even buried, and he wants his clothes?"

Lou and his family slipped into the black limousine without even a glance toward Sheela. Mary and John took Fanny. Sheela went out to the cemetery with Alice and her family. She still couldn't face her daughter's pain and had avoided the little girl since they'd left Stanton's estate.

Fanny hoped they were taking her to heaven in the long black limousine and was terribly disappointed to wind up in a strange place, with a lot of trees and old marked up tombstones. She asked Willie if he knew where heaven was, and he gave her the same silly answer. "In the sky," he told her.

She didn't believe any of them. Heaven couldn't be in the sky. Nothing but clouds there. Heaven was someplace they didn't know about—probably in the earth 'cause that's where they'd put her daddy.

Next day, when Alice took her to the park, Fanny dug a hole and leaned down over it.

"Daddy?" she said softly.

"Oh, child," said Alice.

"Daddy?" Fanny whispered, as she leaned over the hole and wept.

# Chapter Fifty

After the loss of her father, Fanny attached herself to the males who had loved him. Willie was always telling her that her daddy liked to fly paper airplanes. "Look what I got, Fanny," Willie would say and hold the plane up in his hands. "Come on, girl, let's fly these planes."

And they'd run off to the park—twist the rubber bands until they were tight and then let them go. The paper planes would dip and glide against the sky.

*Swishhhh.* They'd laugh as the bright blue wings took flight. *Swishhhh.* Her daddy used to hold out his hands like wings, too. *Swishhhh, Fanny.*

Wilfred kept taking her to the lake in Central Park to put her model boat in the water.

"Look Fanny, look how nicely she sails. What a beauty, uh?"

Fanny always followed the boat with her eyes and ran around the lake so she could send it back in the water before it hit the side. She still didn't believe her daddy couldn't see it, too. She always felt he was watching with her. Standing somewhere close and smiling, even though she couldn't see him.

Her Poppy was always taking her into the garden in Greenpoint and telling her about her daddy's favorite flowers, taking her down to the basement to sit in Julius's old workroom. "He loved fine things," John told the child. "Look at this chair, Fanny. How proud this chair is. Your daddy and I restored it. Look. It's something special, no?"

The little girl touched the chair very carefully and looked around the room. Milika sat at John's feet and followed her every move, stopping every now and then to lick Fanny's hands. The model boats Julius had built were up on shelves, and off in the corner, a lot of old empty frames lined the wall. The room was damp and musty, but Fanny always wanted to be there.

"I think you like fine things, too, Fanny." John smiled at the girl. "Would you like to help me sand down this table and then we'll put a fine coat of stain on it?"

Fanny nodded and showed the gap between her two front teeth, just like her father had.

"I'm going to take it over to that crowded antique store on Greenpoint Avenue and sell it. What do you think of that?"

Fanny took the fine sandpaper out of his hands and copied her Poppy's movements.

"I think you are very much like me, little Fanny. I think your happiness is in your hands. How your daddy would love that."

Sheela sent her daughter off to Greenpoint every other weekend after Julius was murdered. Fanny found it difficult to go at first, knowing that she wouldn't see her daddy, just a lot of empty spaces. But then she pretended that he had gotten permission from heaven to leave and was hiding down in the workroom. That hope made going to Greenpoint bearable.

Her grandmother kept crying all the time, and that made Fanny sad. Even her Poppy seemed very unhappy, but at least he didn't cry all the time. She got to sleep in her daddy's old bed, and she pretended that he sneaked up at night from the workroom to lie down beside her.

Her grandmother was always hugging her. The hugs made Mary cry, and Fanny wanted to get away from her pain, just run downstairs to her Poppy and Milika where everything was quiet.

"Always be kind to German Shepherds," her Poppy would tell her. "Their hearts are very large."

Fanny would kiss Milika's nose and down under her mouth where it felt like velvet.

Her mother never mentioned her daddy anymore, and she never accompanied Fanny to Greenpoint. It was Alice who took her out in a taxi and then picked her up on Sunday. She wanted her mother to take her, but Sheela told Fanny that she couldn't go, she was busy. Fanny didn't understand why she couldn't go until she overheard her grandmother yelling at her Poppy one day because Lou wouldn't let her mother in the house.

"He's boss here?" Mary had said to him. "Since

when is Lou Kerty boss here?"

John told her it was Sheela who felt uncomfortable and didn't want to come.

Mary slapped her husband on the arm.

"When does he tell me I can't see my grandchild? Eh? When does that day come?"

John stood up from his chair and faced her.

"Don't be silly. I say who comes and goes in this house, not Lou Kerty. Do you hear me?"

Mary pointed a finger toward the ceiling.

"Tell that to him. You tell him that he is always to allow my granddaughter in this house. Tell him that."

John insisted that Lou didn't hold any grudges, but Mary's anxiety was not so easily consoled. Fanny had watched quietly as her grandmother slammed the bathroom door behind her and said something very loud in Hungarian.

Stephano Noffe's trial began the day after Julius's funeral. It lasted two weeks. He was found guilty of the premeditated murder of Richard Roth Martin and sentenced to die in the electric chair. Another guest at the party that night had seen Richard Martin being taken out to the pool and testified that he had witnessed the murder firsthand. He had also seen Sheela watching from the patio, but she was not called to testify, even though she had been subpoenaed.

Later that year, James (the Worm) Navarro was found guilty of the murder of Frank Welton and given a life sentence. Sid Bernstein was tried in

December of 1956 and found guilty of fraud. He was fined and sentenced to serve eighteen months in Sing Sing. Rocco Noffe skipped bail and disappeared. Many years later, Sheela heard that he was living under an assumed name in Mexico selling fake artifacts to American tourists.

The murder of Julius Clark remains on record as an unsolved crime.

# Chapter Fifty-One

Most of the money Jack Stanton lent Sheela had been spent on living expenses. Sheela was broke, except for her equity, the General Motors stock she refused to sell under any circumstances. "And after I go through the money? Then where are we? In the street?" she'd ask Alice, who kept reminding her that she was worth something with all that stock she had.

Instead of selling it, though, Sheela used it as collateral and took out a loan. She didn't want to be indebted to Jack Stanton for any more money, and she certainly didn't want to move into his Connecticut estate. She signed a lease on a smaller apartment on the upper East Side of Manhattan. Once she was settled, she had a lock put on a closet in the foyer, and she put all her valuables inside.

She called Margo Sweeny six months after Julius's murder.

"I've got to go to work," she said. "But not as one of the girls."

"My client list will cost you fifteen thousand

dollars, and I'll take whatever you want to give me just to stay out of your way."

"Ten percent on your girls. Nothing on my girls or me. Deal?"

"Deal."

Margo was relieved. She was now close to sixty years old and eager to sit back and collect. She hadn't been running the business as actively as she used to, and Sheela could revive it. Sheela had the means and the looks to make an even bigger success out of it. Margo welcomed what could turn out to be a lucrative transition.

The apartment on the East Side was smaller than the two Sheela and Julius had rented together but was still considered to be a good size for the city of New York, where many apartments were not much bigger than a birdcage. Sheela had two bedrooms, a dining room, living room and a large kitchen. She decided she would go all out and decorate it to please the clientele. She sold off everything that she and Julius had had in the old apartment, all the antique furniture he had loved. She replaced it with pieces that would have made him scowl. She wasn't comforted by anything he had held or sat in, though she wished she could have been. Everything made her cry, made her feel anxious. The changes were what she needed to keep her and Fanny alive. The changes helped her forget that Julius was too far away to help her.

Sheela had the walls in the living room painted dark green. She bought a white sectional couch. The couch traveled like a long sleeping snake around a curvaceous black coffee table that held a potted fake plant. A print of a Salvador Dali painting hung on the wall over the couch, dark and creamy lovers on their way to the moon.

The beige drapes were heavy, and they closed off the light and flowed onto the rug with all the nonchalance of a well-made coat. The bar was black and red and lit from below. The barstools were made of chrome and red leather. A john she barely remembered had given her a lamp that she kept on top of the bar. When the lamp was lit, it revealed a little boy urinating into a lake, illuminating what appeared to be his urine landing in a pool of blue water.

Off in a corner, a black lacquered Chinese cabinet shielded a television set and a phonograph player. The doors of the cabinet were painted a pale yellow and beige, with beautiful Asian women sketched on the front. The women appeared to be gathering flowers from a field. Wispy green vines silhouetted the background, and pale soft colors ran through their kimonos.

In the other corner of the room stood an upright piano. The same Steinway that Sheela had bought for her first apartment. Above the piano she had placed Daniel's box, the one he had painted with the cozy little house in the dark forest. All around the room were large colorful glass ashtrays — pale green and soft blue glass in rounded shapes and little coffin-shaped indentures on the edges, lying in wait for a cigarette.

A large square table, lacquered in shiny black,

dominated the dining room. Six tall wicker chairs sat around it. The backs were high and circuitous. The seats were upholstered in a rich red stripe. Next to the window, Fanny's four parakeets hopped incessantly from floor to swing and chirped like the captured little creatures they were, helplessly resigned to the confines of their cage.

Sheela had a large king-sized bed in her room with a peach velvet headboard and a luscious bedspread that fell before it like a plot of land. The bedspread was also peach with hints of green and blue. The drapes were a muted color and lined in silk. A pale blue chaise stretched sleepily by the window, and a glass vanity table stood against the wall lined with perfume bottles and painted paper boxes filled with body powder. There was a dresser on the other wall, its legs small and curved, accented in antique gold and painted the color of the sky on a bright day. On top of the dresser, from one end to the other, were pictures of Fanny framed in silver.

Fanny's room had a double bed and a cedar chest for her toys. A small cot on the other side of the room was for Alice, and on the wall over her bed two Keene prints of big-eyed children stared out with large, startled eyes. Inside a fishbowl Fanny's turtle slept on a bridge, its shell as green as the carpet that covered the floor.

"Lord have mercy, Sheela Fournier. You can't run no prostitution business right here with the child underfoot."

"She'll be in school all day and then enrolled with that nice Mrs. Humphrey for piano lessons on Tuesdays and Thursdays."

"*Hmph.*"

"She's got her horseback riding lessons on Saturday, and at night she'll be asleep by nine."

Alice put her arms over her chest. Her eyes were squinted, and her lips were held in tight.

"You fixing to expose the child to prostitution?"

Sheela went to the locked closet and opened it.

"Go on. Take anything you want. Just don't leave. Take our ring."

"Shoot. Still trying to pawn that damn ring off on me?"

"Why don't you want it?"

"It's yours. That fool Leroy didn't give it to *me.*"

"I'll give it to you to sell, and I'll raise what I pay you to tend to me and Fanny."

"Ain't enough money on earth make me work in a whorehouse with a little girl underfoot."

Sheela started to cry. "Please," she begged her. "Please. Not for me, for Fanny. She needs you."

Alice thought of the little girl being brought up with Sheela and a bunch of whores sitting around being drooled over by horny men and felt her heart skipping beats as if it might stop. She knew nothing on earth was going to change Sheela's mind. She'd already sunk her money into turning the place into some grade-B movie set. Alice sat down on the big white sectional. "Poor child just lost her father," she said and rubbed her brow. "I've got to watch that child. Somebody with half a brain got to watch that child. Lord have mercy, Sheela Fournier. You know what the hell you're doing?"

Fanny went to a public school, and after school she had a multitude of activities to amuse her. Alice always picked her up from wherever she was and brought her back home. Sometimes "the girls" would still be at the apartment when they returned. Fanny heard them all laughing the minute the elevator door opened. She'd knit her brows, and Alice could see her face get all red with anger.

"*Bang*! *Bang*!"

Fanny ran into her room and grabbed her toy guns. She hid behind the door so she could shoot at the women from behind the archway, just like Gene Autrey did on the television set.

"*Bang*! *Bang*! Go now. Or I'll shoot you all dead."

The women laughed and ignored her. Some said she was cute and tried to engage her in conversation. Fanny turned her back on them and ran over to her mother.

"Hush, darling. Soon. Soon they'll all be gone," Sheela promised.

The girls continued to drink and wink at Fanny.

"Go away."

Fanny hated all these women hanging out in her living room as if they owned it. Only thing she didn't mind was when one of the johns, Fat Alex, slouched all over the couch. Her mother fed him liquor until he practically fell off to sleep. Then the minute she got him to wobble out of the door and find a taxi home, she and Fanny would lift up all the cushions and count all the money that had fallen out of Fat Alex's pockets. It was a funny game that used to make Alice frown and put her hands on her hips.

"Lord have mercy, Sheela Fournier, you fixing to teach that child bad tidings. Bad tidings."

Sheela laughed and winked at Fanny who loved finding Fat Alex's money all over the place, sometimes even in the bathroom.

Fanny watched from behind the door as her mother added up all the bills and then laid them out in stacks on the dining room table. She counted along in a whisper. "One hundred-hundred-dollar bills, fifty tens, sixteen twenties."

Sheela put little rubber bands around the piles and put them away in envelopes that went to the bank every Friday morning. Fanny knew when her mother was counting money that she had to be quiet and stay out of her way.

When Fanny wasn't in school, Alice took her all over the city and kept her out until Sheela said it was all right to bring her back home. But sometimes there would be men sitting around with women when they returned.

"I'm going to run them all over," she'd tell Alice.

"I know, child. I know."

But most of the time, Sheela would be out in the evening when Alice would get back with Fanny.

"Where's my mommy?"

"Your mama's a young woman, honey. She's out

with her friends."

"Where's Willie?"

"Willie will come tomorrow, child. He's got his own friends, too."

Alice put Fanny to bed and stroked her hair until she went off to sleep. Her friends up in Harlem told her not to get too close to the white children, that tending white children was just a job. But Alice loved her Fanny, and it didn't matter what the hell color she was.

Alice picked her head up fast when she heard the key in the lock.

"Get away from that child," she called as Sheela wobbled into the room with an armful of balloon animals.

"Don't you go picking up the child in that state you're in. You fixing to drop her."

Sheela's smile revealed one too many drinks. The balloon animals were twisted into puffy shapes with long rubber torsos and short corpulent legs—Sheela's walk, a sway as jagged as the letter Z.

"Get in bed, Sheela Fournier, 'fore I put you there myself."

Fanny heard her mama squeaking on over to the bed and covering her with scotch kisses. It almost woke her up, but not entirely.

Sometimes Sheela sneaked past Alice and carried her into the big king-sized bed with its green velvet pillows and satiny sheets.

"I'm afraid of the dark," Fanny said as she covered her eyes and lay close to her mother's breast.

Sheela hugged her child tight and made those funny knuckle puppets in the shadows of the room once they were safe and warm under the satiny sheets. Knuckle puppets always made Fanny giggle. They had sinister bouncing noses and short pointed ears, and they brought smiles and shadow wars that ended in exhaustion.

"You're my life, sweet Fanny," Sheela whispered as she reached for a twisted balloon.

Fanny laughed at the squeaky balloon monster and fell off to sleep in the perspicuous assurance of her mother's arms.

# Chapter Fifty-Two

Milika disappeared on the night of March 10th, 1956. The last anyone ever saw of her she was walking west toward Prospect Park, never to be seen again. The following morning John Kuvik's heart stopped, and he died in his sleep. Joe Ganesky said it was as if the dog knew and led the way to heaven.

Sheela sent Fanny to the funeral while she stayed behind in the city. She hadn't seen any of her in-laws since Julius's death, and even though she was fond of the old man she knew she would not be welcomed by Lou Kerty.

John Kuvik was laid to rest beside his son Julius and not far from his first wife, Berta. Fanny stood off to the side of the gravestone and looked at the traffic running on the Long Island Expressway. She wondered if her Poppy would mind all the noise.

The evening of the funeral, Fanny's grandmother held her close. Mary was crying so much that she was difficult to understand.

"I'll never see you again," she said.

Fanny felt so sad she could barely stand it.

"Why, Grandma?"

Mary made her eyes small, like the slats in the shutters that kept out the sun.

"When your father died, all Lou wanted was his clothes, so he and Joseph took whatever they could lay their hands on. Now, Lou wants revenge because he blames Julius, blames him for losing so much money from his pension." She patted the side of the bed. "Come here, Juliana."

The old woman sat her down and went to an old photograph album.

"Would you like a picture of your father when he was a boy?"

The girl nodded, and Mary placed the photograph in her hand.

"That was at his Communion," she said.

Fanny stared at the young boy standing on the front stairs, shyly smiling back at the camera.

"He doesn't look like Daddy." She made a face; her father was much better looking.

"He was such a good boy," Mary said through her tears. "Such a good boy."

Fanny looked around the tiny room. Jesus hung from his cross and avoided her eyes.

"Lou is now head of the family. Men rule," Mary said and kissed her granddaughter on the top of her head.

Fanny noticed that Jesus kept his eyes averted and did not disagree.

Fanny looked at Jesus in the little glass ball on her grandmother's table.

"Does Jesus like being caught in a bubble,

Grandma?"

"Take the snowball, Juliana. You always loved it, no? Take it. It belonged to your papa."

Fanny took the glass ball and shook it. Soon the tiny, captured Jesus was engulfed in snow. She laughed and shook it again.

"I have something else for you, Juliana."

Mary went to a box on top of her dresser and opened it carefully. She handed Fanny a ring.

"I wanted to wait until you were older, but I no longer have a choice. I must give you this now... I..."She broke off and cried.

Fanny was confused and wondered why her grandma was crying so much.

Mary placed a diamond and ruby ring in the young girl's hand.

"It looks like Mommy's ring," the child said in amazement.

Mary laughed.

"Your father had it copied. Took some ring right off your mother's finger and made it look just like this one."

"Oh," Fanny said as she stared at it.

"But this is the real thing. I was saving it for you. Now it's yours." Mary whispered close to her ear. "It was my mother's ring, and now it's your ring. Be careful with it. It symbolizes your past... your roots. Promise you'll cherish it?"

Fanny nodded.

"This ring will be my way of staying close to you." Mary closed the child's hand around it. "Remember me," she said.

Fanny felt a chill in her heart, as if something had been removed, something irreplaceable, and the awareness of that made her nervous.

"Remember your papa, too."

Fanny sat frozen and frightened on the edge of her grandmother's bed.

"Come sleep with me, Juliana. Stay close to me." She held onto Fanny tightly for the entire night.

In the morning, Mary's eyes were puffy and filled with tears.

"I will pray for you," she said again as she hugged the little girl long and hard.

Mary made Fanny her favorite breakfast of eggs and rye toast and a glass of coffee filled with milk and sugar. She put the child's cap on her head and tied it under her chin. She kissed her one more time.

"Bye-bye, Grandma." Fanny started to cry.

Mary stood at the top of the stairs and blew the girl a kiss as Fanny slowly walked out of the door and into the waiting limousine. Her grandmother's ring was deep in her pocket, and her father's photograph was in her hand. The snowball had been carefully packed away in her bag. Fanny looked back only once as the car pulled away.

Upstairs, in the little apartment, Mary sat in John's old green chair and looked out over the garden. She cried so loudly that it carried up to the third floor. Lou turned up the volume on his radio. Rebeka considered trying to get him to change his mind.

"Let Fanny visit her grandmother," she said.

Lou turned away and faced the wall.

"Don't you think we're going a little too far?" Rebeka sat on the arm of his chair and touched his hair.

Lou narrowed his tiny eyes and turned to glare at her.

"I've lost enough because of Julius. I won't lose the house. The old woman will give it to her unless we keep her out. That's the end of it. The whore's little bitch will not get our house!"

Later that evening, Fanny put the little glass snowball next to the turtle bowl so Jesus could watch over the little green beast as he walked over the sharp sandy rocks and miniature bridge. Then she put her daddy's photograph under her pillow so she could send him her dreams.

# Chapter Fifty-Three

Jack Stanton died in 1957. Francis showed up at Sheela's door, just days after his death.

"He was found stark naked under a black silk robe, back behind the house," he wept. "He was lying in the snow, and holding a small bouquet of roses in his hand."

Sheela smiled sadly to herself. "It's been all over the papers, Francis."

"Oh, I haven't been reading the papers. I've been in confinement at the house just wanting to be alone. I've avoided the phone. I've avoided everyone except for that horrid wife. I couldn't possibly avoid her, the bitch. She kept me out of the funeral." He shook his fists in the air. "Told me I wasn't welcome."

Sheela took his hand in hers. She wondered why he had come to her, of all people.

"It was a small gathering. Just family. I showed up at the gravesite anyway," Francis said through sniffles.

Sheela noticed that his eyes were all red, as if

he'd been crying for days.

"I found him in the morning. It was awful but also beautiful. He was just lying there with a smile on his face."

Sheela watched as Francis blew his nose and cried into a soft white hankie.

"Do you want anything from the chateau, honey?" he asked.

Sheela asked for the big bronze Buddha that had been in Jack's bedroom.

"Jack was very fond of you, you know? He called you his beauty with the brains."

Sheela laughed and squeezed the boy's hand.

"He left his wife everything, everything but the chateau and its contents. That he left to me." Francis put his head in his hands and cried again like a small child. "I cared for him deeply, very deeply. I understood him."

Sheela was surprised that Jack did not leave most of his estate to Francis, but she assumed that in the end, Jack had to keep up appearances and that being of his persuasion still made him uncomfortable.

"I worked the beach circuit, all the hotels, but mostly the Fontainebleau. That's how we met. He called for my services." Francis dabbed at his eyes. "And voilà! Magic! Who could have guessed? There was an immediate bond. Oh, there was much more than sex between us. Much more. I wasn't looking for love, you know? I didn't think you could really have that with another man. It was just about business for me, and for Jack, too. It was only about an exchange of favors for both of us, and love was, well, love was unreal, like God, I suppose. Unreal until it hits you. Who knew? Ah, sweet mystery of life. Who knew?"

Sheela sat back in her chair and thought about Julius. Francis dabbed at his eyes again and carried on talking.

"Egocentricity is either adored or the queer one is taken out in the back and shot. Well, I adored Jack, and he treated me like a treasure. 'My treasure,' he called me. He said I was his first and his only love."

Francis took the cigarette that Sheela lit for him and held it between his fingers. She noticed that when he smoked it, he didn't inhale but sucked on it so long that he made the paper all wet.

"I have enough money. Cash Jack gave me, stocks, the house and all the artwork and antiques. I'm taken care of. I would not have wanted it all anyway. Ahhhhh!" Francis put his outstretched hands to either side of his head and screamed again. "*Ahhhhh*! 'Death, where is thy sting?Grave, where is thy victory?'" he wailed, as he put his forehead on Sheela's arm and wept.

Sheela found Francis an apartment in her building after he sold the house Jack left him, and he moved down the hall. He quickly became Fanny's "Uncle Fran." Sheela put the big bronze Buddha in the foyer, so it was the first thing anyone noticed when they walked through the front door, and she burned a rich evergreen incense in the pot under its belly that made Alice's eyes squint and wrinkle up her nose and fan the air frantically with her hands.

Fanny loved her Uncle Fran, though Alice did not approve of all the time she spent with him.

"That boy is queer," she told Sheela. "My Willie not going within three feet of that boy's door."

Sheela glared at Alice. "Well, as I see it," she began, "you two have a lot in common."

Alice put her hands on her hips. "I got nothing in common with no queer boy."

"Yes, you do."

"*Hmph.*"

"No one on God's earth laughs more than colored people and fags. And no one laughs better, either."

"*Hmph*, Sheela Fournier. You don't know what the hell you're talking about."

# Chapter Fifty-Four

Fanny had been calling her "Bulldog" for five long years. She hated her more than any of the others and wished she'd go away, but she kept showing up. Her real name was Laura, and though she was a young woman, her cheeks fell over her bones and her eyes drooped.

"Keep that Bulldog away from me," Fanny said through her teeth. Bulldog sat on the big white sectional sipping her fourth or fifth scotch of the day.

"Don't mind Fanny. She's just a kid." Sheela sent Fanny off with Alice.

Laura scowled. "Your kid should learn to respect her elders."

"Keep her out of my room," Fanny yelled as Alice shoved her fists into woolen gloves and walked her out the door. She was going to spend the night up in Harlem, and although she couldn't wait to get a look at Cousin Clarise Cleary's color television set, she always hated leaving her mother alone with the Bulldog.

It was the night of November 21st, 1958. Fanny would be turning twelve years old in January. She and Sheela were lying on the living room floor watching *Dragnet* on television, talking about what Fanny might want for her birthday during the commercials.

"I want a dog," Fanny said, "a big poodle."

Sheela stood up. "Come on, Fanny, it's past your bedtime."

"What about the dog?"

That's the last thing Fanny remembered saying before feeling the hand on her shoulder, shaking her.

"Fanny? Is that your name?"

Fanny looked up to find a policeman sitting at the edge of her bed.

"Did you hear any noises?" he asked her softly.

"No," she said and looked around for her mother.

There had been a knock on the door sometime after eleven that evening.

"Who is it?" Sheela asked through the peephole. She saw the one Fanny called Bulldog, but she didn't see anyone else. She almost didn't let the Bulldog in, but she ignored the instinct and opened the door.

Two men quickly followed. The white one drew a gun the moment they were all inside, and the door slammed shut behind them.

"Give us the key to the closet!" he shouted.

Sheela started shaking. She couldn't get her feet to move. A thin black man ran back to Fanny's room and pointed a gun at her as she slept.

"Get the key, or we'll shoot your kid," he called out.

Sheela wanted to scream but couldn't, for fear she'd wake Fanny. She tried to think, formulate a plan, but the fear was paralyzing.

"Anything. Anything," she screamed. "Just don't hurt my baby!"

Sheela ran back to Fanny's room. Her legs worked but felt like jelly.

"*Click*," the man with the gun smiled and clicked back the trigger as he kept it pointed at the sleeping child. "*Click, click*." He laughed. "Move, white bitch, the key!"

"Anything, anything, just don't hurt my baby."

"Shut up!" He shoved Sheela out of her daughter's room and back to the bedroom with the peach-colored spread. The handle of the gun felt like an explosion as it hit the side of her head and knocked her down.

"Where's the key, bitch?" Bulldog came into the room and shouted out, "Where do you keep it?"

"No, it's not in here. The Chinese cabinet." Sheela screamed. "It's in there."

"Get it." Bulldog pulled her up by the sleeve.

The white man took her other arm roughly and pushed her into the living room. Sheela felt his hard shoves on her back. She fell to her knees before the cabinet and reached up behind the phonograph needle. The key fell to the floor. Someone grabbed the key out of her hands and gave it to the Bulldog. Sheela's head felt as if it would burst open, as the blood from her wound ran into her eyes.

"Empty the closet," the black man said. "Quickly!"

"Get back," said the other man as he ripped the gown from Sheela's body and forced her into the bedroom.

"What the fuck are you doing, Eddie?" Bulldog shouted.

"Just shut up and get the money and the coats … any jewelry, too. I'm busy."

The one called Eddie raped her while the Bulldog emptied the minks and diamonds into a suitcase, as well as three thousand dollars in cash. Sheela didn't know where the black man was. She prayed he was not with Fanny.

When the white man was through raping her, he slapped her with the back of his hand.

"Don't move, whore," he said and left the room.

Sheela lay very still. Her head throbbed as the hot sticky semen ran down her thigh. She prayed they would leave and not harm Fanny. She listened very quietly. She could not tell if they were pausing by Fanny's door. Sheela reacted quickly, without analyzing her actions. She ran to the window and screamed, repeatedly. She screamed for the police as loudly as she could, so loudly that her throat would hurt her for days afterward.

Startled by her screams, the three intruders ran

out into the street. Sheela heard the front door slam and a police siren howling back at her in the distance. She ran to Fanny's room and quickly closed the door.

The robbers dropped the suitcase in front of Sheela's building as they fled and only managed to escape with a twenty-dollar bill.

It was all over the papers the next day. The *Herald Tribune* had Sheela's picture on the front page, and the *Daily News* wanted to interview Fanny at her school, but Sheela refused to let the reporters near her.

Someone had found the suitcase in the street and emptied it of all the cash. Two mink coats were returned to Sheela but none of the diamond jewelry.

"Our ring is gone," she told Alice. "All of it gone."

Alice told her she was lucky to be alive and sat down and held her heart when Sheela told her they had held a gun on Fanny.

"Lord have mercy."

Sheela's hand shook as she reached for the bottle of Johnnie Walker.

"I have to protect my child," she said.

"What you going to do?" Alice sat close to her and looked into her eyes.

"I don't know," she said, the scotch burning the cut on her lip. "But not here. She can't stay here."

Leda had moved to Brevard, North Carolina, and she and her husband had opened a motel in the mountains. They were doing very well financially, well enough to raise Fanny without taking a dime from Sheela.

"I'll raise Fanny," Leda told her. "Little Buddy would love a sister, and you know how I love that little girl. Your lifestyle, Sheela, well, it's just too dangerous for a child."

Sheela shook her head.

"I can't. I can't give her to you. You live so far, so far."

"You can't subject her to anymore danger, Sheela," Leda insisted.

"I know," Sheela said sadly. "But I can't send her to North Carolina, either."

Alice and Wilfred had offered to raise her in Harlem, and even Francis said he would take responsibility for Fanny.

"Perhaps we should get married and move to Sands Point. We'll become a respectable couple and raise Fanny there. I'll marry you, Sheela. I'll take care of you."

"I can't," Sheela said softly.

Sheela knew she couldn't give her daughter up to anyone, not even just for a short time, and she certainly couldn't move to Sands Point with Francis. She stared at his pink lips and the dainty gold bracelet he wore around his wrist.

"I'm sending her to boarding school," she said. "A fancy boarding school on Long Island."

"She's only twelve years old," Francis exclaimed.

"She'll be home weekends."

Sheela sighed deeply and reached for a scotch. Fanny was her life. She didn't want to send her away, but she had to assure her safety. That's all that mattered.

The scotch burned and coated the ache in her chest, so she barely felt it.

Fanny cried when Sheela told her about the boarding school on Long Island and she vowed she would never forgive her mother for sending her there.

"It's the best school on the eastern seaboard." Sheela tried to sound convincing.

"I won't go!" Fanny screamed.

"It's so clean, like your grandma's. You could eat off the floors."

"No!"

Sheela sat in the darkness and cried softly.

"You'll be home most weekends."

"No!"

"I love you. I'm sorry. Forgive me."

Fanny turned to the wall and listened to her mother's tears. The tiny Jesus looked on from his bubble as if he would help with a miracle were he not so confined to his fate. Fanny was afraid and cried deeply. Her mother had returned to the darkness of the living room and the comfort of the warm scotch in her belly without offering to change her mind.

# Chapter Fifty-Five

Sheela instructed Alice was to go through the mail and separate the bills from anything important. "Always toss the third-class crap," Sheela told her.

Not long after Fanny had been sent to boarding school, Alice noticed a large manila envelope postmarked all the way from North Carolina.

"I think something's come from your sister," she said, as she walked into Sheela's bedroom. "She lives in North Carolina now, don't she?"

Sheela looked up and stared at the brown envelope.

"Open it," she said slowly.

Alice went and got a letter opener and carefully pried away the top flap. Inside was a small note wrapped around three or four sealed letters.

"What is it?" Sheela asked.

Alice pulled out the note tied around the letters and read it quietly to herself.

"What is it?" Sheela asked again.

"Lord have mercy, child." Alice held out the tied

letters to Sheela. "These letters are from your mama, girl! Your sister done sent 'em to you. And what's this? Why, look at this pretty box. It's a music box." Alice opened the lid and listened to the lively tune.

Sheela pulled her head back sharply and said nothing.

"Your mama's letters, girl," Alice repeated, as she put the letters in Sheela's hand. Sheela pushed them away.

"Do you want me to read Leda's note to you, Sheela?" Alice asked carefully.

Sheela nodded her head, agreeing to something she clearly wasn't sure she wanted.

Alice slowly picked up Leda's note and read it aloud:

"'*Dear Sister,*

*I was most surprised to receive Mama's letters from Sister Vincetta after all this time. I didn't open those addressed to you. Can you imagine her keeping them all these years? She said that after Papa died they were sent back down to her. It seems that they'd originally been addressed to the orphanage but must have been intercepted. Can you imagine that? My heart was in my mouth as I read mine. Poor Mama! I'm so glad I wrote to the Sister when I married Bill and she knew how to find me. But the letters wound up with Bill's sister in Kissimmee after we moved up here to North Carolina. They weren't forwarded to me until the poor girl died last year. Why don't you write to*

*Sister Vincetta and thank her? She said she was saving Mama's letters for you but never knew where to find you. I found a photograph of Mama for Fanny. I'm sure she'd appreciate knowing what her grandmother looked like. I was shocked to see the music box. Sister Vincetta was explicit about it going to you. Mama wrote you three letters before she died. I only got one letter. If there were any to Hank or Wade Jr., the Sister didn't mention it.*

*We wish you would visit. Buddy is so cute now and such a good boy. How is Fanny? I miss you so. God Bless,*

*Leda.'"*


Alice looked over at Sheela and noticed that she had her head in her hands.

"Don't cry, girl." Alice said softly and put the letters near her.

"Not now," Sheela said quickly.

Startled, Alice picked up the letters. "What do you want me to do with them?" she asked.

"Put them away," Sheela snapped. "Just put them away somewhere. I'll read them later. And put the music box on top of the piano since someone stole the other box."

Alice placed the music box on top of the piano and took the letters and placed them carefully in Sheela's lingerie drawer. Quietly, she closed it shut. She put the photograph in Fanny's room.

"*Hmph, hmph, hmph,*" she sighed. "If I know the woman, and I surely do, these poor letters ain't ever going to get read."

After much agonizing deliberation Sheela decided that dwelling on the past was an unnecessary expenditure of painful energy, so she never read the letters from her mama. She wasn't even sure what Alice had done with them. No matter, it was time now to concentrate on her daughter's transformation into womanhood.

Fanny's last visit home had proven to be monumental, for she could be heard screaming from the bathroom, "Yuck! Blood!" This pronouncement sent Sheela to the liquor store for a bottle of bubbly to toast her daughter's coming of age. After exclaiming to anyone who would listen that her little girl had finally become a woman, she went off to Bloomindales to upgrade Fanny's "childish" bedroom.

Sheela chose a white four-poster bed, a high matching dresser and a glass vanity table with an outlet for Fanny's hair curlers. She even found a pink ballerina lamp that twirled around to the tune of "I Love Paris." Sheela told Alice that she wanted all of Fanny's old things thrown out to make way for her makeover. Everything had to go. It wasn't intentional insensitivity, since Fanny would be away at school and would not be consulted; it was, in Sheela's mind, simply time to expand her daughter's horizons.

So, everything in Fanny's old bedroom was put on the "good riddance" list.

"Lord have mercy. Those her pets, Sheela Fournier," Alice said angrily as she started packing everything up. "Her parakeets, her turtle."

She looked around at the glossy pictures of the movie stars she had helped Fanny tape on the wall and wished she could send them to Fanny in nice pretty picture frames. On instinct, she took the little snow globe and hid it away in her pocket. Then she tore the pictures from the wall and threw them in the garbage. But at least she'd save that snow globe for Fanny.

"*Hmph!*" Alice said aloud. She got so angry with Sheela sometimes, she could barely stand it. She told Wilfred there wasn't enough money in the world to hear herself called a nigger every time that woman poured one too many drinks in her belly.

"You a nasty drunk, Sheela Fournier. I just may quit this tending your ass." She'd said time and time again.

Sheela cried and sniffled so badly that Alice would have to run for a tissue.

"You fixing to gag yourself, girl. Stop your crying."

"I love you, Alice. You can't ever leave me."

"You can't call me no names, Sheela Fournier."

"I'm sorry. So sorry. I don't remember. I swear I don't remember." Sheela sobbed and carried on so much that Alice always forgave her. Sheela'd throw her arms around Alice so tightly that the two women lost their balance and fell over.

"You mind yourself, Sheela. You just mind yourself."

"My baby needs you, Alice. Don't you forget that."

"*Hmph,*" Alice said aloud, as she opened the cedar chest. "Fanny needs her mama. That's what that girl needs, her mama!"

Alice was surprised to find the beautiful painted music box Leda had sent at the bottom of the chest underneath one of Fanny's old teddy bears.

She smiled as she picked it up and traced the piano that was painted on the top. She thought Sheela had knocked the pretty little box off the piano and broken it days ago. Just the other day she had asked her where the beautiful music box was.

"Honey, you know these women steal everything they can see."

"So, Fanny took it." Alice laughed aloud. Then she heard something in the box slide over to the other end. "Sounds like money. Child must be using this box to save some money in. She going to need a place of her own someday. Get herself out of this nuthouse," Alice said as she opened the box and looked at the three tied letters she thought she had placed in Sheela's lingerie drawer.

"Those letters from her grandma! Why, Fanny must have known that, must have overheard her mama getting drunk and crying over 'em. She must have found those old letters and hidden them away last time she was here."

Alice noticed that Fanny hadn't opened the letters or even untied them. "She must be saving them to read," she whispered softly. Also in the chest Fanny had placed her grandmother's photograph. She'd wrapped it in tissue paper."

Alice smiled.

"And now what on earth is this?"

Alice looked at the tiny piece of velvet, tied around something small. "Lord have mercy." Alice felt the ring in her hand as she untied the velvet. The little white diamonds and dark red rubies sparkled back at her from a small, jeweled crown on a circle of white gold.

"Little Fanny went and took that fool Leroy's ring, too. Well, Lord have mercy. Well, I guess it was her mama's engagement ring, not really Leroy's no more."

After Alice got everything neatly packed away in paper bags, she went out to the living room and showed Sheela what she thought was Leroy's old engagement ring, the one that Julius had altered so it didn't even resemble itself anymore. But she didn't tell Sheela she had found her mama's letters in Fanny's cedar chest. And she certainly didn't tell Sheela that she was taking the letters home and the music box home, just as she had found them, and she was putting everything away for safekeeping.

"The ring wasn't stolen?" Sheela asked incredulously. "I could have sworn I put it away in the locked closet."

Alice smiled and nodded.

Sheela slipped the ring on her finger.

"It's big on me now. It looks different, doesn't it?"

Alice stared at the ring and slanted her eyes at Sheela.

"What you planning on doing with that ring?"

"Wear it. It's our friendship ring, isn't it?"

"I'll take that ring now, Sheela," Alice said.

Sheela held her hand in the air.

"Really?"

"Sure. Why you want to go and wear that fool's ring? Give it to me. I wouldn't have given it back to you if I didn't think you'd let Fanny keep it."

Sheela laughed. "Fanny is too young for a ring like this. She'll lose it in a heartbeat. But I'll give it to you. Here. It's about time you accepted it from me," Sheela said in a pout. "Julius did alter it beautifully, but I've got my wedding ring. I'll never take off my wedding ring."

Alice reached out and slipped the ring in her pocket.

"I called the Salvation Army. You sure you want to give her stuff away? She'll be home for the holidays. She still lives here, and I'm sure she don't want no big ole fancy bedroom. This is her home, and that's her bedroom, and she likes it just the way it is," Alice insisted.

"Fanny is too big for toys and movie star pictures. She's a little woman now, and she needs a fine satin bedspread on her bed and a little glass vanity where she can put her hair up in curlers. Fanny has to grow up. We all have to grow up sometime, let go of the past."

"But they her things in that room, Sheela Fournier. What you going to tell the child? What you going to tell her?"

Angry, Alice wanted to shake the woman till she heard the good sense rattle.

"Fanny won't mind. She'll love her new room," Sheela said quickly and kept her eyes on the scotch.

"*Hmph, hmph, hmph.*" That was all Alice said as the men took the paper bags packed with all the toys and left. The birds were let out the open window, and the turtle was given to the super's boy who promised not to tell Fanny he had it.

That evening, when she got home, Alice handed the little snow globe to Wilfred and put the music box in the dresser that she kept out in the foyer. She wrapped the ring up in the blue velvet and slipped it back inside the box.

"I'm sending this snow globe to the child. Wrapping it up and sending it to Fanny. She's got to have something to keep for herself. Someday, I'll give her those letters. When she's off living on her own."

Wilfred sighed and shook the globe. Jesus opened his eyes to see the snow.

"She fixing to break that little girl's heart. Giving her stuff away. Poor Fanny lost enough in her life. She went and wrapped that ring up in velvet like it was the Virgin Mary's earring," Alice told Wilfred, as she took off her old stiff shoes and got into a pair of slippers.

"*Hmph,*" Wilfred sighed, as he shook the globe and watched the snow fill up the glass and land on Jesus.

"It don't snow in Jerusalem, does it?" he asked her.

Alice took the extra twenty dollar bills out of her pocket and put them under the phone. Sheela always gave her extra money when she felt guilty about something. She went over and sat beside Wilfred and watched as he held the glistening ball to his lips.

"They turn the whole damn world white, don't they?" he said quietly. "They put snow in Jerusalem and blue eyes on a man as dark as me."

Alice smiled and reached for the globe.

"This belonged to her daddy when he was a boy."

Wilfred took in a breath and looked at his wife.

"She wants to throw away that child's mementos. Just like she don't give a damn about that ring or those letters she got from her mama. She give me that damn ring twenty years ago. Should have kept it then. Well, I've got it now.Ain't worth much to me, but it's worth a whole lot to Fanny. I guess she feels it's from her daddy." Alice reached out and took her husband's hand. "Ain't worth nothing except being worn by her mama. The warmth from her mama's finger. That's all the damn thing's worth. Might mean something someday."

# Chapter Fifty-Six

Sheela knew Alice was angry with her. Everyone was angry with her. Sheela opened the door of her daughter's room. But at least Fanny would be happy with her pricey new bedroom set. Sheela was certainly happy with it. She gazed appreciatively at the cool blue walls and the new crisp blue-and-white curtains. Fanny loved the color blue. And she'd surprised her with a new phonograph player. She'd even bought her Elvis's latest album. And of course, there was that beautiful ballerina lamp.

Sheela couldn't believe the money she'd made in the last few years. She enjoyed spending it on Fanny, buying her daughter beautiful things, putting money away in the bank for Fanny's future.

"What's this?" Fanny exclaimed as she stared in horror at the blue room.

Sheela frowned. "You don't like it?"

Fanny turned to her, her mouth frozen in a static gape. "It looks like a girl's room, like it belongs to some frilly twerp."

Sheela was stunned. "It looks like a little princess's room, like it belongs to a movie star."

Fanny sat forlornly on the bed. "Where are my parakeets?" she asked.

Sheela sat beside her. "They got away, honey."

"All four of them?" Fanny yelled.

"It was an accident," Sheela stuttered.

Suddenly, Fanny jumped up and ran to the cedar chest.

Sheela brought her nail to her lip.

"It's empty," Fanny cried.

"Nothing in there important," Sheela said, earnestly seeking her daughter's approval.

Fanny clenched her jaw. "You threw away my grandmother's ring."

"What?" Sheela exclaimed. "What are you talking about?"

"And the letters ...." Fanny started to cry.

Sheela stood up. She was confused.

"Get out of my room!" Fanny hollered and picked up the glass lamp.

Sheela felt as if she might faint. Fanny took the glass lamp, with the dancing ballerina at its base, and threw it. Sheela stepped back as it crashed to the floor, its pieces landing at her feet.

Sheela went to the bar and fixed a drink. She stared at the wall. She wasn't making Fanny happy. *Where is the road to happiness?* Three drinks later, she was even further from the answer.

Sheela was driving a wedge between her heart and Fanny's every time she took another sip of scotch and drifted into some safe reliable distance, a distance her daughter could neither understand nor penetrate. The harm was something Sheela felt but unable to prevent, like the knowledge of falling.

*Will the distance continue to deepen between us? Deepen and hollow until the utter despair of unspoken need settles in my daughter's heart as rage, and in mine as grief?*

Later that evening, Sheela went into Fanny's room. Her daughter had swept the broken glass into a tiny pile below the window. It hurt to see the broken ballerina, as if the vacant eyes on the shattered doll were an extension of something gone, some static ache.

Sheela sat on Fanny's bed. "You awake?" she whispered.

Fanny glared at her. "No," she said.

The ice cubes floated in Sheela's scotch and clinked along the side.

"*Ping*," she said and finished the drink.

Fanny moved so close to the edge of the bed she might have tumbled to the floor.

Sheela smiled sadly as she looked at the vanity table, the pink princess phone. She reached out and stroked the back of Fanny's hair.

Sheela suddenly had an image of the gypsy she had seen when Fanny was nothing more than an anticipation in her womb. The veiled woman's fingers had crawled out ahead of her like knurled clarions as she covered her crystal ball. "Life is not easy for anyone," she'd whispered.

"No, not easy for anyone," Sheela said softly as

she lay down on Fanny's bed.

"Don't bother me," Fanny said as she put the pillow over her head.

"What letters?" Sheela asked in the dark. "What letters were in the cedar chest?" She reached out and took the pillow out of Fanny's hand.

"Letters from Hannah, my grandmother. I put them in that box you had. You would have lost them."

"I told Alice to throw everything away." Sheela felt a sudden sensation of failure landing on her heart with too much weight.

"You didn't know they were there?" Fanny asked.

Sheela shook her head. "No."

"They meant so much to me... Daddy's snow globe, Grandma's ring... Hannah's letters."

"I'm so sorry, I had no idea." Sheela held back the tears. "Grandma's ring?"

Fanny nodded. "She gave it to me, the one Daddy copied for you. Grandma gave me the original."

"I guess the one your Daddy gave me got stolen."

"What was she like?" Fanny turned to her mother in the dark.

"Who?"

"Your mother... Hannah?"

Sheela let the tears fall. "I don't remember," she said.

Fanny was disappointed. Sheela usually talked about Hannah when she'd had one to many drinks.

The piano, trapped in an institution the way she was, that wonderful brogue.

"We're like hearts upon a fragile bough," her mother suddenly said.

"I can't believe you don't remember."

"Shadows on the wall, Fanny. That's what I recall. Shadows."

Fanny closed her eyes. She was tired and disgusted. Sleep would come soon and, so too, the day and the unforeseen perplexity of tomorrow.

"Miracles," she heard Sheela whisper. "They may turn up. Faith in the improbable is sometimes all we have. And then, out of all the shadows, maybe a miracle."

# The End

# Sneak Peak from Book Three of The Fourniers: A Song for You

## Prologue
## 1959

Fanny's bedroom was a perfect square; the walls were the color of a Robin's egg, barely there blue. The windows opened on to city buildings in shades of pigeon grays, parting only slightly to allow the sun to fall across the floor, an intruder in the dusty gloom. The flimsy white curtains fell in a listless dance, moving slightly in the pellucid wind, lazy and lackluster. The toy chest had been placed before the windows, richly oiled in brown tones of cedar wood.

Fanny loved the smell, the cedar chest smells, like green forests. Even with the top closed the rich forest cedar scented the air. It was a good place to hide all secrets, holding back from the world what is most cherished, refusing even a glimpse. But she knew that within the scent of cedar, Hannah's music was near. Her notes stilled by wooden walls, her song, a fragile history.

Music is all that the ghost had, perhaps music is all that any of us have. All traces of Hannah's being, the flesh and blood of her, had been captured in magic by the fading and fragile box, bringing to life what once was. Fanny was afraid to touch the box, to hold it in her hands for it could crumble and fall to pieces. The painted piano was barely visible on the top, bending slightly, like an ear to the outside world. The music still played, obstinate music that could not be stilled. The top of the box opened, and the music hit the air, fanciful and free. Fanny didn't know the song, but it was playful, and it made her smile.

She loved the unknown presence of Hannah Reilly, the warmth of her, the soothing sense of her when she lay close, her words caught up in brogue. It was stupid not to believe in ghosts, they were here on earth, especially clear to children. Knowing is not at all superficial, sometimes knowing is beyond description. The ghost's laughter mingled with Fanny's until their voices were lost to the other, captured and returned. This kind of knowing could never be translated into anyone's conventional understanding, but Fanny's. She knew the ghost was Hannah and the ghost was there.

Fanny had taken the music box: the top of the box was not only bent, it was slightly broken, chipped like a disfigurement of what had once been perfect. There was something sad about it. Fanny knew that sometimes it's all too sad. She knew about sadness, because that's what a life was, more so than not. It is fragile and broken and sad.

One could say she had committed a theft by taking Hannah's music box from its haphazard home, but thievery is a good thing. If she'd stolen a dog from someone who'd abused it, she would be a hero, not a thief. She hadn't stolen a thing, she had only protected the box, rescued it from eternal loss. She knew she had to do what she did. All of Hannah would be gone forever if she hadn't made up her mind to just do it. Her mother would have made the box disappear; like all things disturbing, she'd vanquish it to the bottom of a scotch glass.

One day Fanny would place Hannah's music box right out in the open; she planned it out, she'd be eighteen, only six years away. One day she'd be brave enough to face her grandmother's sorrow. But not now, sorrow is too frightening and too vast to face alone. One day, she wouldn't be alone, and she'd share the abyss of her feelings. For now, though, all that comes to her of Hannah is light and sweet. In the night, when Hannah comes, it is without tears, without weight, it's a soft glow in the darkness of her room. It's a ghost.

Fanny found a photograph of Hannah along with the music box. The box and the picture were so of the times, 1917, 18 … perhaps. The round eyes were blue because she had been told of their color and her hair was a rich, deep auburn, she had been told that too. Hannah was sitting, her shoulders small and narrow. The painting behind her was muted and beautiful, though the photograph itself was black and white, Fanny saw the greens and the deep gold and the swirl of the ornate brass frame. Hannah was sitting, and in her arms, two children. It was so posed, the way it was back then, even before her mother's birth, but back then, it was new to have a photograph as good as this one.

Then, perhaps, only then, Hannah had shed no tears. Fanny placed her grandmother's photograph on a small table near her bed. How does life turn bad, she wondered, when it starts off good?

"I've hidden your music box," Fanny whispered to the photograph. "Don't worry, someday I'll take it out and open the lid and we'll hear the music again. Someday I'll make sure to play the tune over and over, as you did. When I miss you, I'll open the lid, just to say hello."

But then, so suddenly, they were parted, ripped away from one another without any warning at all. It had seemed so violent to lose her grandmother, so cruel. The music box gone; the cedar chest emptied. Hannah never returned after that. Fanny sat and waited but she never returned, never told her where she could be found.

Loneliness came in waves, a fearful feeling. Fanny cried the entire night. Loneliness deeper than the earth can reach, loneliness deeper than the sky extends, was what she left behind.

"Is that what it was like?" Fanny asked.

And for the last time, Hannah whispered, "Yes."

# Acknowledgments

I'd like to thank Lisa Orban, publisher of Indies United, for being so helpful and knowledgeable. When I am ready to pull my hair out she is truly the port in the storm.

Ebook launch has given me two of the greatest covers I've ever had and I anticipate the third in the Fourniers series. Dane is a wizard.

Jayne Sullivan is the best editor I have ever worked with, a true master at her trade, thank you so much Jayne for making Glamor Girl the best it could be.

Deep gratitude to Marianna Young who gives me support and encouragement – my very special cheerleader.

And last but not least, in memory of my father, Julius, whose brief life contributed to this story and to my grandmother, Mary, who needs no ring to be remembered.